AMOUR TOUJOURS

The two naked women had Robert flat on his back. He was frantically aroused. Their hands roamed all over him, their mouths caressed him with quick little kisses and their teeth nipped at the bare flesh of his belly and thighs. Suzette sat astride his loins, his swollen part in her hand, while Gaby arranged herself behind him, sitting back on her heels with his head cradled in her lap. Robert was almost dizzy with pleasure as he stared up at Gaby's small pointed breasts, then at Suzette's full round ones.

'The truth now,' said Suzette. 'Have you ever been had by two women at once?'

Amour Toujours

Marie-Claire Villefranche

HEADLINE
DELTA

First published in 1995
by HEADLINE BOOK PUBLISHING

A HEADLINE DELTA paperback

10 9 8 7 6 5 4 3 2 1

ISBN 0 7472 4633 5

Typeset by Keyboard Services, Luton, Beds

Printed and bound in Great Britain by
Cox & Wyman Ltd, Reading, Berks

HEADLINE BOOK PUBLISHING
A division of Hodder Headline PLC
338 Euston Road
London NW1 3BH

Amour Toujours

Suzette after the show

They say that the Casino de Paris in the rue de Clichy is
built on land which once formed part of the estate of the
Abbesses of Montmartre – and stands on the very spot
where the holy sisters had their chapel. But manners and
customs change with the years – the practice of poverty,
chastity and other formerly esteemed virtues has been
supplanted in the rue de Clichy by the pursuit of pleasure.

The young women who are assembled every evening at
the Casino are not there to pray but to dance. Their
bodies are not hidden in decent black and white from head
to toe like nuns – they are stark naked – except for tall
plumes of ostrich feathers on the head, high heels and
black fishnet tights – and a pretty little *cache-sexe* with
gold sequins, where their thighs meet.

For this is the world-famous Casino de Paris, where the
show-girls are stunningly beautiful and the stage sets are
magnificent. Coloured light cascades down over the
feather-bedecked nudes on a slow-turning glass carousel.
The chorus dance and twirl, legs in the air, thighs
gleaming, breasts swaying.

The stars of the show make a majestic entrance down
the grand staircase. The male stars are sleek in white tie
and tails, the female stars fabulous in *haute-couture*

1

creations from the best fashion-houses in all Paris. The audience listen with a fervour worthy of the nuns' original chapel, if ever there was one here – they applaud and cheer, they cry for more. Large bouquets of flowers are rushed up to the stage as the orchestra brings the final number to a close.

Afterwards, after the final curtain-call and the last wild burst of applause, back in her dressing-room the star of the show sat down with a sigh of *Ouf!* and kicked off her spike-heel shoes. At the start of her act she had made a grand entrance down that famous staircase where the great Mistinguett had once trod, proud to be in the Miss tradition. She had sung five songs and the audience adored her. But then, they always did. This was her fourth week at the Casino – and from the first night she had been a raging success.

This was Suzette Bernard the singer and recording artist. She was twenty-four and her ascent to fame had been meteoric. She was tall, with a beautiful face and body, her hair was a glossy raven-black and she wore it in a fringe on her forehead. She was very famous, all Paris knew of her. Newspapers wrote about her in their columns, magazines sent their best writers to interview her. And their best photographers to take her picture.

One was in her dressing-room now, Pierre-Raymond Becquet, but not to take photographs – he was too famous to be employed by a journal, except occasionally. He was there as an admirer.

In the foyer of the Casino a little publication was for sale, it could also be bought at news kiosks. This contained photographs of Suzette and an account of her life – a version of it, that is to say. Mostly the pictures were publicity photographs, but there was a studio portrait taken by Pierre-Raymond.

Simone, the dresser, poured a glass of chilled champagne for Suzette, picked up the shoes she had kicked off, wiped them and put them away.

'You were marvellous, Mademoiselle Suzette,' she said. 'I was listening to you from the wings. They adore you!'

An unkind person might say it was part of Simone Plon's well-paid job to constantly tell her employer she was marvellous and superb and magnificent. On the other hand, it might well be she was speaking the simple truth. Who could say?

Suzette's dressing-room was filled with flowers, they arrived before every performance. There were huge and showy displays in tall baskets standing on the floor, more restrained and tasteful bouquets sat on her dressing-table and on occasional tables in the room. There were some smaller bunches of blossoms bought from street-corner flower-sellers, for which vases had to be found.

A journalist once suggested, gazing round the dressing-room, that these tributes from the less well-off of her admirers must touch her heart more than all the expensive flower arrangements that she received. It would have sounded good in print – a star who loved the little people. Surely they would rush out and buy her records in even greater numbers, these warm-hearted admirers from the suburbs, the all-important *little* people?

To tell the truth, Suzette sang for men who could afford to buy their girlfriends diamond bracelets, sable fur-coats and similar expensive trinkets. Men of importance who travelled in limousines with uniformed chauffeurs, or drove themselves about in open-topped white sports-cars if they were young. Men whose natural habitat was the sixteenth *arrondissement*, in the Avenue Foch or the Boulevard Lannes, in elegant and luxurious apartments.

She had little interest in suburban dwellers, and none at all in the people she had sprung from – the poverty-stricken Belleville mob, the drunks who beat their women and stole their money. It was ironic that they loved her songs as much as the rich.

Alas for the cause of journalism, Suzette was not sentimental – it could be said she was remarkably unsentimental for a young woman of her background. She cast an eye over bunches of roses, carnations, violets, in vases supplied by the management of the Casino. She twisted her diamond bracelet round her wrist – that bracelet was as much her trademark as her jet-black fringe.

'I love everyone who loves me,' she said with a shrug, 'poor or rich, I sing for all of them.'

Her indifference to the journalist's suggestion did not spoil his story – he printed what he wanted, as they do.

Yes, I adore the little people who send me bunches of flowers bought with their hard-earned money, Suzette was made to say in the newspaper story, *the few francs they spend mean more to me than the thousands of francs rich men can afford to throw away on fabulous bouquets.*

While Suzette sipped her glass of champagne, Simone was down on her knees in front of her to massage her shapely calves. The spike-heel shoes she wore on stage were a fetishist's delight – but they made her legs ache after half an hour.

'That flower garden in the corner was delivered when you were on stage,' said Simone. 'The card says it's from Monsieur Gruchy. He was at the first night party, you

4

remember? That's the third lot of flowers he's sent since then.'

'I remember him,' Suzette said, stretching out her long legs, pleased by Simone's skill in massaging them, 'a tall lean man, very charming, dark hair brushed straight back with no parting. He's some sort of aristo, pretending not to be.'

'He wants to take you to supper, any night, you choose.'

'I took some pictures of his wife not long ago,' said Pierre-Raymond, 'a very beautiful woman, lean and sexy as a leopard.'

One thing was certain, every collection of flowers that came small, large or gigantic, had a note attached. The senders were determined to express their admiration. Only the small bunches from fans up in the gallery were without an invitation to lunch or dinner or supper. And bed, that went without saying.

There was someone knocking at the dressing-room door, someone was always knocking at Suzette's door. She wriggled her toes in her sheer black silk stockings and finished her champagne.

'See who it is, Simone,' she said. I hope it's somebody amusing I refuse to talk to boring people tonight. If they insist, they can come back tomorrow. I don't want supper with Monsieur Gruchy – wherever he suggests. And if it's my agent, or that fat song-arranger, don't let them in.'

'*Bien entendu*,' said Simone with a shrug, 'as you wish.'

'With any luck it will be a handsome and interesting man, who is madly in love with me already,' Suzette said.

'With any luck,' the dresser agreed with a grin. She stood up and went to the door.

'No, wait a minute!' Suzette said quickly. 'Wait while I put my knickers on!'

She was not a superstitious person, not in the usual way. But each evening in her dressing-room before she went on stage, she pulled her frock up and took off her knickers. Her admirers had not the least idea of it, but when she sang she was naked under her elegant frock, above her silk stockings.

She did this because she was convinced it brought good luck – and the curious custom dated back to her early days of struggle to become a singer. There had been a turning-point in her life and career when a young man in a roll-top sweater had taken her knickers down in a doorway in Montmartre. She had come up for a breath of air from the cellar where she was engaged to sing. The young man was from the audience – an unresponsive audience which had almost made her despair. He had followed her up the steps and out into the dark and deserted street.

He was a little drunk and he had her against the wall, they said hardly three words to each other. Afterwards she went back into cellar and sang with a new confidence. She had to sing without knickers then, because the unknown young man went off with them in his pocket.

It goes without saying that there was no mention of this incident in the illustrated publication about Suzette. But it was always in her mind – from that day she was certain good fortune was hers if she sang bare-bottomed.

While Simone stood waiting at the dressing-room door, Suzette got up quickly and pulled open a drawer of the make-up table – in it lay the underwear she took off before going on stage. Here was an utterly charming pair of knickers, designed to excite male fantasies rather than conceal the female body. This absurd little creation was not much more than a tiny triangle of cream-coloured lace, the texture open to permit the gleam of pink flesh to show through.

Pierre-Raymond the society photographer sat astride a chair, arms on the back of it, watching with an amused expression the performance of Suzette putting on her knickers. She paid him not the least attention, he was a part of the scenery, so to speak, like the dresser.

Suzette slipped the knickers up her long sleek legs, elegant in black silk stockings, under her frock and up her bare thighs – she settled the tiny triangle neatly over her *belle-chose* and smoothed her skirt down. This she did with a secret smile – for she was wondering, now she had her knickers on, who might take them off that night . . .

Was there an amusing and interesting man at the door, someone who would sweep her off her feet – and into bed? After taking her creamy lace knickers off. Or would it be some dreary person she had no wish to see? In which case she would go home alone and take her own knickers off. She would sleep in an expensive nightdress instead of naked in a lover's arms.

What was fascinating to the press and her fans apart from her very individual style of singing, was Suzette's background. For a singer it was unusual. Only two years ago she was a show-girl at the Folies Bergère! From which it goes without saying that she was beautiful – no plain girls are hired for that job.

For more than a year she was on stage every evening at

the Folies Bergère, her magnificent body naked. Naked, that is to say, but for a head-dress of white ostrich plumes a metre high, set with glittering coloured glass jewels. And a spangled *cache-sexe*, of course, no larger than the palm of a man's hand.

She didn't appear on stage alone. She was one of a dozen very beautiful young women lined up in seductive poses in front of sumptuously painted scenery. It is well known that show-girls are present on stage to add a certain *je ne sais quoi* to the performance – glamour perhaps. And to give the patrons a sufficiency of gorgeous naked young female flesh to admire and fantasise about.

They were also a living back-drop, these skimpily clad girls, against which the big-name stars sang their songs, or danced or told their jokes. And why not? If beauty is the only talent the good God has bestowed on a girl, she must make use of it while it is hers.

But Suzette formed another ambition, she became determined to be a big-name star herself. It was not so crazy an ambition as some of her friends thought at the time. She had seen the best performers on stage at close quarters, not once but night after night, and she was not overwhelmed by their talent, only by the sheer determination they showed – and their self-confidence.

Naturally, that particular thought of hers was not mentioned in the little publication about her that could be bought in the Casino foyer, illustrated with publicity photographs of Suzette bare-breasted at the Folies Bergère. After all, it is better to be prudent when discussing famous names.

But the little publication did explain that Suzette worked at her ambition and took singing lessons to develop a style of her own. Two sentences in the publication covered that part of her rise to fame – though it must be said in frankness, of the story of Suzette's singing lessons and her first appearance as a singer in a dingy Montmartre cellar, that there is material for a book here! A most improper book, if the truth were told.

Eventually, as may be read in the little publication, she achieved her first success as a *chanteuse* in a night club in the Avenue Montaigne. A plushy private club for important people, not a tourist-trap for Americans. There were more photographs to illustrate this part of her life – there were no bare breasts this time, just Suzette looking impossibly glamorous and desirable in an elegant black velvet evening frock. And with a diamond bracelet round her wrist. Real diamonds at last.

She always wore the bracelet – even in bed with a lover – and took it off only in the bath. It gave rise to various speculations by the press and by her fans. The most frequent conclusion was that it had been given to her by her first lover, which was why she never took it off. Needless to say, the conclusion was not true. It had been given to her by a film-producer named Julien Brocq.

He fell in love with her when he heard her sing at the night club in the Avenue Montaigne. He gave her the diamond bracelet the first time they met. He wanted to make love to her and he also wanted to make her a film star. She had no wish to be in movies – much to Brocq's dismay – but because she liked him she let him take her to bed a few times. None of that was mentioned by the publication about her rise to celebrity. Her brief *affaire* with Julien Brocq and what happened to him afterwards when he became infatuated with two of her friends at the

Folies Bergère – that was a *chronique scandaleuse* in its own right.

'It's a Monsieur Dorville,' said Simone from the door, doubt in her voice, 'he says you have been friends for years. Do you know him? Do you want to see him?'

'Robert Dorville?' said Suzette, her finely shaped eyebrows rising slightly in surprise, 'I haven't seen him for ages! Ask him to come in.'

It wasn't really ages since she last saw him, it was a little under two years. When she was a show-girl at the Folies Bergère, Robert had been her lover. She was half in love with him and he was more than half in love with her, in those days. But, sad to say, satisfactory though he was as a lover, there was a serious failing in his character – he had no faith in Suzette's ability to become a star.

He adored her to folly, he cherished her, he cosseted her, he would do anything for her! But whenever she spoke to him about her ambition, he shrugged and smiled and said nothing. From his point of view there was nothing to say. Eventually Suzette gave up trying to make him understand. And not long after that their love-affair came to an end.

Now here he was again, two years later. He strode toward her across her dressing-room in the lively way she remembered – he was the same Robert, handsome, charming, self-assured, sincere, ready to please. And not very bright.

He kissed her hand, he told her she looked marvellous, which was no more than the truth for she was still made up for the stage and wearing the chic black chiffon frock with a short skirt – a *tutu* almost, but better designed – that showed off her legs. On her slender wrist the famous diamond bracelet, glistening when she raised her bare arm for Robert to kiss her hand.

He was some years older than Suzette. Robert would be thirty-one this year, she calculated. But he exercised daily to keep in shape – he was broad across the shoulders, straight-backed and flat-bellied, strong of leg and with a taut behind. In his apartment he owned weights which he lifted and a chest-expander with a spring. He did press-ups daily on the floor, a hundred times! And then a hundred knees-bends! Suzette had always found this routine too comic to watch.

He had brought her a huge and expensive bouquet of pink roses – red roses would have been presumptuous, in the circumstances. He took the chair she offered and the glass of champagne Simone poured for him, congratulating Suzette warmly on her success.

'You have achieved all you predicted,' he said, raising his glass to her. 'You said the day would come when you were the star and not a show-girl. I remember your words so well – you vowed that one day you'd be on stage in a Dior ballgown instead of five metres of feathers and sequins dragging behind your bare bottom.'

'And without my *nichons* hanging out – I remember saying it,' Suzette agreed, a smile on her face. '*Au revoir*, Pierre-Raymond – we are going to talk about the old days.'

The photographer smiled and bowed and departed. He served no useful purpose here. Suzette and Robert talked lightly but what was uppermost in her mind was that Robert had never had faith in her, he believed she was certain to fail. This had cast a chill on their intimate friendship.

Now she had achieved success and he was here to congratulate her – but he wouldn't admit he was wrong. In Suzette's experience, men never admitted they were wrong, not about anything. It was of no consequence to her any more whether Robert did nor not.

In Robert's mind as they chatted was the certain knowledge he had totally underestimated Suzette in the days they were lovers – he'd taken her to be a show-girl and a charming companion but he'd been blind to the determination that drove her. Perhaps it had been deliberate on his part, he had wanted her to remain just as she was.

Simone refilled the glasses with champagne and Robert said he had seen the Casino show three times so far – that included the first night. Suzette's singing was delightful, *ravissante* – and he kissed his joined fingertips and opened them in a gesture of total and fervent admiration.

'You've seen the show three times,' said Suzette, arching an eyebrow, 'and this is the first time you've come backstage?'

'Well,' he said, trying not to sound downcast, 'I knew you'd be surrounded by admirers and well-wishers. It seemed better to wait until there was a moderate chance of finding a moment when you might have time to speak to me.'

'Monsieur chose his time well,' Simone said from the far end of the room, where she was polishing Suzette's street shoes and taking a close interest in the conversation. 'This is the first evening we haven't had seven or eight gentlemen in here calling on Mademoiselle to invite her to night clubs. It's because it's Tuesday.'

The significance of Tuesday was beyond Robert. He

smiled and nodded his agreement, as if he understood perfectly. And it was beyond Suzette also, who decided it was only something made up by her over-protective dresser. Four or five would-be admirers had called earlier, before she went on stage, each trying to be first with his invitation. None had overwhelmed her, she had smiled prettily at all of them and said she was already committed this evening after the show.

That included the persistent Didier Gruchy, absurdly elegant in black tie and dinner-jacket. He was unused to being refused but it didn't damage his self-esteem. He kissed Suzette's hand and bowed and murmured that he might return after the show – in case she decided to change her plans.

'You've moved from the little apartment in the rue de Rome,' said Robert, studying Suzette's long silk-clad legs, gracefully crossed as she leaned back in her chair. Her frock was so short that her thighs were exposed almost to her . . . to her underwear, since she was wearing knickers now. Robert thought wistfully of when it had been his privilege to kiss those superb thighs. And to kiss the Lanvin-perfumed flesh where those thighs met.

'I phoned the day after your wonderful first night to offer my felicitations,' he said, 'but a stranger answered.'

'I moved to a bigger apartment in the Boulevard Lannes,' she told him, 'it is more convenient. So many people want to see me now – I find it very boring. They come in all shapes and sizes, reporters from the press and the radio, song-writers and their representatives, pro-moters, agents – sometimes it's like being in a railway station at rush hour. But Simone takes care of me, she lets no one in before eleven in the morning.'

Robert looked impressed, as well he might – to live anywhere along the Boulevard Lannes required a very considerable income.

'And Gaby,' he said, 'how is she? Do you keep in touch?'

Gaby Demain was a blonde dancer who shared the apartment with Suzette in the rue de Rome. After the *affaire-de-coeur* between Suzette and Robert ended, he had tried to take up with Gaby. He had always been attracted by her, even at the height of his passion for Suzette. Gaby was moderately encouraging toward him and she went to bed with him a few times, more from curiosity than real desire. But it came to nothing, he was pining for Suzette and Gaby was missing a lover who was on the run from the police.

'Gaby shares the new apartment with me,' said Suzette. 'It is idiotic to part from a good friend for the sake of money, there are not so many true friends about. Did you know she's dancing at the Folies Bergère now?'

'No, I haven't been there since you left the show.'

The comment about the shortage of good friends was painful to Robert. Evidently his name had long since ceased to be featured in that particular category. He shrugged imperceptibly, trying not to let his disappointment show.

There was a more pleasing surprise for him when the champagne bottle was empty. Suzette asked him if he'd like to see her new apartment. If he had the time, she added casually. *Yes, yes*, he said at once, certainly he had the time, it would be absolutely charming to see the apartment.

Naturally, what came next did not live up to his

expectations. Secretly he hoped they would ride in a taxi, where in the dark he could slide an arm round her waist and kiss her cheek softly – in the hope of stirring up old memories in Suzette's heart. A fifteen-minute ride through the streets of Paris while he whispered in her ear – who knows, perhaps she would warm to him again?

Alas for Robert's romantic dreams, there was a long limousine waiting for her at the stage-door. And first she made him turn his back while Simone helped her change out of her stage frock – turn his back! He, Robert Dorville, who had a thousand times kissed every centimetre of her beautiful body! Ah, it was too much, it was intolerable!

And when his back was turned, even the mirror was useless to him – he was looking away from it! There was not even a small glimpse of the breasts he had adored for so long! And – more disappointment for his eager heart – when finally he was allowed to turn again and look at her, she had changed into charcoal-grey slacks and a soft white roll-top pullover! And a jacket of black suede! Robert was outraged, but held his tongue – he viewed the casual attire as a direct affront to himself. Evidently she was giving him to understand he was of no significance to her, so she need make no effort to be glamorous.

In the limousine there was no opportunity of slipping an arm round her waist. It was true he and she sat side by side on the rear seat and a glass panel divided them from the chauffeur. In other circumstances, perhaps ... not this evening. Simone sat on the pull-down seat opposite them and chattered to Suzette about the performance with hardly a pause for breath.

The apartment in the Boulevard Lannes, not far from

the Porte Dauphine, had a view over the Bois de Boulogne to the lake and beyond. It had ten rooms and three bathrooms, though Robert was not interested in Suzette's domestic arrangements. The sitting room was long and elegant, it said *star*! very clearly to every visitor who came in and noted the soft white leather furniture, the shiny black-tiled floor, the white goat-skin rugs scattered here and there, the etched-glass table for glossy magazines and illustrated books.

'Cognac and black coffee,' Suzette said to Simone, giving her the suede jacket to put away, 'then you can go to bed and leave us to talk.'

There was no sign of Gaby, though the Folies Bergère show must have been over some time ago. Perhaps she was with a boyfriend.

The apartment impressed Robert. He wondered if he'd be living here now in luxury if he and Suzette had remained lovers. It was an interesting thought, that. But then Suzette asked him to tell her what he had been doing since they last saw each other. In a way that was encouraging, old friends asked questions like that. But half an hour later Robert was still trying to account for the past two years without letting slip anything that could discredit him in Suzette's eyes.

There was so much it was impossible to talk about to Suzette, the *affaire* with Odette, for example, a fashion model with very green eyes. Odette clipped the curls between her thighs into a neat little heart shape. Then there was the difficult *affaire* with Marie-France Lavalle, who fled naked and barefoot down the the Boulevard de la Madeleine late one night because of a silly quarrel. *Good riddance!* Robert had said at the time, but six days later her husband turned up in a shouting rage – accompanied by a lawyer, fully informed of his wife's infidelity.

And less than a week after that fearful incident Marie-France was back. She arrived one morning in a taxi with a suitcase and insisted she'd left her husband forever! Ah, the problems that caused – problems still not resolved.

There was the business with Madame Sassine, not a love affair really, but a long-running and complicated *liaison*. Happily she visited Paris only four or fives times a year. Otherwise Robert felt he would have aged prematurely. A certain sympathy grew in his thoughts for Monsieur Sassine, a man he'd never met and did not wish to meet.

Then there was the *affaire* with Chantal Tessier, the heiress to a considerable business fortune, but disowned by her father. She adored having extraordinary things done to her, she had a large portfolio of candid black-and-white photographs – they showed a former lover actually doing these things to her. She lent these pictures to Robert so he could study them and understood fully what was expected of him.

Only a fool would have mentioned any of this, when invited to tell Suzette what he had been doing of late. Women are jealous of each other, always and eternally, no lapse of time will ever efface the memory of a rival. Robert chatted inconsequentially, he was amusing, he was interesting. And by imperceptible stages the ambience grew friendlier, then warmer, almost touching upon a certain intimacy of understanding.

He and Suzette appeared to be sitting closer together on the soft white leather sofa, though neither of them had budged even a millimetre. But their heads were close, their thighs touched almost, her hand lay lightly on his hand. Robert paused in what he was saying, another moment and his lips touched her throat – it was the lightest of kisses. Suzette's fingers closed on his hand.

The moment was propitious. Robert's free hand crept up under the white roll-top pullover to stroke Suzette's breasts through her thin satin brassiere.

'Ah no,' she murmured, 'I didn't invite you here for that.'

There was no necessity for her to put it into words. He knew what she meant. The balance of power had tipped very decisively in her favour. The initiative was only his if she permitted it. It was true he was the man and she the woman – that could never change – the strong stiff flesh was his, the soft warm opening for it was hers. But . . .

Back in Suzette's days at the Folies Bergère, Robert had been the one who made the decision to spread her on her back and lie on her belly. But now she was a star and he was a supplicant. A supplicant who had disappointed her before. This truth offended Robert's pride. Truth is often intolerable!

On the other hand, he thought he detected a certain ambiguity in this *no* of hers. He'd never disappointed her in bed, she and he both knew that. Perhaps when she said *no* to him she intended to say something like *There is a certain insolence in your hand stroking my breasts, but it is as pleasant as it used to be.*

And indeed, she found it pleasing to let him continue for the moment. If her mood changed, or if Robert was clumsy or became a nuisance, she could push him away and insist he stopped. That was her right, she was in her own apartment, she was not alone. She had reason to believe she controlled the situation. By now Robert had the brassiere undone and both his hands were up her white pullover to fondle her bare breasts.

She knew his ways well from their time together in the past. In a moment she expected him to push her pullover up round her neck and flutter his tongue over the tips of her breasts. That always felt delicious, the way he did it. She lolled on the sofa, eyes half-closed, and let it happen.

He did what she expected, he did it delicately and very well. In his heart there was a fierce exultation – he was remembering the last time he kissed these beautiful breasts. It was in the morning, about nine, after a night with her in the apartment in the rue de Rome. He woke up first and kissed her until her eyes opened. She'd stretched and rolled on her back, her legs moving apart.

There came an almighty crash from outside in the street while he was fondling her breasts and flicking the tip of his tongue over their russet buds. It was nothing of interest, a collision between two cars on the busy rue de Rome. But Suzette leapt off the bed and ran naked to the window to throw open the shutters. She leaned out over window boxes of yellow and blue pansies, to see the accident down below, so giving Robert a perfect view of her superb bare bottom.

Naturally, in his condition of arousal, there was nothing for it but to jump out of bed to go after her. He hurled himself to his knees, arms round her waist, to press kisses upon the round cheeks that confronted him. Then he bit them, making her squirm and giggle and cry *Non, non, chéri!*

In the street a taxi and a blue car had collided. Both of the drivers were out of their vehicles to stand shouting insults at each other and wave their fists in a menacing manner. Taxi and car had slewed sideways at the crash, blocking the road. Scores of impeded drivers were honking their horns, elbows out of open car windows, and were screaming abuse at the embattled pair.

Robert rose to his feet and leaned over Suzette's naked back. His stiff part lay upright along the crease of her bottom, and a sensation of near-ecstasy flooded through him at the touch of warm flesh on warm flesh.

Suzette sighed pleasurably to feel his fingers moving between her parted thighs. She giggled and asked if it troubled him, to make love with half Paris watching.

'They can't see anything,' he said, holding her open while he slid his stiff part into her.

And that was the last time Robert had had the privilege of making love to her. Not because he'd done it at the window, she had no objection to that. But later on that day he'd been idiotically uninterested when she sang for him to demonstrate the progress she was making.

Now here they were together again, almost two years later . . . almost lovers again . . .

Robert slid off the white leather sofa, he knelt to undo the waist-band of her dark slacks. In two seconds he had them right down – and then off, and her shoes. He ran his hands lightly up the length of her black-stockinged legs, from ankles to thighs. He bowed his head with a sigh of purest admiration and pressed his lips in a hot kiss to the tiny triangle of cream-coloured lace that served as knickers.

How well he does it! Suzette was thinking dreamily. *The fact is that Robert has always been my most satisfactory lover . . . he could always make me scream in delight, I'm sure he still can! What a pity he isn't satisfactory in other ways!*

She felt him sliding her knickers down her legs, the touch of his long fingers between her thighs was thrilling beyond words.

'Suzette, Suzette, Suzette,' he was murmuring. 'I never for a moment stopped loving you, *chérie.*'

Between her thighs Suzette was smooth and bare. It became her routine when she was a show-girl at the Folies Bergère to remove her natural curls completely. For her appearances on stage she and the other show-girls wore interesting varieties of the small *cache-sexe* required by decency. Of black leather sometimes, set with rhinestones, of gold lamé or swan's down. The routine of her days at the Folies remained with her still – between her thighs the soft flesh was smooth and bare and gleaming.

Robert helped her out of the white roll-top – except for her black silk stockings she was totally naked now. He took hold of her ankles and parted her legs, the better to stroke in between and kiss the long pinkish lips. She opened her legs wider in an unthinking act of surrender and surprised herself.

But this is absurd she thought. *He is behaving as if nothing has changed in two years – as if he has the right to make love to me whenever he wishes! He has learned nothing! If it were not a catastrophe it would be a comedy!*

Robert's hands slid under her bottom to clasp the soft cheeks while his tongue probed inside her to find her secret bud. She could feel her flawless belly pushing upwards to meet him, soon she would dissolve into ecstasy under the tongue ravishing her senses.

'No, no, no!' she said firmly. 'It is not as simple as you think, Robert.'

She reached down to grasp a handful of his hair and drag his mouth away from her. He stared up into her face in surprise and his expression was so comic she almost laughed.

'Into the bedroom,' she said, and she pushed him off her and stood up. On his knees still, Robert stared up at the beautiful naked body he adored, his senses whirling. He pressed his face to her belly, he put his hands on her thighs – his attitude was one of supplication, he was imploring her without a word spoken to resume her seat on the white leather sofa . . .

'Bedroom,' she repeated, backing away. She turned and marched out of the room briskly. She left her clothes where they lay on the goat-skin rug for Simone to pick up in the morning, slacks, silk stockings, roll-top, provocative little lace knickers.

The cheeks of her exquisite bottom rose and fell alternately to her steps. Robert stared entranced at this marvellous motion of female anatomy, then with a cry he was on his feet to chase after her.

It goes without saying Suzette's bedroom was as modern and as elegant and as opulent in design as her sitting-room. It called out *star* to anyone fortunate enough to be invited in – *big name star*! To some this might have seemed ridiculously ostentatious or even in questionable taste, but Suzette saw no disadvantage in making her position of eminence clear and unmistakable.

Robert had no mind for considerations of this type. His male part was as stiff as a steel bar in his trousers, jerking strongly and demanding relief. The decor was of no

significance, all he could see was the bed, a very large bed,
and Suzette sitting on the side of it. The glow of her naked
body was emphasised by an enormous black fur bed-
spread she was sitting on.

She was looking at Robert with an amused expression
while he ripped his clothes off. She rested her chin on her
hand and her elbow on a raised knee, she smiled when his
stiffness came into view. It strained upwards so eagerly,
that fifteen centimetres of hard flesh he was so absurdly
proud of! And he knew so well how to employ it to delight
a woman – it was almost possible to forgive his idiotic
male chauvinism. Almost.

Suzette was on her back on the sable fur, Robert was
ready at last, naked beside her, raining fervent kisses on
her body, his eager hand fondling between her thighs – an
instant more and he would slide his belly on to hers. Yet a
surprise awaited him at this most tender of moments,
suddenly Suzette was up off her back and on her knees.
Her hands gripped his shoulders and she was pushing at
him. He stared up into her face wondering what she was
doing – and then it was Robert who was on his back.

Not that he knew it, but she had complained once to
Gaby that in bed Robert treated her like a big doll. That
was back in the days when they were half in love with each
other. *What's so bad about that?* Gaby asked. *I adore it
when a man dominates me and does deliciously brutal
things to me.*

But not Suzette. And that had caused her to part from
Robert, half in love with him or not. In the two years since
then their circumstances had changed remarkably. And
now it was Robert who was on his back and Suzette who
threw a leg over him. She took hold of his stiffness and

guided it up into her – she slid down on it, feeling it penetrate deep into her belly. Now Robert was the big doll. He was for her pleasure, not the other way round.

But this was not really how she liked it, straddling a man. A point had been made. She held Robert round the waist and rolled sideways, taking him with her, until he was on top. *Ah chérie!* she heard him sigh in satisfaction, his self-esteem restored.

He had much to learn, this Robert, though he did not know it. Suzette had conceded the uppermost position, but it meant very little, she did not intend to be his living doll. Her legs came up off the bed and her slender ankles locked over his back like a steel trap.

She moving under him, she thrust her loins and belly at him with fast and nervous little strokes, in effect sliding herself along his embedded flesh and back. And he too went into action, to plunge in and out of her, as was his natural right, or so he believed. But her legs were clamped tight around his waist, her arms were round his neck to immobilise him. *Be still, chéri,* she murmured. *Be still . . .*

Robert stared down in wonder at her beautiful face and he saw that her velvet-brown eyes were shining, her mouth was set in a faint smile. What could he do, even if he had wished to escape, held fast in the trap of her superb body? He was the one who lay on top, yes, but she was the one directing affairs. And she used him until he was squirming about on her belly, gasping and drumming his feet on the fur bed-cover.

Her climax came easily and quickly – she cried out in ecstasy and arched her back off the bed, her fingernails digging deeply into the flesh of Robert's shoulders. At some point during her pleasure he bucked violently and spurted his passion into her – but it was of no importance. To be truthful, it went completely unnoticed by her.

She lay limp and content beneath him, while he was trembling and panting in the fading after-throes of what had been done to him, her mind occupied with lazy but very interesting thoughts. Perhaps she might forgive his male chauvinism, perhaps not. But certainly not yet. First he had to learn she was not a doll for him to play with. If he was capable of learning that first easy lesson, then something might be made of him.

If not, then it would be: *Au revoir, Robert, baise-moi le cul!*

Marie-France finds a lover

Robert was fascinated byy the grand style in which Suzette lived now – and he was also envious. The truth was that Robert was in acute financial distress. It was very necessary to find a large sum of money, or the consequences would be disastrous. The only way he could imagine raising the money was by borrowing for he had no profession, no skills, no commercial ability.

When he saw Suzette's apartment on the Boulevard Lannes there was a flicker of hope in his heart – perhaps she would agree to lend him the money. But when he realised the full truth of the reversal of their respective positions – that is to say, at the moment she straddled him on the black fur bedspread – he knew it was impossible to ask for money without discrediting himself in her eyes for evermore.

He thought she would very likely give him the money – for old time's sake – but she would despise him for the idiocy that had brought him to this ridiculous position. And the truth was that he didn't want her to despise him – he was again more than half in love with her. She did not share this tender feeling – their night together opened his eyes.

But it is well known that women's emotions are

transitory and changeable, Robert hoped he still had a chance – therefore this was not the time to ask her for money.

The reason for Robert's plight was the difficult *affaire* with Marie-France Lavalle, some months before. It was Madame Lavalle who became hysterical one night after they had a little quarrel and ran away into the Boulevard de la Madeleine – barefoot and naked! Robert had run after her, in trousers and shirt he had hastily pulled on. But Marie-France vanished into the night and he went back to his apartment saying impolite things about her.

Her clothes were in his bedroom – frock, underwear, shoes and a summer coat. Apricot-coloured little knickers and stockings – although he was angry with her he slept for several nights with her silk knickers underneath his pillow. She didn't come back for them, in fact she made no contact with him at all. But less than a week later her husband was at Robert's door. He was furious, he shouted and waved his arms about. He swore a great deal and he was a very muscular man, an athlete.

He also brought a lawyer with him, a sharp-eyed man in a suit far too flashy to be worn by anyone of taste or distinction. He knew his business, though, and in negotiation he was a predator of the most savage type. He laid down the conditions upon which Monsieur Lavalle would agree to take no further action against Monsieur Dorville in the matter of outraged matrimonial honour.

Naturally, Robert was not fool enough to put his signature on any document without careful consideration, especially if money was involved. He gave assurances he would think things over, he would communicate with the lawyer, whose name was Lafoy, within the week. Robert was playing for time, of course, to put his own lawyer into the contest against Lafoy. It was repugnant in the extreme, the idea of paying money to the idiotic Lavalle for the occasional use of his pretty wife's facilities.

Robert's lawyer agreed. He assured Robert he would dispose of Lafoy and Lavalle and their ridiculous claim. He advised him to do nothing, say nothing, admit nothing – just leave everything in his hands. Needless to say, this legal advice pleased Robert immensely and in his mind he wrote off the dreadful incident. Then a few days later Marie-France was back. She arrived one morning in a taxi, fully dressed and with a large suitcase of clothes.

She said she'd left her husband. She had thought things over, divorce was out of the question for her on religious grounds – she intended to live with Robert. She loved him and she knew he loved her, in spite of how atrociously he had treated her the last time they were together.

Robert went into a total panic. He wanted to phone his lawyer urgently and ask him what to do – but Marie-France had her arms round his neck and was kissing him. Surely it could do no harm to talk to her for half an hour and make her understand that what she planned was impossible. That was the most reasonable thing to do, persuade her to go away. So they sat and discussed their curious circumstances.

But not for half an hour – not for even a quarter of an hour. Marie-France was an extremely attractive woman, she kept saying she adored Robert – and within ten minutes he had undressed her yet again and they were lying on his bed. She stayed all night. It was after lunch the next day before Robert phoned his lawyer to inform him of this new development. The lawyer was appalled.

He was also apprehensive what Lavalle and Lafoy would make of this latest provocation. Robert shrugged and put the phone down and went back to the bedroom, where Marie-France lay naked, awaiting his return . . .

The income which supported Robert's man-about-town style came from his father. Dorville senior owned a factory in the Sentier district north of the rue Reaumur which made women's clothes. His intention was to teach Robert the business, with a view to handing over to him one day and retiring. But although Robert tried hard, the simple truth was that he was utterly incompetent in business affairs.

The old man did what he thought was best, bearing in mind tax considerations – he made Robert a director of the company, with a generous salary, and asked him to stay away from the factory. This suited Robert very well – he lived his own life, he ate in good restaurants, he chased after women, he had an apartment by the Boulevard de la Madeleine. And, being a dutiful son, he dined at home with his father and mother once a week.

It was through his married sister, Brigitte, that Robert became acquainted with Madame Lavalle. They had known each other since their schooldays, Brigitte and Marie-France, and they had remained friends. Brigitte Dorville had married an accountant who, after the honeymoon in Italy, was absorbed into the family business. Sadly Robert did not find his sister's husband, Daniel, sympathetic. He was certain the accountant regarded him as a drain on the company accounts and an unfortunate item to be got rid of when a convenient moment arrived.

How it came about Robert had no idea at all, but Marie-France married a professional athlete – a cyclist, one of the iron men with huge thigh muscles and strong backs for pedalling up steep mountain roads for 5,000 kilometres in the Tour de France. Till now Jules Lavalle had never won, nor his team – but they had determination and stamina and courage, and it was merely a matter of time . . .

Naturally, this Jules was away from home often – for training and for racing in various stadiums in France and other countries.

Marie-France was the same age as Robert's sister Brigitte, twenty-five – a few years younger than Robert himself. She had long golden-blonde hair which hung in soft waves to below her shoulders. When she was listening to a man saying something of interest to her, she had a trick of tipping her head to the side so her free-floating blonde hair slid partly over her face like an exotic veil. It was very effective when she did it, the suggestion was of modesty waiting to be thrillingly ravished.

Apart from that, her face was enchanting because of her pout. Her full red lips were always pushed forward a little, her eyes were half-hooded most of the time – in brief, Marie-France had a sulky expression which Robert found irresistible.

There was an instant attraction between him and her and it came as no surprise to her when he suggested, in confidence, that he would adore meeting her alone – if that were possible . . . And it came as no surprise to him when she agreed to meet him the next day. What did surprise him was being invited to her home. Jules was away, it seemed. She wrote her address on a strip of paper for him and they parted formally, under the eye of Brigitte and Daniel and their other guests.

Later on he was not so pleased when he read the slip of paper and saw that the Lavalles lived in Vincennes, on the far side of Paris. To Robert, whose life was contained within a circle with a radius of two kilometres from the Place de la Concorde, the far side of Paris was as distant and unknown as the far side of the moon. The Place de la Bastille and the Gare de Lyon were to him the limits of civilisation – to go any further eastward seemed strange and foolhardy.

But the mere fact that Marie-France had asked him to her home after informing him her husband was away – it signified she had made her mind up about him. She wanted him as much as he wanted her, and she was honest enough to accept her own desires and to put them into effect. Robert reflected upon this, with pleasure and anticipation, during the long ride on the Metro next day. A taxi would have been preferable, but expensive.

He finally found the address, off the Avenue Daumesnil: it was a fairly old building but a good one. Lavalle evidently made a satisfactory living out of riding his bicycle. There was no lift but the apartment was only one floor up. And after the hardship and inconvenience of the journey from central Paris, a great prize awaited him! Of that he had no doubt.

And he was right – when Marie-France opened the door she was wearing a long loose batik frock dyed in savage reds and greens – it gave her an untamed African appearance. She seemed like a child of nature, a dweller in an exotic land, where men and women kiss and touch noses and lie down together as part of a greeting. And similar improbable fantasies!

It was obvious from the manner in which the thin cotton frock draped itself over Madame Lavalle's breasts and thighs that she wore nothing under it. And her feet were bare, peeping out from the hem of the frock, her toenails lacquered scarlet. Robert's male part stirred eagerly in his trousers and his smile became ever more charming.

Bon chic it was not, this attire of Madame Lavalle's – but to dress this way to receive a visitor indicated a willingness on her part to admit Robert into her intimate friendship.

The moment the door was closed she was in his arms and up on tiptoe to kiss him. In the circumstances, there was little need for words – Robert embraced her and let her guide him into the bedroom. And it was from this moment on that misunderstandings began between them.

Marie-France's eagerness to be embraced by him was flattering to the male ego. But for all that, Robert wished to make a fine impression on her. Without doubt she would let him throw her on the bed and ravage her on the instant, but that would display a shameful lack of *savoir-faire*. Finesse was called for – Robert slipped to his knees in front of her and put his face between her breasts while he put his hands under her long frock and ran them up her legs to caress her body.

She enjoyed that, although it took her a little by surprise. Robert's fingers confirmed what he had already guessed, she had no underwear. He stroked the cheeks of her bare bottom and said pleasing things to her. Marie-France was impressed – and so she should be – Robert had long experience in the arts of pleasing women in bedrooms. She smiled down at him fondly and her pretty face was half-hidden by her shiny blonde hair.

He eased her down to sit on the side of the bed while he took her bare feet in his hands and kissed them. *Oh!* she said, and her mouth pouted in surprise. Robert ran his hands up and down her legs gently, but only to her knees –

as if to memorise the slenderness of her ankles and the fullness of her calves.

She looked at him without saying a word, but in her dark eyes there was an unasked question. Perhaps she was wondering why he played with her in this way. Perhaps she was more accustomed to being kissed and pushed on her back without further ceremony. A hand between her legs to open them and the weight of a man upon her belly without a pause. But Robert was kneeling to her, and caressing the fine curves of her legs up to her thighs – for by now his fingers had advanced beyond the barrier of her knees.

'Marie-France,' he murmured, 'you are so beautiful – the skin is so soft on your thighs! Ah, how smooth and silky it must be higher up . . .'

Her thighs were together, not pressed close, but close enough to make it impossible to continue his exploration. He stood and leaned over her to kiss her until she lay back on the bed and as she did so her knees separated in a most natural manner, and her legs parted slightly – to the fullest extent possible in the frock.

Robert took hold of the hem and slid the long frock up to her neck. He stared in delight at her pale breasts and their darker buds. He had been in the apartment no more than five minutes and nothing was hidden from him. He touched with a delicate finger the shadowed dimple of her belly button – and then the triangle of curls below. They were a pretty shade of light-brown, these curls, not the shiny gold-blonde of her hair.

Marie-France's breasts were fuller than Robert expected on so slender a woman. The rich creamy texture of warm flesh gleamed and contrasted prettily with the large red circles around the firm buds. Robert sighed in pleasure and his stiff part bounded in his trousers.

The manner in which she lay back on the bed was in itself an act of complete surrender. Robert's heart was bursting with joy at the sight of her warm and tender flesh. Her knees were still only a little apart, but he had a perfect view of the fine and silky curls where her thighs joined.

Marie-France's slim body was immensely exciting, he thought. caressing those superb thighs. And in his natural exultation he assured himself that if opportunity ever served he'd lay her on her back to caress her a dozen times a day. He'd have her naked morning, afternoon and evening, to stroke her shapely breasts – and to feel between her legs, of course!

There was something prophetic in Robert's thoughts just then – not that he could know it, of course. From which circumstance may be seen the truth in the well-known advice to be careful of what one wishes for in respect of women – in case it comes true. And when men get what they most eagerly want, often they do not really want it after all.

But such philosophising was far from Robert's mind when he was making love to Marie-France that first time. His thought was only of what he was about to do to her – to caress her body until she went insane with desire and her legs thrashed about, until she begged him to lie on her!

These fervid thoughts whirled in Robert's head because it had dawned on him that Marie-France's enthusiastic responses to his simple attentions could signify only that her husband Jules was unsatisfactory as a lover.

As Robert's hands roamed over her smooth belly, there

formed in his mind a certain conclusion, right or wrong –
the conclusion that the athletic Lavalle was a coarse person
who used Marie-France's pretty body in an insensitive
manner.

To judge by her surprise when Robert began to caress
her with delicacy and finesse, she was more used to being
thrown down on her back by Lavalle and her skirt flipped
up. Could it be this muscular cyclist pushed up into her with
hardly a single kiss? But that was the way of savages, not
the men and women of the most civilised nation in the
world! And if, as was possible in the circumstances, Lavalle
was done in thirty seconds – *Bon Dieu!* – it must seem no
more than a sneeze!

Naturally, while these thoughts were running through
Robert's mind his hands were not idle – he was taking a
proper advantage of the bounties displayed to him. He
stroked her thighs until a nervous trembling of her legs
informed him that he was starting to succeed in his
ambition to drive her insane with desire. His fingers stayed
away from the patch of light-brown curls. That would
receive its share of attention later – when he had her on the
brink of sweet madness.

He knelt at her feet to kiss her belly and he trailed his
mouth up her delicious body to worship her breasts in their
naked splendour. *Ah!* he sighed – there was a lump in his
throat when he saw how pretty they were, so tempting to
the hands and lips, soft and fine-skinned, their buds proud
and pink-brown.

Still she said nothing. She pouted and her velvet-brown
eyes followed his fingers and mouth as they strayed gently
about her body, caressing, kissing, touching, nipping. And
her eyes grew darker yet, as the emotions Robert evoked

36

became stronger, more demanding. Her knees had separated of their own will and her long thighs were open, the brown curls displayed fully. Within those silky curls, soft pink lips gleamed with moistness.

Needless to say, to caress her affected Robert intensely. He felt as if the tender warmth of her bare body was gliding up through his hands and arms into his heart -- he was on fire for her. When at last he touched the long pink lips framed in light brown curls his stiff flesh jumped so hard he thought he'd gone too far and was spurting in his trousers! *Not yet*, he said with a sigh, *not just yet . . .*

With gentle fingers he teased the tender lips – Marie-France was sighing, her eyelids half-closed, an uncontrollable tremor shaking her legs. Her pretty apricot was slippery and warm and soft beneath his fingertips, ready for him, hungry for him – his for the taking! Robert desired her so much that it was almost impossible to hold himself in check. He was on fire – he wanted to wrench his trousers open and slide his hard flesh into her – every fibre of his body was screaming for him to do so.

But he waited, he caressed between her legs with a trembling hand. Her *joujou* was beautifully warm and so soft to the touch, it felt alive under his fingers – he half-expected it to squirm with passion. And now at last words were wrung from her by the overwhelming force of the sensations gripping her.

'What are you waiting for?' she gasped.

'Yes,' said Robert gently, 'yes, *chérie*, yes – but you are so beautiful I feel this immense need to look at you and to admire you. Do you know how very beautiful you are?'

He opened her with two fingers. He touched her small bud with a careful fingertip.

'So beautiful,' he said, as his fingers held the soft lips apart so she was more widely open and accessible and prepared than at any time in her life before, 'let me kiss you there.'

'*Ah non!*' she exclaimed.

Robert guessed she had never been caressed like that before and she was unsure of herself. But her thighs parted wider when he put his head between them, and then wider still when he put the tip of his tongue to her slippery bud. He flicked his tongue over it heard her give a little shriek. Her legs shook wildly – another instant would bring the massive orgasm he wanted her to feel.

She forced his head away from her with urgent hands as if she was afraid of what might happen to her in the next few seconds. He resisted her push, he felt her knees pressing against him in an attempt to close her legs and guard her centre of sensation.

'What are you doing?' she gasped breathlessly.

'Let me kiss you,' he urged.

From her strange reaction to his caress he was sure that when Lavalle lay on her belly and pushed into her for his thirty seconds of pleasure, her response was equally fast. And pitifully brief no doubt, a shallow twitch of her body, a flick or two of minor pleasure between her legs.

She was taking fright. Robert had invoked in her responses of an unfamiliar intensity, sensations so imperious and dominating that she didn't know what to think.

Give her a moment of respite, he thought, raising his head to smile at her in a reassuring manner. His hands travelled slowly upwards from her thighs to her pretty breasts. The buds were as big and firm as berries on a tree. Because he had respected her anxieties and moved his head away from her *abricot*, she became calmer. She murmured a little in pleasure at the soft caressing of her breasts.

'Do you like them?' she asked, almost shyly.

'They are superb,' said Robert. 'They are entirely adorable! I must kiss them . . .'

Hearing no opposition to the suggestion, he straightened his back and leaned forward to press his mouth against each aroused little bud in turn. And when that elicited a contented sigh, he used his tongue on them. From the tremors that ran through her hot body he knew her excitement was growing feverishly. It was acceptable to her to caress her breasts, it seemed, even though the sensations were the same as when he caressed her elsewhere.

In his mind Robert shrugged. Who understood the psychology of women? Later he was to regret he had dismissed the question so lightly. It would have been prudent to examine it a little, and to contemplate some possible answers . . . for example, what would be Marie-France's attitude to him be after he introduced her to an impossible ecstasy she had not before experienced?

She would adore him, of course, she would want to keep him as her lover. And then? Would she be content to endure the clumsy attentions of her husband, *blim-blam, merci madame!* And await patiently the surreptitious meetings with Robert, irregular and secret *rendez-vous* when she would be transported to paradise by his touch? The answer to that question ought to have been very clear to Robert, and also the consequences that might follow.

But as all the world knows, a comedy of life is that when the male part stands stiff at the sight of a naked woman, the brain is switched off like an electric light – it is not required for the time being. Not that Robert's intelligence ever functioned brilliantly, he was well-meaning and good-hearted but dense to a certain degree at the best of times. And when he was kissing a pair of bare breasts, nothing else in the world existed.

While he was nuzzling at her bosom, he was aware her hands were gliding down her own body, down to her belly. Then lower – until she was touching herself between her thighs! A thrill of delight ran through Robert, his male part swelled so hard and big in his trousers that it became almost painful.

He trailed his wet tongue between Marie-France's breasts, then down her belly. His mouth touched her hands, lying between her own parted thighs. He noted how she held herself open with her fingers, to caress herself with a delicate touch.

'Ah yes, yes,' he murmured. He had succeeded in arousing her so hugely she had no shame in stroking herself, she didn't care if he saw her do it or not! She was open and moist as a rose – the velvet petals turned back, she was Robert's to do whatever he wished. She understood very well he was staring at her and she was offering herself to him, offering her secret self, her warm and slippery self . . .

The thought sent shivers of excitement through Robert, his stiff part leapt in desire and delight at the prospect of sliding between the smooth pink lips – sliding all the way into Marie-France's hot belly.

He put his tongue to the lips she held open and pushed it inside as far as it would go. He slipped his hands between her bottom and the bed and he grasped the soft cheeks. She moaned and squirmed under his attentions. Her legs were open as wide as they would go and her loins began to rise off the bed in rhythmic spasms to meet his darting tongue.

With every passing second the rhythm quickened. Then came her long wailing moans and strong convulsions of her body as her thighs clamped Robert's head between them. He felt the hot soft flesh pressed to his ears and cheeks. He could feel the palpitations of ecstasy within her, again, again, again.

'Robert – what have you done to me!' she gasped. 'Oh Robert – it's too much!'

Robert's brown eyes were bulging from his head – he had taken her to the ultimate of orgasmic pleasure, he had woken her body to its full potential. She could never again be satisfied with Jules and his footling little penetrations, she would demand the crashing sensations Robert could give her!

In his moment of triumph Robert felt his belly clenching in a knot of unbelievable anticipation. He cried out and his fingers dug into the soft flesh of Marie-France's bottom at the instant he spurted his pent-up desire into his underwear! Six or seven fast gushes and he sank forward until his cheek was resting on her belly, a warm wetness spreading under his shirt.

At this moment of vulnerability, Marie-France sat up, all her body shaken by tremors of passion. She tugged her long cotton frock up over her head, her hands were on his shoulders and she pushed strongly at him, and he was taken by surprise and had no resistance. His stiff part was throbbing in his trousers and spurting, he fell away from the bedside, on to his back on the carpet. And Marie-France was off the bed and over him, with her knees either side of his head.

Her *belle-chose* was poised above his face, wide open and very wet, as he had made it. He started in delight at her pink rose, its petals fully spread ... but only for a second before she sat down on his face and those wet pink lips were rubbed quickly on his mouth. Marie-France wanted more, she wasn't done with him!

He reached up with both hands to clasp the hot cheeks of her bare bottom. He writhed beneath her and the final spurt of his climax was as intense as the first. *Yes, chérie!* he wanted to cry out, but her slippery flesh was pressing too close upon his lips for him to make a sound.

His ecstasy faded away in small after-tremors of delight but hers didn't falter or fail. It went on – it went on and on. Her wet *joujou* rubbed at his mouth, wringing unending pleasure from him. His surprise turned to amazement. He had released in her a long-dormant passion, a demon of desire she had never known.

Lassitude was overtaking Robert, his hands slid away from her bare bottom, his arms lay on the floor by his sides. He wanted her to stop now, he wanted to rest and be free of her insistent passion. Surely she would stop now? Run down like a clock and stop, till she was wound up again.

He stared up at her flushed face, her mouth hung open and her breath rasped through it. Her eyes were wide open and wild, she was looking at him as if she meant to eat him alive. He put his hands on her thighs and tried to push her away from his mouth, but she was immovable.

He comforted himself with the thought that the human nervous system was unable to tolerate sustained ecstasy on this scale – in another moment she would collapse and sleep for a week! But he was mistaken, she continued to rub her wet softness over his mouth, she moaned and sighed, her body shook in long spasms of sexual pleasure. He'd let a genie out of a bottle where it had been imprisoned. He released it to serve him – but it had grown so huge that he had become the slave and now was serving his master.

With a last wild shriek she reached the end of her impossibly long orgasm. She sat slumped heavily over his face, panting and shaking. Now she let Robert ease from underneath her, climb to his knees and pick her up, an arm round her waist and one under her knees. With a great effort – his knees were still not strong enough for this sort of exercise – he lifted her up and laid her on the bed. He collapsed beside her, still fully dressed.

Marie-France lay very quiet and unmoving, her eyes closed. It had fatigued her greatly, the formidable orgasm he had put her through. A period of recuperation was indicated – Robert sat up and took his shoes off, then his socks, and dropped them on to the floor by the bed. After another moment's thought, he got off the bed and stripped naked, then lay beside Marie-France again and pulled the coverlet over them both.

He intended to doze for a little while. He did not think that Marie-France would want to make love again that day – not after the most stupendous climax he had ever witnessed. But he wanted to talk to her when she had recovered and he thought he would take her out to dinner that evening. Perhaps she would ask him back for the night.

She lay on her side toward him, her face peaceful, breathing calmly. Robert put his arms round her and kissed her forehead. To his astonishment, she rolled on her back the instant that he touched her. She took hold of his limp part to pull him toward her – her legs parting to offer herself to him with unbounded generosity.

'Make me do it again, Robert!' she said urgently.

If her flattering words sounded any warning in Robert's mind he chose to ignore it. Later on, weeks later, when this *affaire* degenerated into a nightmare, a type of Grand Guignol melodrama involving a menacing husband and a slippery lawyer, he recalled the words Marie-France spoke to him in bed. Of course, though these later events were a tale of tragic horror to Robert, to everyone else the circumstances were farcical.

But that was another place and another time. When Marie-France requested him to make her do it again, he did not hesitate. He kissed her ardently and ran his hand over her warm bare belly to feel the smoothness of her skin.

Her hand lay down between their bodies, holding his male part and massaging it to restore its strength. It took only a little time, and then he was lying on her and she was guiding him into her softness. He pierced her with a long hard thrust, his hands kneading her breasts while he slid backwards and forwards with a vigour that made her moan with delight and jerk under him.

She lay with her knees up and her legs spread wide in desire, her soft little belly quaking to Robert's plunging. Her dark-haired head was thrown back on the pillow, her chin pointing up at the ceiling. Her eyes were staring, seeing nothing, not even Robert's face so close to her own. She seemed oblivious to his presence when he pressed his open mouth over hers and slid his wet tongue into her mouth.

In short, Marie-France was in a world of her own – her pretty body might be on the bed and beneath Robert, but her spirit was elsewhere, soaring through realms of indescribable ecstasy. Her orgasm had already started. In a crescendo of whimpering cries, her back arched off the bed and lifted Robert on her belly. And to him it seemed she was completely open to him – demanding that he plunged to her depths!

Her ecstasy went on and on, longer than he had ever imagined any human being could endure such intensity of pleasure. To sustain it for her, he slowed his thrust, to delay the onset of his own crisis. Her head rolled from side to side on the pillow, mouth wide open and gasping, her hot body writhing under him. She shrieked and wailed, she clawed at Robert's shoulders, her legs thrashed at the mattress.

If ever a horse-breaker struggled to remain in the saddle on a wild mare, kicking and bucking beneath him, then this was how it was done ... But needless to say, the arrival of Robert's own climax could not be delayed indefinitely, not with a mad woman under his belly. He slid his hands beneath her to grip the soft cheeks of her rump, he held on tightly while he swung his loins ruthlessly, ramming her with his stiff and throbbing flesh.

The moment was arriving – he thrust hard into Marie-France's soft and slippery warmth, his belly smacking on hers. As her cries grew shriller, his fingers dug into the flesh of her bottom and he spurted his desire deep into her squirming body. It may well be doubted if Marie-France noticed Robert's passionate tribute – she was too caught up in her own massive sensations.

Robert was very pleased with himself for causing her to feel emotions of such intensity – and for so long! His male ego was flattered. He formed the absurd idea that perhaps he could kill her with passion! He had never heard of a woman expiring in an orgasm but it would be interesting to try the experiment. Not that he wanted Marie-France to die, of course – but vanity drove him on and he kept thrusting into her, right to the moment when his male part lost its stiffness and slipped out of her.

Poor Robert! If only he had known what this most interesting encounter with Marie-France Lavalle would eventually cost him in anxiety and harassment, worry and foreboding, loss of sleep, nervousness and fearful concern – to say nothing of pay-offs to her husband and to the lawyers! If he could have known any of that, he would not have pushed Marie-France to the far limit of orgasmic endurance. But regret after the event is pointless.

Even after his soft wet flesh had slipped out of her, she went on wailing and bucking for some time – several minutes, it seemed! But at last the violence of her movements diminished and by stages she became calmer. Eventually she lay limp beneath him, her belly stuck clammily to his. She looked into his eyes solemnly and said, *You made me do it again, Robert . . .*

When they talked he learned his guess had been accurate – her husband the athlete, was totally unsatisfactory in the bedroom. He made love to her very often but only because he believed it improved his performance on the track. It was more an exercise than an act of pleasure – his idea of how to do it was limited to rolling Marie-France on her back and pushing in without much fuss over preliminaries. *I am only another bicycle to Jules*, she said to Robert with an exquisite pout, *he swings his leg up and is mounted, he pedals for ten seconds and the race is over!*

Fifteen minutes later she wanted to make love again and it began to dawn on Robert that he might just possibly have entered into an intimacy more demanding that he expected . . . On the other hand, her eagerness was probably due to

previous disappointment – she would be content to leave
matters to Robert when she came to understand that
ecstasy was hers every time he made love to her. So he
kissed her and they arranged he would pass the whole night
with her after they had been out for dinner.

That agreed, they rested quietly and talked, each
wanting to know everything about the other, as lovers do.
Robert wished to conserve his strength. He had it in mind
to discover how far he could go that night in driving Marie-
France to sexual frenzy – he had made a woman faint with
pleasure once and he believed it should be possible to
repeat that triumph with Marie-France.

Alas for Robert – his plans did not work out precisely as
he intended. At six o'clock they left the bed to shower and
dress, ready to go to dinner. Marie-France made up her
face with great care and skill and she put on a white frock
that made her look eighteen. At the apartment door,
before opening it, she paused to rummage through her
crocodile handbag to see if she had the key. Her face was so
serious, and so charming, while she was looking for the key
that Robert could not resist putting his hands on her hips
and kissing her.

She smiled at him, she pouted at him, she dropped the
handbag and put her hands on his shoulders to return his
kiss. And then her hands slid down his arms, down to the
uncovered skin of his wrists, where his pulse beat. Her
fingers tried to encircle his wrists, her touch light but very
arousing.

'Yes,' sighed Robert, who was hungry, 'when we come
back.'

'Yes,' she agreed.

She lifted his hands and put them on her breasts. Robert

was unable to prevent his hands cupping those soft delights through her white frock.

'Robert – you *do* like me, don't you, she asked. 'I mean, it's not just a quick thrill and *bon soir*, is it?'

'I adore you, Marie-France.'

He said this to every pretty woman he knew, it was expected.

'Good,' she said, breathlessly, 'because I adore you, too.'

In another instant his back was against the closed door – and Marie-France was on her knees on the polished wooden parquet of the hallway floor. Robert felt her fingers at his trousers, she opened them wide and took hold of his warm but limp male part. She flicked it up and down a few times, he heard her chuckle – and his next sensation made his legs tremble and his knees turn weak! It was the hot wetness of her mouth around his throbbing part ... making him grow long and stiff without delay.

Robert's body was shaking continuously. What was happening in the narrow entrance hall of the apartment was exciting him out of all proportion to the actuality, it captured his imagination in the strangest manner. He was ready to bet money Marie-France had never taken a male part in her mouth before – evidently she was a fast learner!

And he, Robert, his moment of crisis was about to arrive. His body was responding so quickly to Marie-France's unexpected stimulation that he knew he was going to experience the fastest climax of his entire life! His stiff maleness felt bigger and harder than he believed possible – and still it swelled thicker and stronger to the lap of her tongue.

'Oh!' he gasped. 'Oh Marie-France ...'

Her neck was bent, her mouth held his quivering part, and her long blonde hair hung like a shining veil all around her head, screening from Robert's sight what she was doing to him. *Oh* he gasped again, and in his mind was the thought that he was about to spurt into Marie-France's shiny-gold hair.

It goes without saying that this *oh* was not a complaint – nor did it mean he wished her to stop what she was doing. It meant *I adore you, Marie-France* or some equally platitudinous phrase.

She was up on her feet suddenly, very close to him, pressing him to the wall while she hitched up her frock and rolled down her knickers. Her face was so close he could kiss her pouting mouth – her eyes were closed and there was a faraway expression on her face.

'You're going to make me do it again,' she said jerkily. 'You won't leave me alone – I don't think I can stand any more . . .'

But her feet were well apart – she gripped his stiff part and steered it straight up into her moistness. Robert said *oh* again when she bucked her belly at him – and this final *oh!* was more like a squeal. Blind ecstasy gripped him, it churned through him until it felt as if his belly had turned inside out.

He pushed upward, his male part a steel ramrod a metre long! Not more than four seconds had passed from when Marie-France spiked herself on him to the frantic spurt of his desire into her.

For him it was over almost at once, but she was hanging round his neck, sighing and sobbing, her belly thumping against him. He sighed and put his arms round her waist to lessen the heavy drag on his neck, waiting for her seemingly endless orgasm to reach its conclusion. He adored her – and there could be no doubt she adored him. It would require all his endurance to stay the pace with her but it would be fascinating to find out how far he could make her go. Time would tell.

And time told other truths, less entertaining. After she left her husband and moved in with Robert, there was the unpleasant business of the threats and the demand for compensation. Naturally, Robert didn't want to ask his father for the money, he had high expectations when Dorville senior retired, and was reluctant to confess to anything to make his father think him a fool. He had to find someone else to borrow from.

All that was in the future – not the distant future – but the future. For the present he was holding Marie-France tight round the waist while she rubbed her pretty body against him in noisy and extremely satisfactory climax. He was very proud of himself – proud that he had the power to reduce a woman to this sobbing ecstasy. Poor foolish Robert.

Gaby discovers a new pleasure

Backstage at the Folies Bergère, Gaby found it easy to make new friends. Perhaps this was influenced by her friendship with the celebrated Suzette Bernard – gossip soon spread the story that Gaby shared a luxurious apartment, in the Boulevard Lannes with the singer. Some shrugged, some winked and many were of the opinion that Gaby was a lesbian. Even when they saw with their own eyes handsome men collect her at the stage door after a performance, their opinion remained unchanged – the fixity of any belief grows stronger in proportion to its absurdity.

Women need women friends, of course, so they have someone who understands when they complain about their men friends. Suzette had filled this role in Gaby's life, and Gaby in Suzette's, for all the time they had shared the small apartment in the rue de Rome – but things were different now. Although they still shared an apartment, the demands on Suzette's time were pressing and days could pass without an opportunity to sit on a café terrace with Gaby and laugh over their adventures.

Another reason why Gaby found it easy to make friends was her cheerful disposition – and because she was beautiful. It is unjust and deplorable, no doubt, but it is a

simple fact of life that beautiful women have more friends
than plain ones. Not only men friends, but women friends
too. There is a kind of reflected glory in being seen in the
company of a great beauty, it is as if a little of the quality
spreads to the companion.

It goes without saying that there were no plain women to
be seen on the stage of the Folies Bergère. Patrons do not
pay money to see plain women expose their breasts and
thighs, not when it is possible to see good-looking ones. Yet
even in this select band of young women, Gaby stood out
from the rest. Partly it was her silvery-blonde hair, but her
slim and shapely body had much to do with it -- her high
pointed breasts, narrow waist and legs that seemed to be
several metres long.

It was not to be considered a surprise when another
dancer at the Folies Bergère assumed the role of friend and
confidant for Gaby. Her name for stage purposes was
Loulou Mongolfier and she was twenty-five, a year older
than Gaby. She was tall, slender, lithe and vivacious, all the
qualities a dancer must possess. Her hair was a rich dark-
brown shade of red and she was an amusing gossip. She had
a boyfriend who made a lot of money selling used cars from
a site on the Boulevard Raspail.

When this boyfriend heard that Loulou's new friend
shared the apartment of Suzette Bernard, top of the bill at
the Casino de Paris, naturally he wanted to make good use
of the connection. A profitable scheme took shape in his
brain – a scheme to sell an enormously expensive limousine
to Mademoiselle Bernard. Not that he had such a vehicle
but, after the way of his profession, he knew where he
could lay his hands on one.

All that is another story, unedifying and ludicrous.

Besides this car salesman, Jacques Colombe, there was another in Loulou's life. This was widely known backstage, although not in detail. But it was generally understood there was someone of importance to Loulou, someone who shared her apartment. Beyond that, all was speculation and rumour. No one had met the mystery someone.

And no one had been to Loulou's apartment, not even the boyfriend Jacques, it seemed. He had not the least suspicion of anyone in Loulou's life beside himself. Her colleagues backstage kept very quiet about it when Jacques was about but indulged their fancy freely at other times. One theory said Loulou was hiding a husband who dare not go out, perhaps he was the hooded Clichy rapist the police were after. Or perhaps he was a victim who lost all his arms and legs in the war or in a terrible traffic accident. Those who held this view claimed that he lay helpless in bed while Loulou fed him daily with a spoon and made love to him astride.

Another version had it that Loulou was ambidextrous and lived with a woman. She was never able to decide which she liked best in bed, they claimed, hard flesh or soft flesh, and so she went with Jacques Colombe as well as the woman who lived with her. A variation of this story claimed that Loulou's lover was a hard-hearted older woman who prostituted Loulou to the car-salesman. For cash, of course. Alternatively . . . but these rumours changed from day to day. None of them were taken seriously.

It was after some time, when Gaby and Loulou had become good friends, that confidences were exchanged. They were sitting one day on the terrace of Le Dome café, under the awning, chatting about old boyfriends.

Gaby made Loulou laugh with an account of her

complicated love-affair with a lawyer named Claude. He was a good-looking man with a thin black moustache, like an old-time film star. He loved Gaby to desperation and showered expensive presents on her, taking her for weekends in luxury hotels. He used to make the most tremendous scenes if he found she'd been out without him – he would rage and bellow for a quarter of an hour, then break into tears and beg forgiveness. By good fortune he made his young wife pregnant and disappeared from Gaby's life.

In response to this tale, Loulou told Gaby about the boyfriend she had before Jacques the car salesman – a stage magician who called himself Maxim the Great. He had wanted her to give up her dancing career to be his assistant.

'I really liked Maxim,' she said, 'so I tried it for a month or two, just to please him. The assistant he had before me must have been forty – she'd been with him for years. She wore corsets and a long evening frock on stage because her figure had sagged. Maxim dressed me in silver tassels and the smallest *cache-sexe* I ever saw in my life. I might as well have been naked on stage!'

'That sounds interesting,' said Gaby.

'He put me in a big glass box and made me vanish, he sawed me in half – that sort of thing. The audience applauded but it was because I was almost naked, everybody had seen the tricks before a hundred times. But you can imagine that, after dancing in some of the best cabarets in Paris, it was boring for me to stand about handing Maxim his props and taking doves from him when he made them pop up out of a top hat.'

'Being sawn in half – didn't you find that interesting?'

'Only the first time,' said Loulou with a shrug. 'When I

knew how it was done, it was boring, twice a night and a matinee mid-week. But I'd fallen for Maxim, so I put up with it. It was his profession and I was loyal to him. Until one terrible day!'

'Don't tell me his saw slipped and he cut you across the midriff?' Gaby exclaimed in horror.

'Worse than that! By chance I found out he was still meeting the assistant before me – the middle-aged one with the drooping *nichons*! He'd been having her for fifteen years and he didn't want to give her up! Twice a week he visited the cheap hotel where she lived and made love to her! Can you believe it?'

'Oh yes,' said Gaby, 'men are comedians, all of them. They do the most stupid things and never know why they're doing them.'

The exchange of confidences continued, Gaby told Loulou about a past boyfriend named Raymond who was more or less permanently stiff and so ridiculously proud of it that he boasted to every woman he talked to, even strangers he'd just met, that he was a five-times-a-night man.

'That could be very embarrassing,' Loulou commented, 'hearing the man you're out with telling someone else what he is capable of. I suppose his idea was to tempt them into trying him out.'

'No, he never strayed while I was with him as far as I know. It was just insane pride, he wanted the world to know.'

'And could he really do it five times a day?' Loulou asked.

'Not very often,' Gaby said with a grin. 'Twice was his usual and three times at weekends.'

'Then his boast was a lie? You can't believe a word men say. Not when the subject is you-know-what. They tell lies to make themselves sound more important.'

'What he did before I knew him, I can't say,' said Gaby, 'but on one occasion he managed it five times with me. Though, to be truthful, after the third time he was so slow he exhausted me – by his fifth time I was half-asleep and didn't care if he could do it again or not.'

'Too much can be as bad as too little,' Loulou said, nodding her pretty head. 'I knew a man three or four years ago – he saw me on stage and fell for me. You'd never believe what he got up to!'

'Yes, I would,' said Gaby.

So Loulou told her about a building-contractor named Poitiers who saw her dancing at the Moulin Rouge and was so taken by her can-can that he claimed he couldn't live another day without her.

He was in his fifties, this Bertrand Poitiers, a plump man, almost bald, who spent money like water and wanted to do the strangest things to Loulou.

'Ah!' said Gaby, greatly interested. 'What sort of things?'

'You won't believe me,' said Loulou, 'I never really believed it myself, even though it was me he did things to! You see, he had lost interest in ordinary love-making, I'm sure he couldn't do it any more. At least, he never did with me.'

'What did he do?' Gaby asked, her eyebrows rising.

'Mostly he wanted to paint me. He'd make me strip stark naked and stand on a bath towel in his sitting-room while he daubed colours all over me.'

'He was an amateur artist of some sort?'

Loulou shrugged.

'The result never seemed very artistic to me,' she said, 'but what do I know about it? He'd paint one *nichon* bright blue and the other green, then red and yellow zigzag stripes down to my *lapin*. Every time was different, you see, according to his mood – he'd do my backside in black and pink spirals, for example, a purple zigzag down my spine, one leg in orange with white rings and the other leg black with scarlet diamonds – crazy stuff.'

'It must have taken hours,' said Gaby, fascinated by what she heard.

'An hour and a half, perhaps, to cover me from head to foot,' Loulou agreed. 'He used very fine brushes that tickled, though he didn't mean to. Sometimes I could hardly stand still because I was giggling so. He got all indignant when that happened, and so I tried hard not to.'

'He saw no comedy in painting you all over?'

'Far from it,' said Loulou with a grin, 'it made him excited. He always left my *lapin* till last and he painted it a shade of mauve, never any other colour. I kept it shaved, of course.'

'And that was the entire performance?'

'By the time he got to the last bit of me, he was red in the face and shaking like a leaf. He'd stand back like an artist to look at his work – he'd be puffing and panting. Then he doubled over and I knew he was doing it in his underwear.'

'Ah, I understand now,' said Gaby.

'After he'd got his breath back he took photos of me with a flash camera,' Loulou informed her with a certain pride, 'every time he painted me, two or three times a week. He had an entire album of photos of me painted all different ways. I've got some, I'll show them to you sometime, if you like.'

'An interesting man,' Gaby said, her head on one side. 'A pity he's middle-aged and fat.'

'He was very good to me,' Loulou assured her. 'He took me out everywhere and bought me anything I asked for.'

The world went past the café terrace, tourists arm in arm carrying guide-books and maps, businessmen in suits with briefcases. A white-aproned waiter hovered near the table where Gaby and Loulou sat, not only because if they ordered something else he could expect a bigger tip – but for the very natural reason it is always pleasing to be close to attractive young women. As these two were indeed attractive – Loulou in a dark green silk summer frock, Gaby in a slim-cut dark skirt and a blue-and-white striped top, open at the neck and with elbow-length sleeves.

After these confidences between them, Gaby felt able to tell Loulou about Lucien Cluny, a gangster she had been in love with two years before. The only other person in the world she'd ever talked to about Lucien was Suzette, her dearest friend. Lucien was a fetishist, as strange in his desires as Loulou's building contractor with his paint box.

Shoes and knickers, these were Lucien's obsessions. He passed much of his time prowling in women's shoe shops and in lingerie departments of the big stores. High-heeled shoes fascinated him – the higher the heel, the more exciting! He was recognised in all the better shops the moment he entered – if another man had appeared so often and been so interested, the management would have sent for a policeman.

But Lucien was a valued client who spent lots of money buying knickers and shoes for his girlfriends – or so he explained it. He was made welcome in the shops he visited, even though it was impossible for him to conceal the long bulge in his trousers as he handled shiny new shoes or tiny lace-edged knickers.

'He made you wear the shoes and knickers he bought?' Loulou enquired. 'Then what? Did he touch you?'

Gaby grinned at the recollection and in a few words described a favourite pastime of Lucien's. He'd take her to his apartment and show her his most recent purchase – perhaps a tiny pair of knickers, a wisp of finest black lace, nothing more. He'd want her to undress completely and put them on, and walk up and down the room while he admired her.

For this he took off his jacket and sat in an armchair in the sitting-room. It goes without saying that Gaby walking about in only her high-heeled shoes and tiny black knickers was a vision to heat a man's blood to boiling. Her long sleek body swayed to her step, but her taut little breasts did not roll about – they pointed pertly upward and forward.

She rolled her hips at each step, so making the cheeks of her bottom slide up and down against each other. It did not require much of this before Lucien was red-faced and panting.

When she thought he was ready, she stopped in front of him to raise a leg and stretch it out straight. Lucien's thighs opened wide, he slid his loins forward on the beige cushion. Gaby put her foot against the bulge in his trousers. She was wearing his choice of high-heeled shoes, perhaps red, perhaps white glacé.

Through the sole of her shoe she could feel his hardness,

and how it throbbed. She pressed, Lucien's mouth opened in a silent shriek of ecstasy, his eyes rolled up in his head. The jerking beneath Gaby's foot announced the spurting of his desire in his underwear. When he removed his trousers it could be seen he was wearing women's knickers, fine silk and lace, soaked through.

'Really?' said Loulou, eyebrows raised. 'Did he wear them every day? Or did he just put them on when he was in the mood for playing games?'

'He always wore women's underwear when I was with him but on other days I do not know.'

Sadly, the money Lucien spent on his obsession was obtained by criminal means, although he had never told Gaby how. The police had been on his trail for years and eventually the evidence was enough to arrest him – but his connections were so useful that he knew of the impending arrest in time to catch an airplane at Orly.

'You really fell for him, the way you talk about him,' Loulou said. 'Would you still be with him, if he hadn't gone away?'

'Probably. But who can say? To be honest about it, I enjoyed his bedroom games. I've never met anyone like him.'

Loulou glanced round to make sure the waiter wasn't too close and lowered her voice to a confidential murmur as she told Gaby about her brother, who lived with her. He was two years older than her and he was, she said in almost a whisper, a *transvestite*, who loved to dress as a woman.

'Just sometimes, I suppose?' said Gaby.

'When he started it was knickers and silk stockings under his trousers, but he gradually got worse,' Loulou explained. 'Now he'll only wear women's clothes, nothing else ever.

It's become an obsession with him. Naturally, I have to buy the clothes for him. He won't leave the apartment except dressed as a woman but he's so timid about it he rarely goes out any more. And when he does, it's only late night, for a stroll.'

'He's left-handed, I presume,' said Gaby with a little shrug, 'but this coyness is unusual. All the transvestites I've met go to Madame Arthur's cabaret in the rue des Martyrs – you must know it. They dress up as girls in elegant evening gowns and go on stage to sing a song and wiggle their bottoms.'

'Marcel would never do that,' said Loulou. 'The place is full of business men from the provinces out for a good laugh at men dressing up as women.'

'I suppose,' said Gaby with a little shrug. 'There were a lot of foreigners when I was taken there. Many of them had no idea what was going on or perhaps they were too drunk to understand – they thought the artistes really were girls.'

'You see, Marcel's not left-handed,' said Loulou, still very confidential and muted in tone. 'He was married for three years to a girl he adored. She left him because she said she couldn't go to bed any longer with a man wearing a nightdress and frilly knickers. He still misses her.'

'That's very sad,' Gaby commiserated.

'Hearing about your friend wearing knickers under his clothes made me think – my poor Marcel may be more of a fetishist than a transvestite.'

'Or both,' said Gaby, 'is he good-looking?'

'Extremely – when he's made up he's as pretty as a girl. And he's let his hair grown longer than mine.'

It was that word fetishist that struck a chord in Gaby's heart. It stirred happy memories of Lucien. She asked if it was possible to meet Loulou's brother. By now Loulou had confidence in her discretion and understanding and said she would speak to him about it.

So it was in this strange way that Gaby was invited, a day or two later, to meet Loulou's brother, the transvestite recluse. The invitation from Marcel, charmingly phrased and written, was delivered by Loulou – who also passed on a certain stipulation of importance. Of importance to Marcel, that is, though to Gaby it was a little amusing. She was requested to remember that the name of the person she was to visit was Marceline, not anything else.

The apartment was not far from the Jardin des Plantes in an anonymous building in an unremarkable street. In fact it was the sort of ordinary home Gaby had once shared with Suzette in the rue de Rome, before Suzette achieved wealth and celebrity. Certainly it was a considerable contrast to Gaby's present apartment in the Boulevard Lannes overlooking the Bois. Finding herself thinking in these terms, Gaby realised how easy it was to become accustomed to living in grand style – but what happened when the music stopped, so to speak?

She and Suzette were the closest of friends, no doubt of that, but in the natural course of things a day would surely arrive when Suzette fell in love and decided to marry. And then there would be changes in the domestic arrangements. But all that lay in the future – there was no necessity to borrow troubles from tomorrow.

While Gaby climbed up two flights of stairs to the apartment, she began to wonder if what she was doing was sensible – or was it a formula for disappointment and regret? She paused with a hand raised to knock on the door and almost turned away. Then with a quick grin and a shrug she rapped briskly. Gaby was adventurous – and some-times scatterbrained, according to Suzette.

The door was opened by Marceline in person – Loulou was out with her car-salesman – a tall and slender figure in a stylish blue and white silk frock. Marceline's hair was long and waved, down to the shoulder and curled under, the same tint of chestnut-brown as Loulou's – no doubt the same dye was used. And, Gaby noted, Marceline had breasts slightly larger than her own, and good legs.

The first ten minutes were difficult, as might be expected in so edgy a situation. Gaby and Marceline sat and chatted warily sizing each other up. They were both conscious it could turn to embarrassment, or that it could decline into the farcical. Both were very pleasantly surprised to find how easy the other was to talk to.

Finally, when relations were established, Gaby was shown the rest of the apartment. As to the bedrooms, there was little to choose between Marceline's and Loulou's, both were decorated to a frilly feminine taste. There were more jars and bottles on the dressing-table in Marceline's room than Loulou's: lipsticks and face creams, nail varnish in seven different shades of red, face powders, three or four different eyebrow pencils, perfume sprays and crystal bottles.

Marceline saw Gaby's interest and asked for advice on make-up – so far Loulou had been the only guide on the subject. And one could always learn from a friend. Gaby smiled agreement and sat Marceline before the mirror. She smoothed away the lipstick, which to her way of thinking was a little too emphatic, and wiped the neatly plucked arched eyebrows. She took the long-handled brush and used it to put a shine on Marceline's long chestnut hair.

Marceline chattered away, watching the mirrored reflection as hair was brushed, eyebrows redrawn, lips painted, fascinated by this personal attention. The chatter began to slow and to fade, and Gaby realised with secret amusement that to be treated as a woman was making Marceline aroused.

So much so that in a while the mounting desire was too strong to repress. Murmuring little words of endearment, Marceline put an arm round Gaby's waist, and pulled her gently down to sit on the blue-and-white striped lap.

'*Oh la la!*' said Gaby with a smile. She was hoping this was the beginning of the marvellous experience she was looking for. A smooth-skinned and perfectly manicured hand was on her knee – then up her skirt, sliding over her silk stockings to touch the soft bare flesh above. A warm mouth pressed in a gentle kiss on her neck, just below the ear. So far, so good.

Gaby had come visiting in a pink linen summer suit and a silk blouse, its two top buttons left undone to show her creamy skin down to the valley between her pointed breasts. She had removed the jacket before starting the make-up demonstration. When she felt the hand between her thighs it occurred to her that this was not the usual overture to seduction. If she was sitting on the knee of any man friend, he would almost certainly have started by putting his hand into her blouse to feel her breasts.

'Just girls together,' Marceline whispered and Gaby giggled.

It was obvious where the centre of Marceline's interest lay – the hand up Gaby's skirt was slipping into her knickers, which were small and flimsy and almost no hindrance at all to exploring fingers. To begin in this particular way raised some curious thoughts in Gaby's mind. But who could be bothered with thinking at such a moment? She parted her thighs a little, to permit those gentle fingers to caress her *joujou*.

'Ah,' Marceline whispered, 'you shave it bare like Loulou – knew you would. So do I – I find it very exciting.'

A fingertip probed gently, making Gaby sigh and then smile a little. What Marceline meant by *so do I* could wait until a more fundamental matter had just been resolved.

'Well, that's one question answered,' Gaby said. 'Loulou told me you weren't left-handed, but I wasn't entirely convinced, not until now.'

The fingertip insinuated itself further and found Gaby's bud.

'The truth is,' said Marceline, with a sorrowful sigh, 'I'm a lesbian.'

That made Gaby laugh and protest it was impossible.

'You must understand that I'm as much a woman inside my skin as you are,' said Marceline, 'although an unkind fate has given me certain parts that women are not born with. To add to my complicated physical and psychic condition, I am strongly drawn to women. And so, viewing the matter logically, I am a lesbian. How else can you explain it?'

'I don't want to explain it,' Gaby murmured, giving herself up to the tremors of pleasure the fingers between her thighs were provoking. Yet for all that, she found she was unable to turn her thoughts away from certain speculations on Marceline's process of arousal. Was there a stiff male part straining and throbbing under the silk frock, purple-headed and engorged, ready to push up between any convenient pair of spread female legs?

Whether that was so or not, it was indisputable the caressing fingers in Gaby's knickers were achieving their purpose. Around her waist an arm held her tight, supporting her as she began to pant in feverish excitement. And an instant later Gaby shrieked in delight as she reached her climax.

When she was tranquil again, she slipped off Marceline's lap, took the hand that had teased her to ecstasy, and led the way to the broad matrimonial bed. Without a word said, they paused and kissed briefly at the bedside, holding hands. An enquiring glance passed between them for a moment, as if to ask *Shall we do this? Are we about to make a mistake?*

Such questions can never be answered in words, of course. The two of them lay down together on the softness of the bed, half-lying and half-propped on an elbow to face each other. As their warm breath mingled, so did the perfume dabbed on throat and on wrists, under the arms, behind the knees. And other interesting more intimate places. Gaby's was Lanvin, Marceline's Chanel.

'You are a woman inside your skin, you told me,' said Gaby, a smile of acceptance on her pretty face. 'Well then, *chérie*, you shall be a beautiful lesbian for me.'

They lay close, their hips and thighs touching lightly while they kissed and caressed with tenderness. Gaby was initiating the love-making, Marceline was passive yet also voluptuous. She sighed -- for in both their minds now Marceline was *she*, a sigh through half-open lips painted prettily. *Her* hand lay on Gaby's thigh, a long-fingered hand with painted nails. But now it made no move to glide higher, to insinuate itself again into Gaby's little silk knickers, as it had before.

Marceline's velvet-brown eyes were half-closed, she lay still while Gaby had her way with her. Was Marceline regretting this strange affair she had committed herself to? Did Gaby's touch bring pleasure or disappointment? As for Gaby, what strange thoughts ran through her beautiful head? What curious emotions was she experiencing as she kissed and fondled this woman-man?

Marceline murmured and sighed, her body jerked delicately to the touch of Gaby's hand under her blue-and-white frock. A long gasp was heard when the fingers caressing her through the sheer silk stocking crept up her thigh. Her long leg twitched at the instant Gaby's hand reached warm bare flesh.

'Ah, *chérie*,' Marceline murmured, 'you will drive me mad . . .'

'All the times I've been made love to,' said Gaby with a grin of pure amusement, 'I know what pleases a girl best.'

In truth, men's hands had been sliding up her skirt to stroke her thighs ever since she was fourteen. And she adored to be caressed lasciviously above her stockings, on the soft and smooth inside of her thighs. And then higher yet, but with finesse, up to the ultimate touch of fingers at the soft join of her thighs.

Who was better qualified than Gaby to cast that familiar age-old sexual spell over another woman? Or cast it over Marceline the pretty transvestite?

After the stockings and the bare flesh, there was silk again, the fine silk of flimsy knickers under her fingers. To preserve the illusion for Marceline, the fragile illusion that

Marceline was a woman – Gaby did not feel any higher. Not yet. The dream could continue for a little longer – the strangely perverse and yet luxuriant dream they were sharing.

Fleshly reality had receded for a moment – it was held at bay by pure enchantment, it was kept at arm's length by an unspoken but shared pretence that between Marceline's legs a loving hand would find the same soft lips as lay between Gaby's thighs. Tender lips that parted – not a length of stiff flesh rearing up to demand access and gratification. The reality was not yet not while the dream held Gaby and Marceline entranced.

Gaby's fingers found silk between open thighs, she felt the trembling of Marceline's legs, she heard her sighs of pleasure. Then Marceline sat upright on the bed and kissed Gaby's mouth, before struggling out of the thin silk blue-and-white frock.

Her eager undressing revealed a black lace corselet, a close-fitting and elegant garment shaped to the body and nipped in at the waist, curving out for the hips. Marceline's body was pale-skinned, as if never exposed to sunlight, a milky white against the corselet's black ribbon-straps over her shoulders – slender and rounded woman's shoulders, Gaby noted.

The corselet's full cups seemingly supported round breasts – Gaby put her hands on them out of curiosity and squeezed. What was inside responded naturally to the pressure, but it was not the feel of warm springy flesh through lace cups, it was a spongy substitute.

She squeezed them harder, smiling at Marceline, knowing there were no pink-brown buds inside the cups to tease – a pity that. No buds to caress with her tongue and make them stand firm, as her own were standing now, aching deliciously to be touched and kissed.

The hollows above Marceline's collar-bones were deep and most inviting. Gaby put her tongue in them, then licked up the long throat to the throbbing pulse in the neck. A shudder of delight ran through Marceline, she whispered wordless endearments. Gaby slid her fingers into Marceline's mouth and smiled to feel them licked by a warm tongue.

She put her hands into Marceline's smooth-shaven armpits, she teased her with gently tickling fingers. The sensual perfume of Chanel 5 rose fragrantly from the warm and tender hollows under Marceline's slender arms.

The corselet ended at the hips, the lacy edge lying across a a flat belly and just concealing the button. From the corselet there depended long black suspenders to support silk stockings. A strip of bare flesh, then shiny black knickers contained the secret of Marceline's sexuality.

And evidently this was a secret which caused Marceline to be discontented. Why the transvestism otherwise? Why this elaborate attempt to appear a woman, to *become* a woman, to *be* a woman?

These speculations had no place just then, reason is never required when passions run high. The pleasure of the moment is of dominant importance – to satisfy hot desires overrides every other consideration, only the urgent need to attain a climactic release has any sway in a mind enflamed. The visual elegance of what was presented to Gaby's glance only added to the pressure – below the ivory lace edge of Marceline's knickers were thighs as gleaming-smooth as Gaby's own.

They were slender and shapely, these thighs – most amiable to the touch of fingers or the kiss of a warm mouth. But they were a little too lean and taut, perhaps, to keep the secret hidden for long from a close scrutiny. Attractive, of course, but they lacked the luxuriant curves of a woman's thighs.

While Gaby undid the suspenders, Marceline lay back, propped on a well-shaped elbow, face pressed to Gaby's superb breasts, murmuring in desire.

'No, turn round with your back to me,' Gaby suggested.

She did so and Gaby pulled the black knickers down until she had bared the cheeks. Marceline bent forward to exhibit them fully. They were small and lean and lacked the fullness and roundness of a woman's bottom, but there were dimples where the spine ended. Gaby stroked the cheeks, she enjoyed the feel of smooth unblemished skin. She ran her fingers up and down the long crease.

When she had stroked Marceline's bottom as much as she wanted and told her to turn over again, Marceline's face was flushed a deep pink – was it the pink of arousal, could it be the colour of shame? Was some residual shadow of masculinity put to shame by what Gaby had just done?

It made no difference which it was, sexual shame and arousal are so close together in the human soul that one changes easily into the other. Gaby slid her hand under the bottom edge of the corselet and stroked Marceline's smooth belly. Whatever emotion had caused her cheeks to redden, she was suffused by excitement now – she kissed Gaby's mouth avidly.

The long dream was fading, its purpose was fulfilled for both of them. Fast-rising sexual arousal that could not be repressed a moment longer was recreating the reality of

male and female. And therefore of male and female parts –
those parts devised by Nature to fit each other, one
to enter, one to receive. Hot desire was transforming
Marceline back from a woman into a man.

She was a *he* now – a slender young man wearing silk
knickers and stockings. Gaby pushed him onto his back to
touch the front of the thin knickers for the first time. She
smiled a little to feel, under her palm, the long bulge of stiff
male flesh.

'*Ah chérie,*' Marceline moaned pleasurably. It was time –
time to move beyond the tender dream and encounter the
satisfaction of fleshy reality.

Gaby slid Marceline's flimsy knickers down – to see what
was there – and the subtle perfume of Chanel reached her
nostrils. Marceline had dabbed it generously in his groins
and over his belly before dressing in his summer finery. Just
as Gaby did herself whenever she dressed to go out,
dabbling fingertips drenched with expensive perfume down
between her thighs and between her small pointed breasts.

There was a second tiny garment worn inside Marceline's
silk knickers. It was a type of thong, made out of a strong
elastic material, shaped to contain Marceline's secret and
conceal it. It was of a sturdy design to ensure his maleness
was kept close tight to his belly, aroused or calm, soft or
hard, so there was nothing to see under a fancy frock to give
away the sly mystery of his sex.

So tight, so implacable – it was like the chastity belts used
in the Middle Ages by mistrustful barons and chevaliers
riding off from their chateau and wishing to guarantee the
fidelity of their wives, Gaby thought.

But what possible chastity did transvestite Marceline
wish to preserve? Evidently he wished to keep prying male

fingers out of his silk knickers for he had been adamant that he was not left-handed. And this she now believed, more or less.

With some difficulty she dragged the confining garment down below Marceline's hips. And up sprang his stiff part, long and strong, purple-headed with passion. There was no thicket of dark brown hair round the base of it, belly and groins had been shaven bare, the shaft and pompoms beneath were smoothly naked. *Mon Dieu!* Gaby marvelled to herself. *To go so far – to imitate a woman! What devotion to a bizarre ideal. This must have been learned from Loulou, who does it for the stage as I do myself. But how incredible!*

And with that, Gaby hoisted her skirt and pulled off her own tiny knickers. She knelt over Marceline, sitting on his thighs to pin him to the soft bed.

Though his true physical nature was fully exposed, Marceline continued to play the female role. He disregarded the evidence of the quivering flesh now standing in plain view. He lay still and waited, his eyes shining and his belly trembling, just like a woman on her back, waiting to be penetrated by her lover.

Gaby parted the moist lips between her own thighs with her finger and thrust Marceline's jerking flesh up into herself. It slid in smoothly, making her quiver with delight. There were no more ambiguities after that entrance into softness, after that reception of stiffness.

In spite of the adopted name, Marceline was a *he* and Gaby was most surely a *she*, although the usual position was reversed and he lay under her while she drove her belly down on his.

But what of it? The parts were joined in incipient ecstasy,

hardness inside softness. Gaby was moving upon him, making his stiff flesh slide in and out of her. There had been no time for her to chat at length to Suzette since the night Robert visited the Boulevard Lannes, so she didn't know yet how he was used in much the same way as Marceline. But for a different motive – he was being taught a lesson in humility. Marceline had no need of that – the pleasure lay in making use of him.

'*Chérie, chérie,*' Marceline moaned, 'I shall love you forever – let me be with you always . . . I devote my life to you . . .'

And well might he say so! To be made use of in this intimate and delightful manner – what triumph! To be exploited sexually by the beautiful dancer Gaby Demain, what a fantastic adventure for him – or for any man! This was a privilege for which half of the males in Paris would fight duels to the death with each other – or perhaps up to the threat of injury!

Gaby slid her shapely loins briskly up and down, enjoying the feel of hard flesh advancing and retreating between her thighs. She had always insisted to Suzette that she adored being dominated by a man, that she wanted the weight of a man's body lying upon her belly, holding her down and helpless, controlling her while he used her for his brutal pleasure.

Perhaps she believed it. Suzette smiled and shrugged when she heard Gaby make this claim. Now she was mounted on Marceline in dominating style, Gaby was thrilled to realise that she enjoyed being the one in control. True, it had been pleasurable when he pulled her down on his lap and put his hand up her skirt – very pleasurable. But what she had experienced then did not compare with what she felt now. He had given her a little orgasm, quick to arrive and soon over.

She felt sure that what was going to happen to her soon would be stupendous! The strange thing about it was there was no man lying on her belly ... and not even Lucien on his knees with his arms round her thighs, gripping tightly, holding her still, his head under her skirt, his hot breath on her bare thighs ... She was doing it to a man – controlling him, using his body for her own pleasure.

'*Je t'aime* ...' Marceline moaned, almost past coherent speech.

'Ah, you will never escape from me, my little transvestite,' Gaby gasped, 'not now I've found out how exciting this is!'

Since the first time she permitted a man to spread her on her back and get between her legs, she had delighted in love-making in many forms, with many types of men. The sensations she felt now, mounted on Marceline's belly, were new and strange. And so immensely exciting that she knew it would be over all too soon.

When she felt her pleasure about to arrive, she paused in her up-and-down movements, hoping to prolong the thrill. Marceline moaned and jerked under her, trying to continue the rhythm. But his legs were held together by the silk knickers and *cache-sexe* down round his knees. His furious jerking achieved nothing, but it tired him quickly and he stopped.

He was panting and breathless when he reverted to the female role – the passiveness he preferred. His brief moments of masculine assertiveness were over and done with, he lay still and waited for Gaby to do what she liked with him. It was he who felt that delicious weight of a lover's body on him, not her. He felt the soft gliding of her moist flesh up and down his throbbing part, he stared wonder-struck into her beautiful eyes, hardly able to breath for the strength of his emotion.

Gaby could not restrain herself another instant – she rode up and down on him eagerly – and she gasped in exquisite torment as her climax hit her. She was crying out shrilly and at each spasm of ecstasy her body jerked as if she were stabbed with a knife. Marceline moaned as he felt his pleasure overflow in his belly and spurt up into the shaking woman sitting over him.

'No, you will never escape me now,' Gaby cried out, incoherent in her long-devastating orgasm. 'I'll have you every day – till you're no good for it any more!'

'Yes!' Marceline wailed. 'Yes, yes!'

Suzette at a party

Suzette was never certain who it was brought Charles
Desjardins to her dressing-room at the Casino de Paris one
evening. Seven or eight admirers were standing about,
champagne glasses in hand, all chattering loudly, no one
paying attention. One was a woman in a man's dark-blue
suit, with a very short haircut and a massive bosom. Two
were journalists, hoping for some fragment of gossip to
print. It was probably Pierre-Raymond Becquet, the
photographer, who had brought Desjardins.

Robert Dorville was there in the over-full room, leaning
a hip against the wall, a slightly displeased expression on his
face. In the past two weeks he had stayed three times with
Suzette in her apartment, had lunch with her twice, and
been shopping with her once. He had to admit to himself
the unfortunate truth that he had not succeeded in
reinstating himself in her affections, not to the extent he
desired.

To be truthful about it, she was treating him as a valued
old friend, called upon to accompany her when there was
no one more interesting available. And invited to pass the
night in her bed on occasions when no one more exciting
had turned up. This was an uncomfortable realisation for
Robert's male self-esteem. But what could he do? he asked

himself with a mental shrug. If he confronted her in his injured pride, she might well raise an eyebrow and tell him not to come back again.

That would be more painful than his present miserable and displeasing position. And for a simple reason – since the night of their reunion, that first night she had taken him to her apartment to make love on the black fur bedspread – ever since that night, Robert had been aware that he was still more than half in love with her.

He tried to be with her as often as she permitted but it was not enough for him. He came to her dressing-room after the show every evening but the dresser did not always let him in. This evening she had admitted him with a smile of welcome – and all these other people as well!

In the middle of this confusion Suzette was half listening to Didier Gruchy, looking absurdly elegant in black tie and dinner jacket. He was leaning over her as she sat at the mirror to put on her diamond ear-studs, and he was smiling and murmuring to her in a confidential manner that made poor Robert jealous and angry. He felt sure that she and Gruchy were lovers, though he had no evidence for this belief.

Suzette was fiddling with her ear-stud and paying little attention to Gruchy's nonsense, signalling in the mirror to Simone to refill her glass and almost listening to what one of the journalists was asking her. All this – when another voice at her shoulder asked permission to introduce Monsieur Charles Desjardins.

'No, alas,' she said in reply to the journalist's question, a sharp-eyed little man in a shiny blue suit, 'I regret there is no one of importance in my life at present – the demands of the theatre are too urgent for any man to compete, however charming he may be.'

It was fortunate the room was too noisy for Robert to hear so distressing a statement, he might well have gone out and thrown himself into the Seine to drown! The journalist scribbled down Suzette's answer and was pleased with it. Even if he guessed it was a statement previously rehearsed with Suzette's press agent to be used on such occasions.

'How truly sad,' said someone behind her. She turned to smile at the man who had been introduced to her, Charles Desjardins. Her smile was polite to begin with, then became friendly – she liked what she saw. He was a man in his thirties, tall and strongly built with very dark hair which was already receding, long-nosed and humorous of expression. He wore rimless spectacles with gold side-pieces – the curved glass caught the light and shone when he moved his head. Suzette noted his expensive dark-blue suit and his thick-woven silk tie.

'For one so very beautiful and so very gifted – and so famous – to admit there is no one of importance in her life,' he said with a lift of his eyebrows, 'this is a national disaster!'

The journalist was lurking, notebook at the ready, hoping for yet more precious quotations. Suzette ignored him.

'You must not believe everything you read in the newspapers,' she said, offering her hand to Desjardins, who bowed and kissed it. Then he explained that in addition to the honour of meeting someone of her distinction and beauty, he had another reason in coming to make her acquaintance.

In brief, he had been requested by the editor of the esteemed and scholarly publication *Les Cahiers d'Autrement*, which as all the world knows is read by every person in Paris with the least pretension to learning or culture, to write him a long article about Mademoiselle Suzette Bernard, *chanteuse extraordinaire*.

This was not a show-business piece, he need hardly say, but an article assessing her as an important cultural icon of a Paris still recovering from the social ravages of the war. In preparation for this, he had bought her records and listened to them, he had been to the Casino three times for her performance. It went without saying that he found himself utterly enchanted.

Suzette bestowed her most ravishing smile on him and asked if he wanted an autographed photo of her. She had several dozen in a drawer for these occasions and he accepted it with a curious smile. Then, seeing how the other admirers were pressing to have a word with her, he excused himself politely and slipped away – but not before inviting her to a party in four day's time.

Suzette thanked him gracefully, she couldn't promise, but she would try to be there if only for ten minutes. Of course, this was only to be courteous, she had no intention of accepting. An average of nine invitations a day reached her, mostly by mail.

'Another scribbler like you,' she said to the journalist when Desjardins had gone. 'Which paper did he say he writes for?'

'You don't know who he is?' the journalist asked.

'So who is he – a politician?'

'No, he's an academic, an intellectual. He teaches history at the Sorbonne and writes books.'

'He thinks I'm an historical figure? Like Josephine?' said Suzette, raising her shoulders in surprise.

'He writes for the intellectual magazines. You're a cultural icon, you heard him say that. I expect he'll send you a copy of the article – but whether you'll understand it, that's another matter.'

'I saw you writing in your notebook – are you going to print what he said to me?'

'Naturally. You're news, he's news – and him and you together that's real news. Are you going to his party?'

'Professors and their wives? That's not for me.'

'There won't be many of those there. Desjardins knows all the right people, there'll be politicians and film stars and famous writers nobody's ever heard of, publishers and booksellers and diplomats from foreign embassies, and rich socialites like your friend Monsieur Gruchy.'

'Yes, I shall be there,' Didier Gruchy murmured, 'I am at all the important parties, of course. The Minister of Culture will look in for twenty minutes, I imagine – we're old friends.'

'Evidently Charles Desjardins is not a hard-up professor from the suburbs,' said Suzette thoughtfully. 'But who reads history books?'

'His books aren't about history. He writes about politics and sex and calls it the history of today. Because he's a professor people take him very seriously. There's more sex than politics in his books, but just enough politics of a scandalous type to make himself seem an expert. Personally, I call it all fiction, he's a romantic novelist at heart.'

'You're one to talk about fiction,' Suzette said with a grin, 'I never believe a word I read in your newspaper.'

'That's different, we're not professors and don't claim to

be – we're simple reporters keeping the public informed of what is going on in the world.'

'You're a very cynical person, Monsieur Dalmas.'

'The worst of it is, Desjardins probably gets paid as much for one article as I get for a month's work. You ought to go to his party – you'd fit in well, if you don't mind having your bottom pinched by intellectuals.'

'Is it any different from having it pinched by businessmen?' she asked, beckoning to Simone to bring her mink coat.

'When a businessman pinches your bottom, you can be sure he wants to take you to bed. But if an intellectual pinches you, it doesn't necessarily mean that at all – he might want to discuss existentialism or Marxism or something equally absurd.'

'Then if I go, I shall watch out for my bottom,' she said.

Naturally, she went to Desjardins' party – where is the woman who could resist, after everything the newspaper man had said. She arrived late and last after her Casino performance. It was after eleven when her shiny black limousine delivered her. It goes without saying that Desjardins' apartment was on the Left Bank, where else would be appropriate for an academic of his renown?

More precisely, the apartment was in St-Germain-des-Pres, and, specifically, it was located in the Place Fursten-berg. There in this enchanting little square of trees, wrought-iron balconies, antique shops, medieval buildings and classical residences, Desjardins installed himself in a large and airy apartment just one floor up from the street.

Perhaps the Minister of Culture had looked in after the Opera – or a film premiere, the opening of yet another art gallery or some other worthy cultural festivity – to congratulate Charles on his birthday and drink a glass of champagne with him. If so, the event was over by the time Suzette made her grand entrance, though the crowd in the sitting-room was undiminished. For the occasion Suzette wore a little black frock of moiré satin – cut straight across and low, strapless, of course, and sleeveless – the hem only a centimetre or so below her perfect knees.

Her jet-black hair was glossy, the fringe on her forehead was neat and crisp. She wore a pendant round her long slender neck, an antique cameo set in dull gold; the fine gold chain was just the correct length for the oval jewel to dangle where the swell of her breasts began. On her wrist she wore the famous diamond bracelet.

There were thirty or forty people in the room, talking and laughing. They all turned to look at Suzette when she came in – another woman might have felt intimidated by so many inquisitive stares but to her it was another audience for her grand entrance. She had the sublime confidence that comes from knowing every man in the room wanted to make love to her. And that every woman envied her – though they would never show it.

Charles Desjardins kissed her hand, glowing with pride and pleasure to think she had accepted his invitation and increased his standing with his other guests, simply by being present. He was dressed in a casually elegant style – a roll-top white silk shirt with midnight-blue jacket and trousers. Informal, perhaps – but very expensive, Suzette thought – and intended as a statement about himself.

There was music playing from a large radio – dance music, but no one was dancing. They were too busy talking and waving their hands in fierce, emphatic gestures to support whatever they were holding forth about. It was that sort of party. Most seemed to be drinking Scotch whisky, a foreign drink Suzette had no great liking for. She asked Charles for a glass of champagne instead.

Didier Gruchy was there, as he said he would be – and not for him the casual style of his host. Didier was elegant and formal as ever in dinner jacket and black tie – it occurred to Suzette that she had never seen him dressed any other way, and that was because she only ever saw him in the evenings at the Casino de Paris.

Presumably Didier changed from day clothes into dinner jacket at some fixed hour every evening. If she ever wanted to see him dressed otherwise, it would be necessary to accept one of his repeated invitations to lunch.

But did she want to meet him *tête-à-tête*? she asked herself – and she shrugged the thought away when Charles took her arm and led her round the room to meet his guests, or at least the more important of them. In truth he was showing her off, in a state of elation at being able to claim so beautiful and famous a woman as his friend.

As far as Suzette could see, there were no film stars, as the cynical journalist suggested, and no actors, but there were two or three politicians, a professor or two and people introduced as writers. The interests of the rest were not clearly identified. Some of them looked well-to-do, some looked very intelligent, a few both – including Pierre-Raymond Becquet, who seemed to be everywhere Suzette went these days.

Didier Gruchy's wife was there. Suzette shook hands with her, in slight surprise. She had assumed Gruchy was married, for the obvious reason that a man of forty without a wife could only be left-handed and in that case he would not hang about in her dressing-room.

Madame Gruchy was a slender and elegant woman in a grey satin Dior frock that cost a great deal of money. A few years younger than her husband, thirty-five, perhaps, her wavy hair was a rich shade of walnut-brown, her nose long, thin and aristocratic. A woman of breeding and composure, a woman to be taken seriously, Suzette considered. Did she know her husband turned up several times a week in Suzette's dressing-room at the Casino, bringing flowers and perfume and bonbons?

If she did, she gave no indication of jealousy or antagonism. Suzette stared into Nicole Gruchy's dark eyes and discerned no glint of dislike, merely a hint of secret amusement. She hadn't been to hear Suzette singing at the Casino, she informed her, a charming smile on her thin-cheeked face, but she had bought all her records and she adored every one of them – *Rue de la Paix* was a favourite of hers.

It was a favourite of everyone's, of course – the song had been an instant hit when the record was released and had lifted Suzette from night-club *chanteuse* to star immediately. It was a simple little song, all her songs were simple and lucid and memorable A woman strolls alone along the elegant Rue de la Paix, in high heels and a silk frock, a pale mink wrap around her shoulders. She looks into shop windows as she walks, in the boutiques and the jewellers she sees pretty silk underwear, beautiful frocks and diamond bracelets. But there is sadness in her heart because she is alone, her lover has left her.

Before Madame Gruchy drifted off to speak to someone else she made it clear she knew all about her husband's infatuation with Suzette. She tapped Suzette on the wrist, with a knowing smile she said, *If you want my husband,*

*mademoiselle, please have him, but it would be courteous to
return him in good condition when you've finished with him.*

'You're too kind,' said Suzette, determined not to be put
down, 'but I have no interest in him, I assure you, madame.
Any impression you have to the contrary is mistaken. I fear
he's one of those sad creatures who lurk at stage-doors
hoping to be noticed.'

'That describes him perfectly,' Nicole agreed, but there
was a catty note in her voice now. 'Men are tedious and
predictable – all they ever want is to get you on your back
and lie on top of you, panting and moaning. To a person of
discrimination this is unspeakably *déclassé*. But perhaps
you don't agree? You have a less rigorous view, no doubt,
in the entertainment world. But Didier may fit in with that
quite well – he is as shameless and absurd as every man I've
ever known.'

Suzette said nothing and Nicole smiled her unamused
smile before sliding gracefully away. *So I've been warned*,
Suzette thought, *who does that insolent woman think she is!*
But she forgot what Nicole Gruchy had said when Charles
steered her to one side and, with great enthusiasm, told her
about the article he was writing for *Cahiers de Whatever*.
She listened carefully, flattered to be written about by so
intelligent a man, but, just as the journalist Dalmas
predicted, she did not understand what Charles meant.

'Do you like my singing or not?' she asked, puzzled.

'The singing is an immediate part of it,' he replied,
pushing his spectacles up his nose with one finger, 'but your
appearance is of parallel significance. To put it simply, we
must examine the concept of. *Frenchness* as it has been
proposed by historians and poets – we need to chart the
tensions which the concept itself inspires.'

'Why?' Suzette asked.

'The question is of fundamental importance – who speaks for a nation's consciousness? Who determines what a nation's identity is – the rhetoric of politicians? Or the icons of the people?'

'You think I am some sort of symbol of France?'

'That is the question to which I shall address myself closely in the article I am to write.'

Suzette shrugged and Charles did what every man at a party does when he has the attention of the most beautiful woman present – he began to court her, the intention being to get her knickers off in due course. But being who he was, his approach to this age-old and well-understood social ritual was over-elaborate.

'I view the extremes of theatrically induced desire,' he said with a solemn grin, 'as experience at the frontier of conscious awareness, and so not entirely dissimilar to Greek tragedy with its empathy for the sacred. This experience of desire may have the potential of opening a way to the numinous, which is beyond experience.'

'Yes?' Suzette said vaguely.

'I am sceptical about all experience,' said Charles, smiling in a most encouraging manner. 'The truth is – I am permanently dissatisfied in the face of ungraspable aspirations . . . I'm sure you take the same point of view.'

'But of course,' she replied, noting that he was looking down the front of her frock. Now she knew what he was talking about. And he noted that she had realised his interest – and he smiled at her. She smiled back at him. He took her bare arm above the diamond bracelet and led her inconspicuously out of the crowded sitting-room.

The kitchen was also crowded – several people were

sitting on the table eating soft cheese spread thickly on chunks of bread torn from a baguette. The bedroom was too obviously occupied – from outside the door they head a woman's voice shrilling with encouragement and a man's voice groaning *chérie, chérie!*

'We mustn't interrupt so very intense a discussion of logical positivism,' said Charles with a grin, and Suzette agreed with him. In the book-lined study, where his important thoughts were set down on paper, two couples sat in the dark at opposite ends of the room, girls upon men's laps, mouths joined in lingering kisses, men's hand up skirts. Charles apologised for putting on the light at a pivotal point in a close discussion of dialectic materialism, switched it off again and withdrew.

These intellectual activities took Suzette by surprise – they would have been unremarkable at a party for her friends of the stage, but by these highly educated people? Dalmas had been in error to suggest a hand on her bottom was only an invitation to a discussion. Charles' hand was on her bottom, he was fondling it affectionately – but not for an instant did she think that he wanted to ask her about literature or politics.

The guest bedroom was also occupied – the key had been turned in the lock to prevent interruption of whatever important theme was under examination there. But there was a small room beyond, a storage room without furniture. Charles led her into it with a quick look left and right to make sure they were unobserved. He closed the door and turned her back against the wall – with a step forward his belly was pressed to hers and he kissed her.

'Is this research for the article about me?' she asked.

'But of course,' he said, removing his spectacles and sliding them into his breast pocket behind the white silk handkerchief there. He felt under her arm for the long zip down the side of her black satin evening frock and slipped it down.

'I suppose undressing me can be considered a form of literary research,' she said, 'but no one's ever called it that before.'

With the zip open, he was able to pull the front of her frock down to bare her breasts, it was impossible to wear a brassiere under that frock.

'Suppose someone comes in and finds us like this?' she said. 'Will academic research be a good enough explanation?'

Charles was stroking her fleshy delights delicately, making their buds stand up.

'No one would believe me,' he said. 'I shall say you dragged me in here because you are crazy about me and can't wait to get your hand into my trousers.'

He hadn't turned the light on, there was no need for it. Only a little illumination came in through a small window. It seemed to Suzette that Charles' eyes, so close to her own, were myopic and unfocused. Without his glasses she guessed he could hardly see her – his pleasure was that of touch, not sight.

'Why are you doing this to me?' she whispered with a grin – the answer was very obvious, but she was curious as to what he would say.

'As I tried to explain,' he said a little breathlessly, 'this expedition beyond the frontiers of sensation may open a path to the numinous.'

His hand was between her knees, she felt it sliding up

under to touch the smooth flesh of her thighs above her stockings.

'Surely,' he continued, 'there have been times in the ecstasy of the orgasm when you have become aware of the infinite silent spaces of the macrocosm and simultaneously of the microcosm?'

'Frequently,' she sighed, wondering what he could possibly be talking about.

His hand moved higher between her thighs until his fingers were in her tiny silk knickers – and it was his turn to sigh and wonder as her secret was revealed. His fingertips caressed the smooth bare-shaven lips between her legs, his mouth hung open a little and his eyes looked totally blank. Suzette moved her feet apart on the uncovered wooden floor to open her thighs – and she felt the tip of a finger easing its way inside her.

'This is more than I could have hoped,' Charles murmured. 'We shall reach the frontier I spoke of without difficulty. Perhaps we shall pass beyond it.'

He had both hands between her legs to slip her knickers down towards her knees, making her accessible to him. She gasped at the sensation of two fingers stretching her open to uncover her bud. And she gasped again when a third finger slid into her, to caress her bud with great delicacy.

While he was thus pleasantly engaged, she undid his trousers from waistband to seam and put her hand in through the slit of his underwear. *Talk is cheap*, she was thinking, *nothing beats action – are these intellectuals up to it? Do they only discuss it – or do they get on with it?*

The size and stiffness of the hot male part in her hand were satisfactory. *Ah bon*, she sighed and shrugged her bare shoulders in the dark. Charles's mouth found hers again in a long kiss as his fingers fluttered between her thighs – she was sighing into his open mouth when he raised her satin frock to her waist.

She was trembling against him in eagerness as she pulled his stiffness out of his gaping trousers and guided it between her legs. She was open and very ready for him – he pressed straight in with a strong straight thrust.

'Ah,' she sighed, 'ah!' to his in-and-out movements. And he, his open mouth over hers to capture her tiny sighs of delight he too sighed *Ah! Ah!* in time with his own deep and rhythmic thrusts.

In Suzette's mind was the memory of being pleasured against a wall in Montmartre not so very long ago – the night her career as a singer was launched. She moaned pleasurably and pushed her loins at Charles to meet his thrusts, he had slipped his hands behind her to clasp the bare cheeks of her bottom.

'Where is your frontier now?' she gasped, she held his face between her hands and stared into his blank brown eyes.

'We have almost reached it,' he said jerkily, moving faster, 'we shall cross it together, hand in hand, *chérie*, we are there now!'

Yes! she thought, *but not hand-in-hand, Charles* as she felt his fingers clenching tightly on the flesh of her bare bottom.

She squealed faintly, bumping her belly against him, and a long spasm shook her like a leaf in a storm. He spurted triumphantly into her, ramming her with his male part so furiously her back thumped heavily against the wall.

When the last kisses and tender words had been exchanged and clothes rearranged, they made their way back to the main party in the sitting-room. It need hardly be said that Charles was as exhilarated as if he had drunk several bottles of champagne, he had made love to the beautiful star! The scepticism he claimed as to the value of all experience seemed to have been effaced – at least for the present.

'And the famous frontier?' Suzette asked, her arm in his.

Being who he was, naturally he was unable to give the obvious answer of a favoured lover. Instead, he replied that she had raised an interlocking series of further questions by her question and these they must discuss in some detail at the earliest opportunity.

The music playing on the radio was one of Suzette's records – her first big success, *Place Vendome*, a charming love-song of a jewellery shop and a diamond bracelet. For some time after that recording she had found it strange and disorienting to hear her own voice coming out of a radio – just as, more recently, she found it strange to see her own face looking at her from street posters advertising the Casino de Paris.

These feelings had soon passed, she accepted she was a star – and therefore not entirely in control of her own destiny.

By one in the morning the guests were beginning to drift away – to night clubs, perhaps, or to someone's bed. Perhaps even to their own beds, some of them, the married ones. Suzette sipped champagne and chatted to whoever looked interesting and sober. Charles had persuaded her to stay the night with him. He had so much to tell her, he said, so much to ask her.

But it was almost two o'clock when the last guests took their leave – a thickset man with short-cut hair of at least fifty, who looked like a retired boxer (but Charles said he was an academic publisher of European distinction) and his companion, a thin blonde girl who had disproportionately large breasts and was obviously not a day over sixteen.

'She's a publisher's assistant?' Suzette asked as the oddly assorted couple went down the stairs to the Place Furstenberg.

'Of course,' said Charles, 'a most important assistant, as I understand it. They say he can't do anything without her.'

'But he can do everything with her, is that it?'

The sitting-room smelled of cigarette smoke and whisky and of too many people. With an arm around each other's waist, Suzette and Charles made their way toward his bedroom. The light was on and the door ajar – Charles gave an exclamation of anger at the sight of the rumpled bed. The sheets had been dragged sideways and hung down to the floor on one side. The pillows were skewed across the bed, there was a smear of bright red lipstick on one of them.

'That perfume!' he said sharply. 'It is her!'

Suzette caught sight of a trifle of lace showing from under a pillow. She tugged it out – and held up a pair of scarlet silk knickers.

'Her?' she said. 'Who do you mean?'

He snatched up a pillow and buried his face in it, breathing deeply.

'Pauline, that *salope*!' he said furiously. 'She has done it deliberately, bringing a man here to my bed!'

He hurled the pillow to the floor and kicked it right across the bedroom. He grabbed the scarlet knickers from Suzette – she wondered if he would bury his face in those too – and with a cry of rage he wrenched at them with both hands to tear them apart. But the silk was stronger than his rage, he achieved nothing except to make himself appear even more absurd.

'*Salope!*' he cried out and flung the knickers to the bedroom floor – and then trampled them underfoot.

'This Pauline is a friend of yours,' said Suzette, disturbed by the outburst and its implications.

'Not a friend,' he said, still enraged, spectacles flashing, 'my former wife.'

'You are divorced?'

'We are separated. I did not invite her to the party but she came with another friend – I could hardly turn her away without offence to him. This is how she persecutes me!'

'It appears this friend does not mind offending you,' Suzette said with a little shrug. 'He discussed – what did you call it, *positive logic*? – with your former wife. Very positively, judging by the state of the bed.'

'I shall make him pay for the insult to me!' Charles said in a tone indistinguishable from a snarl.

'No doubt,' said Suzette indifferently. 'I must be on my way, if you will find my wrap, please.'

Charles looked at her appalled.

'But you promised to stay!'

'That was before I knew you are in love with someone else, an ex-wife! I cannot stay here now.'

'Love her? I hate her!' he cried. 'I despise her!'

'Truly? Then why are you insane with rage when she opens her legs for another man?'

'She can do it with him whenever she chooses, for all I care. She can do it with as many men as she likes! But to persecute me by doing it here – it is too much!'

'As you say, Charles. However, I am leaving now.'

With a long inarticulate cry of desperation he hurled himself at her bodily, his arms wrapped round her waist and he bore her over backwards on to the bed.

'What are you doing!' she shrieked. 'Let me up!'

The expression on his face was set and serious as he slid his hand under her black satin frock and up between her thighs. His knee was between her legs, forcing them apart. His fingers were in her knickers, prising her smooth petals open. It was evident he had no experience of violating a woman. Suzette had grown up in the slum area of Belleville, where girls of twelve were seen as prey by the more degenerate inhabitants. She had learned how to protect herself when she was very young.

Charles was so intent on what he was doing with his hand that he had left himself exposed to a crippling blow – if she jerked her knee up sharply between his legs he would roll in agony on the bedroom floor. But did she want to stop him? she asked herself, as he flipped her frock up and revealed her underwear, a wisp of *crêpe de Chine* chemise so fine as to be almost transparent.

His arms were locked round her thighs to hold her helpless on her back – he was panting with excitement and she felt his hot breath on her bare thighs. And between her thighs, on the bare-shaven smoothness! His tongue touched her, then it was pushing into her, probing, flicking, till she moaned in delight.

Her knickers were looped around her thighs, hobbling her and making it impossible to kick him, even if she wished to do so – she was far from certain now! He was unable to spread her legs enough to slide into her . . . It was Gaby who insisted she adored being dominated by a man – Suzette was the one who objected to being used like a big doll. Yet the deliciously brutal things Charles was doing to her were exciting her. Flushed with passion he hooked his entire hand in her fragile little knickers and tore at them.

It was his good fortune they were less sturdy than the bright red satin ones his ex-wife had left under the pillow to taunt him – his anger had been defeated by those! Suzette's tore much more easily. He ripped them from her body and she screamed loudly to hear the delicate silk tear – the scream was more expressive of sexual arousal than fear.

He pulled her legs up in the air, his hands clamped round her ankles. His trousers were open, he had one knee on the bed and his stiff male part was rubbing on the smooth flesh between her legs. She screamed again as he penetrated her and continued to scream, staccato, to the feel of his male stiffness advancing and retreating between her thighs. This was what Gaby meant by being dominated, to be held helpless on her back and controlled by a man using her for his brutal pleasure.

He was sheathed in her, he held her ankles tight to hoist her legs up and keep her flat on her back while he was plunging and gasping. Her arms were spread wide on the rumpled bed, fingers scrabbling at the sheet. The ex-wife's perfume was very strong, the woman must drench herself with it, she thought.

Without warning, Charles' moment of crisis arrived and he stabbed passionately into Suzette's slippery depths. Her head jerked up off the sheet and she screamed again – her body bounced up and down, rhythmic contractions of her belly gripped his spurting part and massaged it in nervous little spasms.

When she had recovered the power of, rational speech

she smiled up at his red-flushed face and said, 'What a brute you are, Charles. No wonder your wife ran away from you if that's what you used to do to her!' But on that topic he had nothing at all to say, this learned professor who could talk convincingly about anything. And soon afterwards he helped her up off the bed to undress her and himself. Then they were back in the bed smelling of another woman's perfume, cradled in each other's arms.

He kissed her face and stroked her naked back, his male part limp between his legs.

'You are a beast, Charles,' Suzette murmured in his ear, 'you ravished me – I hate you for it,' and she fell asleep.

It was after eleven when they woke the next morning. Charles made coffee and brought it to her in bed, which now smelled of her perfume, not the other woman's – although the other perfume was still there, overlaid rather than obliterated, for anyone who really wished to find it.

She got into the bath while Charles was shaving. He had put on a pair of azure-blue pyjama trousers when he went into the kitchen to make coffee. He had a good back, Suzette decided, as she lay in the scented water and watched him: a straight strong back, smooth-skinned and hairless, although he had an extensive patch of dark chair on his chest. Some men were hairy front and back, she knew – in particular Julien Brocq, the film producer who had given her the diamond bracelet. Julien's body was hairy all over, like a gorilla.

Charles was smooth, except for the patch on his chest and the thicket of curls between his legs. In some inexplicable manner, when she thought about that part of him, the thought seemed to transfer itself into his mind. He turned from his mirror with a grin and stared at her. He wiped his face with a towel and said he would help her. He smiled at her – his smile was charming – took off his spectacles and laid them on the side of the basin.

And there he was, down on his knees beside the bath, wearing just his blue pyjama trousers, a creamy lather of soap between his palms to wash Suzette's breasts, his hands encircling their fleshy fullness with great affection.

'They are very beautiful,' he said. 'If I had known you when you were at the Folies Bergère I would have been madly jealous, just thinking about the other men seeing these charming breasts on stage. It would have made me furious!'

Suzette smiled, her eyes half closed with pleasure, while his sensitive fingertips caressed her until her buds were firm and pointing boldly upwards. The hot water gave her body a glow that was enchanting – breasts, belly, thighs – all of her from neck to toes. Charles kissed her shoulders, his tongue flicked out to taste the lavender bath-essence on her skin.

When he had washed her breasts to his satisfaction he slipped an arm into the water and about her waist to assist her to rise up on her knees. She giggled to note that his hands trembled a little when he took the ivory-white soap and rubbed it over her superbly rounded belly. His hand moved in a slow and circular motion, the circles getting large, until she was covered with a mousse of scented lather from her thighs up to her breasts.

Needless to say, his hand slipped down the curve of her belly to the soft bare flesh between her legs and caressed her there.

'Suzette,' he said, sounding a little confused, though happy 'I have never known a woman like you before.'

His slippery fingers opened the smooth lips between her legs.

'What!' she said in pretended surprise. 'I thought that you were helping me bath before I dress and leave – but this – this has nothing to do with leaving.'

'But you are so very special to me,' he breathed, 'I want to be certain you understand that.'

'Oh, I understand very well that I am special,' she said, a mocking smile on her face. 'I think I found that out when I was fourteen and a boy wanted to put his hand up my clothes.'

'Dirty little beast!' said Charles. 'Ah, if only it had been me! But I was so carefully brought-up that at fourteen I had no idea of the pleasure a girl could give a boy. Tell me, I must know – did this little criminal succeed in touching you?'

'I wanted him to,' she said, almost gasping, her eyes closed and her legs well apart for Charles to stroke her. His rhythmic touch was having its desired effect – little spasms of pleasure shook her belly. He was leaning against her wet shoulder, both hands playing between her thighs – in front and behind together in a tender caress.

'Ah, Charles,' she moaned softly, her loins shaken by passion between the two hands.

'*Je t'adore!*' he murmured, his hands registering her body's little spasms. 'From this day forward I shall assassinate every man who looks at you with intent to defile you in his mind – I will not have them undressing you in their imagination!'

She allowed herself to sink slowly back into the water under the firm guidance of his hands, until she lay full-length, her rounded knees up and apart – at once Charles slipped into the bath with her, sending waves of scented water slopping over the edge of the tub to the floor.

His pyjama trousers clung wetly to him, his stiff male part was standing out eagerly to find its way between Suzette's thighs as he slid on to her belly. Her long legs shuddered and kicked, sending more water spilling to the floor, when she felt him slide into her. Her mouth opened for his tongue to enter, her hands pawed at his face.

'Oh yes, *chéri*!' she moaned through an endless kiss, as his hard flesh thrust in and out, bringing her to a delicate climax an instant before his own.

When her eyes opened at last and stared into his, it was with an amused and yet wary look. She was thinking about what he had said – his wish to kill anyone who looked at her as if he meant to undress her in his thoughts. That was ridiculous, of course. Every man who saw her stripped her naked in his imagination, it was the way men were.

It had no significance – for all Suzette cared they could put their hand in their trouser pocket and stroke themselves while they pictured her beautiful naked body in their imagination. It was absurd to object to the secret fantasies of others, even if she was the principal actor. The only men who were permitted to see her naked body in reality, not in daydreams, were the ones she chose for herself.

Charles Desjardins was a highly intelligent man, a professor, a writer, he surely must understand that much. Or perhaps not – sometimes intelligent people could be remarkably stupid. And it was possible, to judge by his actions last night when he found a pair of knickers in his rumpled bed – that unreasoning sexual jealousy had driven Pauline to leave him. If that was so, then the intimate friendship between him and Suzette would be brief.

He slid off her sideways with a contented sigh and rearranged their bodies to lie face to face, belly to belly in the warm lavender-scented water. He kissed her lightly and caressed her wet breasts, his eyes myopic and vague.

'*Je t'adore*, Suzette,' he sighed. 'I don't want you to go – I can't let you out of my sight now. We'll dry each other and go back to bed, yes?'

'No,' she said softly. 'I have appointments this afternoon. But you can come and get me from the Casino this evening, after the performance, if you want to.'

'And you will stay here with me all night, *chérie*?'

'No,' she said again. 'You can come to my apartment and stay with me all night.'

Were these the first signs of jealousy? she asked herself. This wanting to be with her all the time and not wanting to let her out of his sight? Or just the usual lover's exaggeration? She put a hand into his sodden pyjamas to hold his soft part. When he was totally satisfied he would perhaps become less possessive.

It was easy enough to find out.

Robert is displeased

Robert remembered Madame Sassine only after he'd tried without success to borrow money from everyone else he knew. Not that he ever really forgot her, no man who'd undressed Madame Sassine and got into bed with her could dismiss her completely from his mind – that was humanly impossible. She never permitted any man who'd had the pleasure of her to forget about it.

She was rich, of course, but she was not generous. Robert did not consider her a source of funds, not until he was facing the ultimate disgrace. To take her knickers down was not an exploit to undertake frivolously.

In his financial difficulties he had gone to all his friends for urgent assistance. And this was as embarrassing for them as it was for him. No one likes to be asked for money by a friend and it is worse if related by family. The annoyance is not just a question of calculating if the money can be found, from what source or how quickly. The awkwardness lies in the necessity to invent a reason for being able to say, with great regret, *no*. A plausible reason, that is.

Eventually Robert was compelled to accept that he knew no one who could produce the necessary money for him.

No one that is to say, except Suzette. She had it and she would very probably lend it to him if he asked.

But he didn't want to ask her – it might bring to an end the fragile friendship they had re-established. To lose her again, probably forever this time, was more than he could contemplate. Not that she had invited him to stay with her overnight for two weeks now. . .

He had a dark suspicion Suzette had taken a lover and he was fairly certain it was Didier Gruchy, that damned idiot who hung round her dressing-room at the Casino almost every night of the week. There was something about Gruchy which grated on Robert's nerves. To think of him kissing Suzette's breasts was enough to make Robert grind his teeth together and break out in a temper.

It goes without saying that if any good friend assured Robert his suspicion was entirely wrong and Suzette had no interest in Gruchy, he would not be believed for a moment.

During these sombre moments Robert remembered Madame Sassine. He didn't want to get into bed with her – but when desperation is only a moment or two away, what can one do? He phoned her.

Madame Sassine was a foreigner, from somewhere at the eastern end of the Mediterranean, where women are sensuous, hot-blooded – and demanding. Her husband was a businessman of importance, a cosmopolitan person who found it necessary to travel frequently to Paris and Zurich and London and New York.

His wife went along with him on his endless travels, probably because she was bored at home with her family and preferred to live in luxury hotels and go shopping.

When in Paris the Sassines stayed at the Hotel George-Cinq, in the same suite every time. When Robert phoned, not knowing if they were in Paris or not, he was lucky – he was put through immediately.

Madame Sassine pretended not to know who he was. This was to spite him – months had passed since the last time he had called to see her, she had been in Paris several times with no sign of him. If the truth were told, Robert had promised himself never to see her again after the last encounter. Alas, the situation had altered dramatically.

'Robert who?' she kept saying on the phone, knowing very well who he was. It took all of Robert's tact and patience to soothe her resentment at being dropped abruptly, six or seven months before. It required all his ingenuity to invent a moderately convincing lie to explain his long absence . . .

Eventually he soothed her feelings to a degree – at least she acknowledged him as someone she knew – though she made it sound distant and casual. It was fortunate she couldn't see the broad grin on his face while they were talking. He was recalling some of the many times he'd made love to her in her hotel suite – in the bedroom, in the sitting-room, in the marble bathroom.

Ah, the infinite capacity of women to persuade themselves they are forever in the right – that night is day and white is black and this was a chance acquaintance talking on the phone, almost a stranger. Not someone whose stiff male part she had taken in her mouth often enough, someone whose clever fingers had probed her every aperture, someone who had ridden her on more than one occasion so hard and fast that she had fainted clean away under the intolerable pressure of long-drawn-out ecstatic sensation.

Naturally, when this almost-stranger suggested calling on her that afternoon she found several excellent excuses to refuse. A fitting with her *couturier*, an unbreakable promise to see a friend about to fly to Athens, her husband's imminent return . . . and so on. But Robert was a persistent man, he accepted each excuse in seeming good faith and talked it into nothingness.

In the end, Madame Sassine was driven to the final excuse – a dreadful cold that had confined her to bed for two days now and made it impossible to see anyone except the doctor. Robert must really excuse her, it had been pleasant talking to him, perhaps he would phone again next week . . . and while she was saying this she dropped her voice to a husky croak to lend some credibility to her untruth.

At his end of the line Robert grinned again and said how very fortunate it was he'd phoned that day. His Grandmama's cure for colds was infallible – the old lady had been famous across half of Paris and she cured sufferers the best doctors had given up as dead. He would call round at the Hotel George-Cinq in about an hour with a bottle of Grandmama's cure-all. Running nose and streaming eyes and all other nasty symptoms disappeared rapidly after it was taken and a complete recovery was guaranteed before nightfall.

And while Madame Sassine was thinking of an answer to that he said *au revoir* and put the phone down. It was going to be hard to persuade her to lend him the money his future depended upon, that was clear, but he was hopeful. By nature Robert had always been an optimist. He knew he was attractive to women. The first barrier was behind him, he'd got her to agree to see him. After that it must be possible to get a hand up her skirt. And then – then she would surely wish to assist him in his hour of need.

As a matter of record, Robert's Grandmama had for years had a cure for colds, which she made everyone in the family swallow. Heaven knows what she put in it, the dominant flavour was clove and castor oil. It was effective – taken twice daily it cured a cold completely in a week. But on the other hand, sufferers who didn't take it also got better in a week.

Evidence of that sort made no impression at all on Grandmama Dorville's confidence in her remedy, she insisted that the cold would become worse without it, develop into double pneumonia or worse – and everyone knew what that led to.

It was out of the question to give Grandmama's cold remedy to Madame Sassine. Robert had no idea what went into it and so was unable to make any – and he had no wish to call on the old lady to get a bottle. Besides, it would be impossible to kiss Madame Sassine smelling of Grandmama's medicine – love-making would be too repulsive. It was necessary to improvise – he took a bottle that had contained hair-tonic, washed it out and soaked off the elaborate Pinaud label – filled it with a mixture of cognac and port wine, adding a very generous dash of Amer Picon. He tasted the result warily. It would pass, he thought.

He dressed carefully for the *rendezvous*, it was important to make a good impression. He put on his newest suit – an elegant tan colour – a thick silk tie in pale blue, brown silk socks and highly polished shoes, a jaunty hat with a brim turned down on one side. And with the small bottle of

Grandmama's cold cure in his pocket, he took a taxi to the hotel.

Robert was desperate. He had to pay off Lavalle and his ferret of a lawyer to make amends for Marie-France's unforeseen transfer of her affections from her husband to her lover – otherwise the cyclist was threatening to bring the matter to the attention of Robert's papa. After making the round of his friends uselessly, Robert had borrowed the money from his sister Brigitte's husband.

Afterwards, of course, Robert realised he'd only made matters worse. He had put himself completely at Daniel's mercy. The man had the soul of a calculator, he was just waiting for Dorville Senior to retire so he could take over the family business. Robert had expected ownership to be shared between himself and Brigitte, with Daniel acting on her behalf. But now he'd given his brother-in-law the perfect proof for Papa that his son was incompetent. Why not leave him out of the arrangements? Daniel would ensure he received a monthly payment to live on. . .

To avoid any of this, Robert had to repay Daniel quickly. Then there was no question of incompetence, merely a brother helping a brother out temporarily. Which brought him here to the Hotel George-Cinq, assembling his charm and courage to take advantage of Madame Sassine.

There was a long wait when he tapped at the door of the suite – and this he had expected. Madame Sassine wasn't going to make things easy for him. After a time he heard footsteps inside and the door was opened a few centimetres.

'Ariane,' said Robert, his voice vibrant with enthusiasm.

'It is delightful to see you again. I have brought you the medicine I promised.'

'You must not come in,' she answered throatily, 'I'm sure you would catch the cold from me. Tomorrow perhaps. *Au revoir.*'

But Robert had his foot firmly against the door to prevent it being closed in his face and he brought all his charm to play, flattery, smiles, gestures – he positively radiated *bonhomie*. After five minutes of that, every woman gave in. It required only three minutes to induce Ariane Sassine to open the door for him.

She was keeping up the pretence of having a cold. She wore an expensive silk dressing-gown in orchid pink and claimed that he had dragged her out of her sick bed to answer the door. Robert apologised as he kissed her hand and insisted Grandmama's cure would soon put her right. Not that she returned to bed. She led the way to the sitting-room and sat down on a Versailles-style gilded wood and tapestry upholstery. She took the small bottle he held and unscrewed the top to sniff the contents.

'Be brave,' Robert admonished her, 'hold your breath and take a good swig.'

She had little choice, without admitting she had lied to him about the cold. She took several good swallows from the bottle, gasped and said it was *very* strong. Robert sat down on a chair facing her, his stylish hat in his hand, and chatted of nothing much. It was necessary to get her in a good mood before he approached the subject of money. And it was not long before she allowed her grudge against him to drop – he was too interesting and amusing a companion to dislike for long.

He persuaded her to tell him something of her recent

travels with her husband, though it was obvious she had seen nothing of Rome or London, other than expensive shops and restaurants. She insisted that of all the cities she knew, her favourite was, of course, Paris.

'For the elegant clothes, naturally,' he said with a smile of understanding.

'And for the men,' she said, 'nowhere are the men so charming as in Paris.'

During their conversation Ariane had taken several more sips of Grandmama's medicine. It seemed to be having a satisfactory effect – her croakiness vanished completely, her face took on a healthy glow. And her pink silk dressing-gown slipped away from her crossed legs, to display a stretch of bare smooth thigh.

Ariane Sassine was almost forty, and plump, as the women of the eastern end of the Mediterranean usually become after they have passed their eighteenth birthday. But she spent a lot of money on her appearance. She had very dark hair, perfectly in place in spite of her claim she had been ill in bed. Her legs were shaved, her eyebrows trimmed to a fashionable curve, her upper lip plucked.

Down between her thighs, as Robert knew well, she had a thick dark fleece of curls. It wasn't on show yet, but if her orchid-pink dressing-gown slipped much further, it would be exposed to his view! Naturally, she was aware of what he was thinking as he looked at her uncovered thighs – and fortified as she was by Grandmama's cold cure, she meant to take every advantage of his susceptible nature.

To dispose of any lingering doubt as to whether or not he was stiff inside his trousers, she leaned back with her arms spread out along the back of the Versailles-style sofa, so calmly that Robert found himself staring all of a sudden at the brown curls where her thighs joined. There were not so bushy as last time he saw them. She had clipped them, or had had them clipped by her beautician. It was a neat oval now, her patch of dark-brown hair, pleasing and exciting to look at.

He realised at last that Ariane had in mind what he had in mind and this disconcerted him. He knew her too well to imagine that she had forgiven him on the spot. Ariane was very conscious of the power of money, she knew the advantage it gave her over others. She was a selfish woman and she made everyone do what she wanted. Robert decided it would be prudent to show a little reluctance and try to find out what she was planning. He doubted sincerely if it would be to his benefit.

He murmured that he ought to go and apologised yet again for disturbing her when she was unwell. He promised he would return on a more convenient day, after the cold cure had done its work – and he said other meaningless but polite things.

Ariane listened and said nothing. Her knees had moved apart a little, perhaps a hand's-breadth, and she was stroking the clipped brown curls between her bare thighs. There were rings on every finger of her hand, rings with priceless gem-stones. Robert was trying hard not to stare, he knew his will-power would collapse under the strain of watching Ariane finger herself so casually.

'While you have neglected me for the past year it has been my good fortune to meet a very charming young Frenchman,' she said with a malicious smile. 'His name is Pierre. He is absolutely tireless – *mon Dieu*, he leaves me crushed and half dead.'

She was exaggerating, of course, to annoy Robert and

make him feel small and useless. It was not a year since they met, only about seven months. And Robert's male pride refused to consider the possibility that this Pierre, or anyone else, could perform better than he did. Robert shrugged in disbelief. This was not well received by Ariane.

'Aren't you interested in what Pierre has been doing to me?' she asked, her tone slightly huffy.

'I do not wish to be told,' he said. 'You have made it clear enough that the friendship between us is finished. You've found someone else so there is nothing more to be said.'

'Well, you deserted me,' said Ariane very reasonably. 'It was not precisely a question of choosing one over another.'

'You are a free agent. The choice was yours to make.'

Robert was trying to meet her eyes while he said these harsh words. He was trying to hang on to the shreds of dignity and to remain composed. But it was impossible, her fingers moving over her neat tuft of curls had the effect of a powerful magnet, drawing his gaze to it.

'I see you still want me,' she said with a sideways smile of ill-will. 'The jealousy is plain in your voice, Robert. Can it be possible in some odd way you feel I am deceiving you with Pierre? That would be very comic, in the circumstances.'

'What nonsense! I have no claim on you. You may do whatever you please. It means nothing to me, nothing at all,' he said, a tremulous note in his voice signifying that the words were untrue.

Her legs opened a little wider. The dressing-gown had slid so far open that she was naked from her slippered feet right up to the tied belt across her round belly. And this position exposed the pink lips below the clipped brown curls she was stroking.

'You used to tell me often enough you adored *this*,' she said with a pout, her fingertips gliding over the exposed lips. 'Now you can't even be bothered to look at it.'

Her accusation was completely untrue and she knew it. He had been unable to take his eyes away from *this* from the moment she had uncrossed her legs and parted them. They both knew that, he knew she knew it, she knew he knew she knew it. Robert shrugged again and smiled – why not do what she was inciting him to do? He had nothing to lose, perhaps everything to gain.

'Well,' he said with a smile, 'so you have been deceiving me with another. How often do you let him deceive me?'

It was Ariane's turn to smile.

'I know you suffered when you thought it was all over between us,' she said, 'but I want you to know I have forgiven you.'

'How charming!' Robert said ironically, though his irony was wasted on her. 'You understand me and so you can forgive me for my long absence. And I understand you, *chérie* – I know you have no scruples, you do whatever your nature prompts you to do, you have no regard for anyone. Many would find this abominable, but to me it is an interesting part of your charm.'

He stood up and held out his hand, meaning to take hers and kiss it as a gesture of reconciliation. Ariane let him kiss it, then grasped his hand tightly and pulled herself to an upright sitting position on the sofa, her feet drawn back and firmly on the floor. Looking down from above, Robert could see a long way down inside her silk dressing-gown. In his face there must have appeared some hint of his appreciation of what he observed, for Ariane smiled broadly up at him.

'You want me to take my dressing-gown off,' she said happily.

Truthfully, Robert was not certain what he wanted. Naturally, he wanted to make love to her now he was aroused, he wanted her to *lend* him a large sum of money. But who could say what might be exacted in return? The commonsense part of Robert wanted to to get away from her, to say goodbye and get out of the suite. He was anxious that her enticements might well be a prelude to embarrassment of some sort. Ariane was unreliable, no one could ever guess what she would do next.

In the end the question was settled for him by simple idiotic male pride – which throbbed stiffly in his underwear and overruled the intelligent part of him. Ariane's wanton exposure of thighs and dark-brown curls had raised him to a fever pitch of desire.

'I think I must take your dressing-gown off,' he said, 'for a close look to see if any damage has been done by the person you allowed to touch you – some clumsy clown picked up in a back-street café, I suppose. It's a month or two since I last looked at this and that. Especially *this*.'

'You've had the pleasure of seeing it enough times,' she said archly, as she pulled the knot loose in her belt. 'You'll know what to look for.'

She opened the pink silk dressing-gown wide and leaned back, her body fully exposed, her thighs well apart. Robert wanted to seize the initiative from Ariane – so far the suggestions were hers. He was pleased with his comment about a *back-street clown* – he thought it was very good. It established him as a person of importance and discernment.

While he was congratulating himself on his wit and cleverness Ariane watched him with a faint smile on her face and the pink tip of her tongue protruding. Robert leaned forward to run his hands over her plump breasts and down her belly.

The dressing-gown had come undone, it fell away to lie on the sofa. Ariane had a curious expression on her face, to an extent it was intense interest but there was something else as well – something Robert was unable to interpret. He smoothed her hair back from her forehead and kissed her while he turned his urgent consideration to her expression and what it foreboded.

She smelled absolutely delicious. Up from her warm body arose the expensive fragrance of the essences and soap and creams she had showered with and rubbed into her skin afterwards. Ariane paid careful attention to her face and body. She bought every cosmetic preparation on sale to keep herself young, fresh and unwrinkled, smooth and desirable.

She spent hours every day in the application of these aids to eternal beauty, these elixirs and essences for each part of her – her face, neck, breasts, arms, hands, thighs, knees, feet. An ancient queen such as Cleopatra, relying on asses' milk baths, henna and beehive jelly, would have been astonished by Ariane's preparations.

And in addition there were also the many hours she passed at the hairdresser and with the manicurist, to say nothing of the twice-weekly massage.

To enable himself to examine her more closely, Robert removed his elegant tan jacket and threw it on the floor. Then his tie. He decided it was necessary to be nearer still to the object of his interest, much nearer, and for this purpose he knelt on the floor. Ariane was eyeing the bulge in the front of his trousers and grinning like a well-fed cat about to catch a song-bird.

Her plump thighs were well open as Robert slid his palm down her belly and clasped her between them. And while his interest seemed to be focused on the feel of her brown-haired *this*, she opened his trousers. At once his male part jutted out, pointing up at the sitting-room ceiling.

Take your trousers off, she suggested, 'otherwise they'll get creased if you kneel in them like that.'

'That's true,' he said, 'it would be a pity to go out wearing creased trousers.'

He stood for a moment while he slipped his trousers down – he had to take off his shoes to get them over his feet. He felt it was too comic to stand about in a shirt and no trousers, so off came his cream silk shirt. After that, all he had were his blue socks and striped underpants – and it seemed needlessly formal to retain his underwear when Ariane was naked. Or virtually so. Especially in the curious atmosphere of exploitation and mutual distrust they had established between them. So he removed them. And because it was grotesquely suburban to make love with socks on, he pulled them off too, and dropped them on the heap of his clothes on the floor.

'Have you finished inspecting me yet?' she enquired, when he knelt down naked to confront her again.

'Visually, yes – for the moment,' he said, 'I find no bruises or scratches, no obvious sign of misuse. But might there be any internal signs, I ask myself? There is only one way to know.'

He eased himself forward to press against her broad belly. At once her legs opened very widely indeed – one

116

long strong push and he had her impaled on his fifteen centimetres of stiff flesh. It was evident that she was as aroused as he was.

'Five minutes ago you weren't interested in me,' she remarked as she stroked his face thoughtfully.

'But I was! And now we're good friends again, I have decided to change my plans and stay with you, *chérie*, all afternoon. Or as long as you permit me, depending on when you expect Monsieur Sassine to return.'

Her arms clasped him to her scented breasts, her feet rose up from the floor, her legs twined over his back to clasp him very firmly to her plump belly.

'I'm so pleased we're friends again,' she sighed while he was riding her with nonchalant ease. 'I've always adored you, dear Robert, impossible though you can be at times.'

'Impossible – me?' he murmured as he slid in and out of her warm flesh with the confidence of familiarity. 'If you say so.'

'But of course you are,' she sighed, her soft belly quivering to little tremors of sensation running through her, 'you leave me alone for months and then arrive on the least convenient day possible. But that's typical of you, *chéri*. Not that I mind too much, I know you too well to expect you to make things easy.'

'Not so many months,' Robert gasped, thrusting into her with the vigour of a true lover, 'and you knew I would return.'

'It seems like a very long time,' she said breathlessly, 'too long, *chéri*, much too long! I am a woman – I need love!'

'Yes,' he panted, 'you need delicious things doing to you all the time, every day, you've told me so yourself often enough!'

He was thrusting into her with short sharp strokes now, close to the moment of crisis.

'Always!' she murmured, her belly shaking under him, 'always *chéri*! Ah, how I adore it when you do these brutal and lovely things to my *petite chatte*.'

'I'm going to turn her inside out,' he gasped and his passion jolted into her in long ecstatic spasms. Her babbling became a long cry of delight and her bottom heaved up off the cushion as the delirium of release took her.

Later, when the power of rational thought returned to him, he recalled something she had said. He was lying on her belly, her head between his hands while he kissed her several dozen times. He was wondering how much longer he should wait before bringing up the somewhat delicate topic of a large loan.

'Why is today inconvenient?' he asked. 'Is Monsieur Sassine expected back soon? If so, I must leave at once.'

'No,' she soothed him, a hand stroking his bare chest, 'he is in Marseilles for business and will not be back today at all.'

'Good, good,' and Robert's anxiety disappeared.

'But suppose he found out you'd been here,' she said somewhat coyly, 'what would he say if he guessed you'd done this to me? What could I possibly say to him?

'You would have to tell him the truth,' said Robert, sounding very sincere. He was brave now he knew there was no chance of a confrontation with an enraged husband. He smiled at Ariane and fondled her breasts.

'No!' she exclaimed in pretended panic. 'He'd be furious if he ever found out I'd let you do things to my *petite chatte*. He wants her all to himself, he's a hot-blooded man!'

A sudden thought struck Robert – not a clever thought, but in his difficult circumstances it was a way out of his most urgent problem.

'Leave him!' he said. 'Come and live with me, *chérie*, let me love you night and day.'

She would have a lot of money if she left Sassine, and Robert believed he could influence her emotions to the point of giving him the money necessary to pay off what he owed. Get her to his own apartment, have her on her back for two or three nights and days with her legs apart – love her into imbecility and ask for the money when she was too far gone to know what he was talking about!

'Robert!' she said, 'I could never leave him! Not even for you, *chéri*! But what a marvellous suggestion – I shall cherish it always!'

'What a pity!' said Robert, and he eased out of the wet grip of her flesh now he was limp again, 'But I adore you, Ariane, I want to be with you day and night, I want to be drunk with love-making! I believed you knew how I felt, why did you lead me on if you did not feel the same about me?'

Ariane crossed her legs and looked at him in an odd manner, a malicious little smile hovering about her red-rouged lips.

'Lead you on?' she said, 'I led you on? I did no such thing – you were the one down on his knees interfering with me while I was trying to conduct a sensible discussion. I only wanted to explain the impossibility of anything between us now I have met Pierre. You weren't listening. I don't believe that you heard a single word I said – you were too busy grinning and pulling my dressing-gown off!'

'That's not true!' Robert said. 'You know it's not. You

were sprawled on the sofa with your legs apart, touching yourself to make me excited! You'd decided you were going to make me do it to you – you were playing cat and mouse with me!'

Then it occurred to him this was not the best way to go about persuading her to lend him a lot of money. He smiled at her to take the accusation out of his words and kissed her warm belly.

'And I loved every second of it,' he added, to make sure that she understood he had only been teasing, 'I would love to do it again!'

Ariane put her hand between his legs to hold his softness and stroke it in an encouraging manner.

'Little monster!' she said, affectionately. 'Do you know you have ruined my *petite chatte* by your brutality. The poor little thing – she can tolerate no more, she must rest.'

'Ah, so warm, so wet,' he murmured, caressing those soft lips in her neatly clipped oval of dark-brown hair, 'so adorable!'

'Maybe she can do without her rest,' said Ariane, never one to put off a pleasure when it was offered, 'come into the bedroom with me and we can lie down properly.'

Robert knew the bedroom of the suite well from past visits when her husband was absent. The broad bed on which many a time he had ridden her to squealing ecstasy – there it stood, ready and waiting. And this was the same bed on which she made Sassine do it to her every night – according to her account.

Truth to tell, the marital relations of the Sassines were too mysterious for Robert to understand. Ariane said they made love every night without fail – she insisted on it as her right as a wife. But she also claimed that Sassine went off in the daytime with very young blonde French girls. He liked sixteen-year-olds. And she herself had lovers – Robert had been that more or less, for some months before he tired of her difficult personality.

Before him there were gigolos, he knew that because when they first met she had mistaken him for a paid man and tried to give him money. Now there was this Pierre person – a gigolo for sure who took the cash and gave her satisfaction two or three times a week. She had told too many lies about her relations with her husband for any sensible view to be reached – that was Robert's eventual verdict. In the meantime, there was the bed. . .

Ariane kicked off pink velvet slippers trimmed with marabou feathers while Robert undressed her – which took two seconds because all she had on was the orchid-pink dressing gown, and that hung loose from her fleshy shoulders. He held her naked waist between his hands and kissed her heavy breasts, flicking their buds with his tongue. After a moment or two of that she flung herself on the bed – it creaked under the sudden impact of her weight.

Robert stared down at her, his male part twitching and jumping in eagerness. Ariane was overweight, that was true, but ah, her creamy-white skin – there was so much of it to feel and touch. To fingers and tongue her body was always warm and smooth and very exciting. He had more than once licked her from her throat to the cheeks of her bottom!

And her superb breasts, big and soft, russet--tipped! And her belly, domed and wide, a warm and fleshy mattress for a man to lie on while he stabbed into her! Such thighs, well-fleshed and full, and the skin silk-smooth when kissed. All of Ariane's body lay spread below him in its delicious plumpness, ready for him to mount and use for his pleasure.

Between the parted thighs, dark-brown curls stood out against creamy skin, the neat oval framing long pink lips that were open and slippery with desire. Robert lay down beside her. He stroked her belly and between her thighs until she sighed.

'Ruin my *petite chatte*, Robert,' she begged him, throwing her legs wide, 'be brutal – burst her wide open! Finish her off!'

At once he was between her legs – she drew them up until her knees almost touched her breasts. Robert balanced himself above her on straight arms and legs, so they could both look down and see him plunge into her. Ariane gasped to observe his long hard part slide into her soft wetness, and Robert moaned pleasurably to see the slippery sheen on the skin as he pulled out and the drove in again.

She was ready, she was more than ready, she was desperate for him to ravage her and spurt inside her and release her from the fierce sensations he was provoking. *Yes*, she moaned, *yes chéri, do it now!*

Twenty or thirty lunges and his body convulsed. He cried out as his climactic passion spurted into her. Her arms round his neck clamped his face to hers and her tongue was deep in his mouth as she squirmed under him in her orgasm.

A quarter of an hour later, as they lay side by side, she was handling his soft part again, rolling it between her fingers.

'I wish I could make it stand up again,' she said. 'I know it can, if you want it to.'

'But of course,' Robert murmured. 'It will, I promise

you. In a very short time it will be stiff – but is your darling *joujou* able to withstand another onslaught?'

Needless to say, the question was not meant seriously. Ariane had formidable capacities in this respect. But it flattered her in some strange way, the pretence that male sexuality destroyed her. If the truth were told, Ariane could wear out two or three strong young men, one after the other, without a rest between.

'I wish you could ruin her again,' said Ariane, and her hand slid up and down his stiffening part. Robert rested his head on her shoulder and cuddled close, he stroked down her perspiring belly until his hand was between her legs and he felt wet lips against his palm.

'I wish you could stay with me,' Ariane said, 'but you chose a day that is inconvenient. You should have come yesterday.'

'You said that before, but I don't understand. How can it be inconvenient if Monsieur Sassine is away all day?'

His proud part was hard in her hand now, thick and throbbing eager to resume the game of intimacy with Ariane's hot body.

'I'm expecting Pierre at three-thirty,' she said, her fingers sliding on his stiffness. 'It must be that now, or very nearly. He will be at the door in a moment.'

'Send him away!' Robert cried in despair. 'Ariane – get rid of him! Lie on your back and let me love you again!'

But she slipped from his grasp and off the broad bed. Robert stared in horror and disbelief while she put on her orchid-pink dressing-gown and tied the sash loosely round her ample waist.

'You cannot leave me like this!' he said in dismay, his hand indicating his length of swollen and jerking flesh. 'It is not human to abandon me in this state – Ariane, come back here!'

She smiled fondly at him and strolled out of the bedroom. He was furious. He jumped off the bed and ran after her, naked and barefoot, ready to throw her down on the carpet and ravish her by main force to relieve the tormenting pressure she had deliberately provoked. But, he reminded himself in dismay he still needed Ariane's goodwill, he needed her money!

His clothes lay scattered on the sitting-room floor, where he had dropped them. Ariane was by the window, running a hand over her dark hair, smoothing it back from her forehead. Through the thin silk of her dressing-gown her breasts looked huge and very exciting. Robert moaned and tried not to look at them.

'Ariane,' he said hoarsely, 'there is a matter of importance I must tell you about, I would not be exaggerating to say it is a matter of life and death. I beg you most sincerely to get rid of this person Pierre and let me talk to you.'

'Impossible,' she said with a smile that was malicious. 'What you want, dearest Robert, is to get me on my back again. I have no objection to that, not in the least. But at the present moment I have other arrangements.'

The prospect of borrowing from her was receding and would go beyond recall if Robert annoyed her now. He looked ridiculous – standing naked by a Versailles-type armchair, his hair ruffled and his fifteen centimetres standing sharply upwards. He made a huge effort to control his natural anger.

'It is not a question of love-making,' he said. 'I am serious when I say there is a matter of supreme importance to discuss – when will be convenient, Ariane?'

'Come tomorrow,' she said lightly, 'but in the morning, about eleven, not before – I like to sleep late. My husband is flying back from Marseilles by the afternoon plane, he will not arrive here before six. Does that give you enough time to discuss your important matter? And for other matters?'

When she said *other matters*, she touched her body through her dressing-gown, at the point where her thighs met. There was no possible doubt what she wanted from him in return for listening to whatever he had to say.

'Very well,' he said, 'tomorrow it shall be, though now would be far better for you and for me.'

There was a discreet tap at the door to the hotel corridor, a knowing sort of tap that hinted at shared secrets.

'It's Pierre,' said Ariane, 'you should have gone when I told you to. Now you and he will meet – and that will annoy both of you.'

She said it with a sharp little smile that indicated it would not annoy her in the least to see the two men facing each other across her sitting-room, the one who'd just served her purpose and the one who was about to. She would enjoy seeing the two of them discomforted.

Robert tried one last time. 'Tell him to go away, Ariane, and I will love you all day and all night and all tomorrow morning. Besides, if you take him to bed now, he will know at once you have been with someone else – you are wet and aroused!'

'What of it?' she said casually. 'He takes my money and does precisely what I tell him to do – it's of no interest to him if I have been with someone else or not.'

Robert's suspicions were confirmed, this Pierre was a gigolo. He was paid for doing to Ariane what Robert had

125

just done for free, and he was probably paid very well. It was unjust, when Robert was in urgent need of money and wasn't given it. The summons at the door was repeated, this time not a tap but a quick drumming of fingers, discreet but a little more forceful than before.

'Take your clothes and go,' said Ariane and she moved toward the door to open it and let the stranger in. 'You can dress in the bathroom if you are embarrassed to be seen naked by Pierre. I'll take him into the bedroom so you can slip away.'

'But, but. . .' Robert babbled, his stiff part shaking as if it was admonishing her gravely.

'*Au revoir*, Robert, it has been very nice, seeing you again. I shall expect you tomorrow at eleven.'

She spoke over her shoulder, she was at the door, her hand on the knob. Robert scooped up his clothes and shoes and dashed to the bathroom. He forgot his jaunty hat, it had rolled behind an armchair out of sight.

Charles writes an article

For three days Charles Desjardins hardly let Suzette out of his sight. She was flattered at first, as every woman is flattered by the thought of a man adoring her so very desperately that he refuses to leave her side. But this close attachment confirmed her mild fears that Charles was by nature difficult.

On the other hand, this good-looking young academic was unlike the men she had known before. His difference was to his favour, Suzette made allowances for him she would never dream of making for anyone else.

The evening after his party he arrived at the Casino de Paris to take her to supper after the show. She took him back to her apartment in the Boulevard Lannes for the night and presumably he was impressed by her modern surroundings, though he kept his opinion to himself. He left at nine, saying he had a lecture to deliver. Suzette turned over in bed and went back to sleep.

That evening he again presented himself to her dressing-room at the Casino and they spent the night in his apartment. And again the next day – the pattern seemed established for a lifetime! Whenever Suzette asked him how the article he was writing about her was progressing, he said he was working at it but he never let anyone see his work until it was completed.

There was one other topic on which he was silent – his former wife, Pauline. Naturally, Suzette was interested to know more of this determined woman who had insulted Charles by making use of his bed during the party; and leaving her underwear beneath the pillow, to make absolutely sure he didn't miss the point. His answers to Suzette's questions were brief and noncommittal.

They were married for three years, he admitted that much, and they lived together in the apartment in the Place Furstenberg. It was she who deserted him, he was insistent on that point. He was less clear on the reason why she had moved out. *Was she in love with another man?* – that was Suzette's next question but there was no real answer. Charles turned pink in the face and shrugged in a meaningless way.

What did she do, the former wife? On that he was prepared to be forthcoming – eloquent almost. Pauline had been a teacher of philology but she had given that up to become a writer. A teacher of what? Suzette enquired. Charles looked at her with eyebrows raised, the circle he moved in knew all about such things as philology and etymology and ontology and ethnology – and every other *ology* worth discussing.

'Philology,' he said, 'is the branch of learning that deals with the origins of words and language.'

This conversation took place over a decidedly late breakfast one morning at the Brasserie Lipp, on the Boulevard St-Germain, only a short walk away from Charles' apartment. They ate sweet croissants, warm from the oven, with hot chocolate.

'Words – very useful for a writer,' said Suzette. 'What does she write?'

'Fundamentally her novels are concerned with women and their suffering in the turbulence of intellectual life in Paris today – in some part they are autobiographical, of course.'

'Are they good stories?' Suzette asked, slightly puzzled by the drift of this. 'Have any of them been filmed?'

'You must read one of her books,' said Charles earnestly. 'No brief summary can give you the feel of them, the characteristic atmosphere, the ambience which is particularly Pauline's own. A good starting-point is the novel that won the Prix Flaubert. It is a most significant book for our times – *Women in Chains*.'

'Ah, that sounds interesting,' Suzette said. 'You remember my friend Gaby – well, she had a boyfriend who liked to tie her up naked when he made love to her. Though he didn't use chains, he used those thick curtain-ropes they sell in furniture shops.'

Charles stared at her goggle-eyed. She grinned and continued.

'Gaby says she found it exciting, being trussed up like that, and being handled and bundled about like a parcel. But to me it sounds uncomfortable, bent over double with your hands tied to your ankles and your elbows tied behind your back – what do you think, Charles?'

Before he could offer his opinion, Suzette remembered more. 'He used to gag her with a long silk scarf. And from what she said, he'd arrange her in the strangest positions before he was ready to do it. Sometimes he'd haul her about for half an hour, face up, face down, bottom up, legs over a chair, sideways on a table – he was very inventive.

Claude, his name was. I think he set a new record, and Gaby is the only person I know who's been had in every possible position there is – twenty or thirty, she says.'

'She is mistaken, there are only sixteen,' said Charles, sounding very authoritative.'

'Are you sure of that?'

'The sixteen positions were drawn by Marcantonio Raimondi early in the sixteenth century. They were published in a little book sometime in the eighteenth century and some of the original engravings survive here in Paris in the Bibliotheque Nationale. And some in London in the British Museum.'

'Formidable!' said Suzette, raising her eyebrows. 'But after all, surely you cannot regard what some old Italian believed as more reliable than my friend who has personally experienced all the varieties?'

He said nothing to that, but from his silence she guessed his loyalty was to old books rather than real life.

'I think it is enchanting your wife writes about sexual games and bizarre positions for love,' said Suzette. 'Did you and she try these out on each other, when you were living together?'

'No, no, you misunderstand,' Charles said, a black frown upon his brow. 'It is not a question of bondage and sexual practices – the title of Pauline's book refers to the chains of the mind, the chains society and history, religion and biology devise to bind women and restrict their freedom.'

'How do you mean?' Suzette asked, puzzled by the thought she was not free to do whatever she pleased. 'Men think they have a right to lie on top every time, is that it? How boring!'

Shortly after that he changed the subject. But Suzette found it interesting, his attitude toward his estranged wife. Here he was defending her books as if they contained the secret of life and the universe. And yet there was a clear image in her memory of him stamping her knickers underfoot while he was calling her a slut and a bitch.

And she could remember how he snatched up the pillow to sink his face in it and breath Pauline's perfume. She concluded that whatever Charles believed, he wasn't finished with his ex-wife. In his anger he'd said she could make love with all the men she liked – it was nothing to him! But why was he angry then? Yet on the other hand, he'd made love to Suzette in that bed where Pauline's perfume lingered . . . his emotions were complicated!

And as if to prove how very complicated, after three days and nights of being with her almost every moment, there was no sign of him the next day. He didn't come to the Casino, there was no phone call, no flowers. Only a little note to say he was behind with his urgent work and simply must catch up. Suzette thought it strange, but she had come to realise that the priorities of intellectuals were not the same as her own.

She left him alone for a whole day, she let Robert stay with her that night – dear uncomplicated but not very bright Robert. He would never write about her in a publication for the highly intelligent, but what of that? He adored her and he was a good lover. Of course, if she had known about Robert's problems over money, she would have given it to him on the spot. But he said nothing, not wanting her to see how big a fool he had been.

The following day she decided Charles had been allowed enough time to do his writing – *Bon Dieu*, how long could it take a man to scribble a page or two about her singing and to say that she was charming and beautiful? Her friend Michel Radiguet, who was a poet, never needed more than a couple of hours to write a poem which could be turned into a song for her. And every one became a hit when she sang it on stage and sold thousands of records.

Charles Desjardins had to be urged to write faster, so he had more time for other things, such as friendship. Suzette decided she would take a taxi to his apartment on the Left Bank immediately after lunch that day.

As she had supposed, Charles had been occupied with his short article, presenting the thesis that she was a cultural icon of some significance. The majority of those who went to the Casino de Paris to hear her sing and see the nude dancers would not be much wiser after they'd read it than before. Except that it was to appear in a publication the public in general ignored and so no harm would be done.

A journalist like the too-cynical Dalmas would have finished the article in an hour, handed it in, forgotten it and gone for a drink or two in any nearby bar. But professors do not work at that pace. They ponder, they compare, they deliberate, it takes time. Charles in a open-necked shirt and casual trousers sat in his study, surrounded by books and journals, tap-tapping away at his typewriter. When the doorbell rang, he was annoyed by this break in his concentration. He looked at his wristwatch, it was a little after midday.

He expected no one – could it perhaps be Suzette come to look for him? Women are very short of patience, everyone knows that unfortunate truth. It would be necessary to make her understand he must not be disturbed when he was working. Gently, of course.

He got up to go to the door, arranging a polite smile on his face. To his astonishment he heard footsteps in the apartment, his study door opened – and there stood his ex-wife Pauline.

That was how he described her to himself in his mind, she was his ex-wife. But the truth was they were still married and she was still his wife. Nothing else was possible, only seven weeks had passed since she moved out of the apartment in a rage.

'Of course!' he said, having solved the problem in his head. 'You still have your key. I must ask you to give it to me.'

'What a greeting!' she said, rolling her eyes upward in mock despair. '*Bonjour*, Charles – how are you? I shall give you the key, if that's all that troubles you.'

Pauline Desjardins was a tall and slender woman. She wore her walnut-brown hair close-cropped to her head in what evidently was a form of political statement about herself, or a sexual-political statement perhaps, or even a sexual-aesthetic statement. She had a firm chin and large brown eyes: her eyebrows had been entirely removed and replaced by the thinnest of black pencilled lines. Her complexion was pale and lustrous, in short she was a bizarrely attractive woman.

She was wearing a grey raincoat with the collar turned up and a Hermes silk-scarf round her head. Charles had been engrossed in his writing all day and had not looked out of the window and seen it was raining. He recognised Pauline's chic grey raincoat, he'd bought it for her, it had been very expensive. She pulled the silk scarf from her head and stood staring at him – he knew she was waiting for his question.

Even knowing that, he couldn't help asking it.

'What do you want, Pauline?'

'I've come to collect the knickers I left here by mistake the other evening,' she said, astounding him by her shamelessness.

'There was no mistake about it,' he said grimly. 'It was done on purpose, to offend me.'

'*Ah chéri*, do my little red knickers offend you?' she asked, she was laughing at him. This made him more enraged.

'Who were you with in the bedroom?' he demanded. 'Tell me – was it Jules Ferraud?'

'It's interesting, the way you put that question,' she said. 'Who was I with? The implication is that I was the subordinate participant in the event. Do you really believe that, Charles? It would be more correct to ask it the other way round: who was with me in the bedroom?'

One inconvenience of being an intellectual is it gives a more exaggerated respect for reason and logical argument than is at all necessary in this imperfect world. Charles could understand her point and recognise the truth of her position. Therefore he apologised, which meant he had conceded the argument – whatever it was. Pauline shrugged her shoulders in a little gesture that expressed a conditional willingness to overlook his lapse this one time. Charles returned to the battle, as yet unaware he had already lost it.

'Who was with you in the bedroom?' he asked angrily.

'What is that to you?' she retorted. 'You told me you never want to see me again. I shall live my life as I choose.'

'Not on my bed!' Charles exclaimed.

'I'm not here to discuss that,' she said very calmly. 'I came for my red satin knickers. Hand them over, please.'

'You dare to insult me!' Charles said.

'Insult you? A simple request – I fail to see where there is any offence in that. You are behaving very badly.'

They were standing, during this confrontation, in the middle of Charles's study, halfway between the door and the desk and a metre apart. He had no intention of asking her to sit down – he wanted her to leave.

'It is you who have behaved badly,' he countered, 'and as for the knickers, I threw them away.'

Pauline laughed at him.

'That is a lie,' she said, 'you adore me too much to throw my knickers away, you always have and you always will. But you are too stupid to know it.'

'Adore you?' he gasped in amazement. 'I detest you!'

'Yes? And when your overdeveloped girlfriend isn't here you sleep with my knickers under your pillow. Have you asked her to put them on? No good, *chéri* – she can't get into them, she's got too much backside to get into my size. I must say, Charles, since you've started to live alone your taste has deteriorated – all that flesh, those big breasts and behind! Perhaps you've found your true level at last, with show-girls.'

'This is outrageous,' he said, overwhelmed by the attack. 'Do you imagine a star like Suzette Bernard needs your underwear?'

Pauline's eye was caught by an illustrated booklet lying open on the desk by the typewriter – Charles had bought it at the Casino for the background information on Suzette, to make use of it in his learned article. By chance the publication lay open at a full-page picture of Suzette in her Folies Bergère days – her magnificent body naked and her arms held out artistically. That is to say, she was naked but for a tiny *cache-sexe* no bigger than a man's hand and a head dress of white ostrich-plumes, at least a metre tall.

'To judge by that picture you have lying on your desk,' said Pauline cuttingly, 'she has every need of my underwear because she has none of her own. Have you given her mine – you might as well admit it.'

'Certainly not!' he exclaimed, his voice strained.

'Then what have you done with them?' Pauline returned to the main question. 'Have you defiled them? Yes, that's it – you've been making love to them.'

'This is intolerable – I'd rather die than do that!'

'Would you? You felt very differently when I was in Holland last year to address the students at Leyden. It was less than a week but you made love to every pair of knickers I didn't take with me. And three pairs of silk stockings as well!'

'I loved you then,' he defended himself. 'I missed you by day and by night – what could I do in my desperate need but turn to something that had been very close to your body?'

'But now things are different? Well, times change. I suppose if I look under the pillow I shall find your girlfriend's fancy knickers, to keep you company when she is busy elsewhere. What an idiot you are, Charles.'

To understand women is to pity men, that is well understood – but to understand men is to excuse women. Charles ran round the desk, where the typewriter stood forlornly with a half-covered sheet of paper sticking out. The brilliance of his analysis and his interpretation of the relevance to contemporary thought of icons of mass culture exemplified by a certain beautiful singer – this was all forgotten in the turbulence of his emotions.

He pulled open a bottom drawer of the desk with a savage jerk and snatched out the red satin knickers that lay concealed by a folder of press-cuttings. His face was flushed – it was almost the same colour as the underwear. A lingering trace of Guerlain perfume arose from the silk, adding to his confusion.

Hardly able to speak coherently, he came back round the desk, holding out the knickers at arm's length to Pauline.

'Take them and go!'

'Good – I knew you'd keep them,' she said with a little smile – her voice as friendly as if she and he were reconciled. 'I'll be off then, and leave you to your work.'

But if Charles took her words at face value, he was due for a further shock. She undid the tight belt of her raincoat and she opened the buttons all the way down, then she slipped it back on her shoulders – and stood with a charming smile on her face to let him see she was naked under her chic grey raincoat. Except for a white satin suspender-belt to support her stockings.

'Pauline – what are you doing!' Charles exclaimed, utterly astonished to think she had walked in the streets and ridden in a taxi naked. Her long slender body was openly revealed to him, the little patch of walnut-brown curls between her thighs which he knew so well. After his intensive attentions to Suzette, his three days and nights of caressing and kissing and piercing the smooth lips between her legs, to see Pauline's little brown fur coat again was highly arousing.

'What are you doing?' he asked again, his head spinning.

'Putting my knickers on,' she answered, holding her coat wide open and making no move to take the bright red garment from his hand.

Visible round her neck, now her raincoat was open wide, was a long loop of green beads, seeming to glow a little against her pale skin. Charles knew those beads – they were jade – and they were an expensive present from him to her in the days when he adored her. He stared at her bare breasts – they were small and pointed, the russet buds turned upwards. He glanced down to the curve of her stomach, cut across by the white suspender belt, and he remembered what it was like to kiss that soft belly.

Unseen by him, there was a sly little smile on Pauline's lips while she watched the very familiar expressions flitting across Charles's face. She advanced toward him, he retreated, she took another step, he moved a step back – this stealthy pursuit came to an abrupt stop when he backed into his desk.

He was trapped, Pauline came closer yet and sank to her knees on the carpet at his feet. Without saying a word, she undid his belt and wrenched open his trousers, slipped a hand in between his shirt and his belly.

'No, no,' said Charles in dismay.

He was struggling to discover a rational basis for Pauline's actions. He was far too influenced by intellectual arguments to know that women rarely make use of reason when it is a question of a man. Meanwhile her hand was moving up and down his stiff male part with familiar ease. He stared down through his gleaming spectacles at the delicious sight of Pauline's pert little breasts bouncing up and down to the easy rhythm of her clasped hand, her jade beads jiggling about between them.

'Pauline, Pauline,' he sighed, the pleasure making him forget for the moment that he hated her, '*je t'adore!*'

'No you don't' she said, 'you detest me – you said so.'

He didn't hear what she said – or if he did, the meaning was lost on him. He stared at her in rapture and fascination as she rose to her feet, her hand keeping firm hold of him. She pushed him backward until he was half-sitting on the edge of his desk, his legs splayed – and before he could even speak her name she had pressed her bare belly against him and impaled herself upon his throbbing stiffness.

The position is more usually reversed – the woman sits on the edge of a convenient piece of furniture, or on a ledge or a low wall if the act takes place out of doors. Charles remembered he had once made love to Pauline in this way, disgracefully enough because the setting was the esteemed Bibliotheque Nationale, in the rue de Richelieu. The millions of books said to be there in the library, the priceless old manuscripts – these lost all their interest one Wednesday afternoon when Pauline removed her knickers in a secluded and dusty corner and perched on a window ledge for Charles's attentions.

But reverse the positions and the man is at a disadvantage to the woman – she is the one with her feet firmly planted on the floor and his thrusting movements are restricted. In effect it was Pauline who was bouncing vigorously against Charles. She pulled his spectacles off and dropped them on the desk top, she stared at very close range into his vague eyes.

'I've missed you so much,' Charles murmured, his hands on her shoulders.

'What a lie!' she said calmly. 'You've got a girlfriend. You don't need me for anything.'

She speeded up her rhythmic assault on his sensibilities and he moaned in pleasurable sensation. He knew he was no more than a second or two from spurting his desire into her. But that was not what Pauline intended. She had left him when she discovered he was having a ridiculous affaire with one of his students at the Sorbonne – a nineteen-year-old girl with straggly hair right down to her waist.

She wanted him back. Pauline thought a week or two alone would make him realise what he had lost and run to implore her to return. Instead, he had taken up with this entertainer from the Casino de Paris! Stronger measures were evidently required to compel him to understand what he was throwing away.

'Pauline!' he gasped, his belly clenching in the first spasm of ecstasy.

'Yes, Charles,' she said, her tone casual.

The expression on her face was mocking, she was staring into his eyes – and his eyes were bulging with the sudden impact of overwhelming sensation.

'Yes?' she said again, as if asking for an explanation.

As she spoke, she pulled away from him sharply. His male part bounded upward and spurted his passion over her bare belly.

'Ah, ah, ah!' he gasped, shock, disbelief, chagrin, mingling in his exclamation. No sooner were his orgasmic spasms finished than Pauline had the handkerchief out of his trouser pocket and wiped herself with it.

That done, she took a step away from him and removed from his nerveless hand her scarlet knickers – he had clutched them with fierce emotion throughout his *martyrdom*. She held them at eye level and examined them, front and rear, as if assuring herself before putting them on he had not made use of them in secret to discharge his sexual desire for her.

'Thank you, Charles,' she said politely and balanced herself with a hand on his shoulder, while she put the knickers on. She was smiling and he was watching in stunned silence as she slid the red satin up her legs and over her hips. The contrast with her white suspender belt was piquant, even Charles in his state of confusion appreciated that.

He looked at her uncomprehendingly. She buttoned her raincoat to conceal her smooth-skinned naked body from him and drew the belt tight round her waist.

'Are you going to offer me a cup of coffee?' she asked him. 'Or are you too busy to bother with me?'

'Yes, yes, of course,' he stammered, finding his voice again. The truth was he wanted her to stay now, he wanted to take her into the bedroom. But the coldly polite look on her face didn't inspire him with hope that she would agree to that.

She followed him from the study into the kitchen, the kitchen she knew so well. She didn't sit down, she didn't look as if she wanted to sit down – that might make Charles too confident. While he occupied himself with boiling water and filter papers, she went to the window and looked out. She leaned her cheek on the rain-streaked glass, thinking her secret thoughts. When the hot water was dripping through the filter, Charles came across the kitchen and stood in silence behind her to look out of the window over her shoulder.

The view was miserable – a small courtyard below and another building opposite. A curtain twitched at a window on the first floor.

141

'The old cat across there is still spying on the neighbours,' she said. 'She can't possibly see anything of interest.'

'It is the fondest wish of Madame Loussier to witness one day an act so scandalous that she will interviewed and photographed for the newspapers and become famous. She has waited for years but she has not lost hope. A violent murder would please her best. Failing that, she would settle for a brutal rape, I suppose.'

'She will be disappointed again,' said Pauline, 'she will see neither here today.'

'Are you so certain?' Charles asked in a melancholy fashion. 'I am an outraged husband, no one would deny that – my bed has been defiled and my honour has been spat upon. Who would think it surprising if I was driven to murder you?'

'Pah!' Pauline exclaimed. 'If anyone here is outraged it is me – you drove me away by your infidelity! I ought to stab you to death with a kitchen knife! Or better yet – perhaps I shall punish you by cutting your pompoms off – that would give Madame Loussier the scandal she is waiting for!'

The curtain twitched again, it was just possible to discern a figure standing behind it.

'Ah no,' said Charles. 'It is you who deserve to be punished. You came uninvited to my party, you let Jules Ferraud take your knickers off and have you on my bed – do not deny it!'

'I deny he took my knickers off,' Pauline said with a giggle, 'I took them off myself.'

'Pauline, Pauline...' Charles sighed, feeling that his heart was breaking. He slid his hands round her waist, as if to hold her still while he wreaked some terrible revenge on her. And at the same time he pressed closer to her.

'A *crime passionel*,' he said sadly. 'No court will convict me when the truth is told. I shall strip you naked, Pauline, and I shall strangle you with my hands. And when you are dead I shall carry you into the bedroom and arrange you on your back on the bed and make love to you one last time. Do you understand me? I shall part your legs and ravish your still-warm body, like a madman! Afterwards I shall dress and go out and get drunk in a bar until I have the courage to surrender myself to the police. I shall make a full confession.'

'This is an interesting storyline for a novel,' said Pauline in a thoughtful tone. 'What a pity I shall not be able to write it because I'll be dead.'

Charles ignored her remark.

'When they come to the apartment to check my confession,' he said. 'They will find you dead and naked, strangled and raped, and your red knickers will be stuffed into your mouth.'

'Such depth of passion!' she said mockingly. 'I'm terrified, Charles!'

His fingers fumbled with the buckle of her raincoat belt – it came undone eventually. His hands trembled as he unbuttoned the coat all the way down, they were at her throat, encircling it with a firm and steady grip. But he did not throttle her, he was showing her how easy it was to do so, he was proving to her that his emotions were intense enough to contemplate murder. Or perhaps it was to himself he was trying to prove these things.

'Now there's something for Madame Loussier to spy on!' said Pauline. 'Rape and murder together! Ah no, you said it was the other way round, murder first and then rape. Not that I have an objection, you understand, but will you explain to me the basis of this decision? To be logical, dear Charles, if I am dead it cannot legally be rape, since there is no longer any resistance to you then.'

Charles made no reply. His hands slid down from her throat to stroke her breasts in the undone raincoat. *Salope*, he whispered in a melancholy tone. He held her with one hand while he opened his trousers – his male part was stiff again, it jerked out and stood upright. Both hands were on her breasts, to squeeze them tightly, while his quivering part was pressed close to her raincoat, it lay upright along the crease between the cheeks of her bottom.

'Has my last hour come?' Pauline asked, her tone mocking. 'I only came here for my knickers.'

The smooth material of her coat imparted pleasant sensations to the hot length of hard flesh pressed firmly to it – Charles slid up and down slowly, his hands clasped over Pauline's small pointed breasts. His face was against the back of her head, his lips touching her short-cropped hair. He craned his neck to try and kiss her ear, he wanted to nibble the lobe and push his tongue into it.

'If I must die,' she said, 'it will be for love spoiled. I am a victim of male dominance, the stupidity I have fought against for so many years.'

'Resign yourself,' said he in a hoarse whisper, 'I must have you, Pauline – I will not be denied!'

He reached down to drag her raincoat to the side, uncovering her bottom in the red knickers. She breathed out sharply as his fingers pushed between her thighs.

'Charles, this is not what I came for,' she said, she sounded not only disinterested but noncommittal. But he squeezed himself against her taut round bottom – only the thin red satin now separated his hot flesh from her.

'Look!' she exclaimed. 'She's staring at us – she's opened the window!'

It was true, the window opposite was open, the curtain drawn aside, and Madame Loussier's face could be seen, peering out in a short-sighted but inquisitive manner. Charles kissed the back of Pauline's neck while he pulled her knickers down her thighs.

'She can't see anything,' he said dismissively.

Pauline said nothing, her raincoat hung wide open as Charles' hands caressed her body. It was obvious the neighbour could see her breasts above the window sill and the hands stroking them. At least there was no view below the waist. Though no one could be so foolish as not to guess what Charles was doing to her.

'So it's to be rape first and then murder, is it?' she said. 'Perhaps it would have been more interesting for you the other way about. I notice you did not consult my wishes but you have always been a selfish man. I thank God there is a witness to my ordeal! Madame Loussier will achieve the celebrity she craves and I shall be remembered by those who read my books as another victim of male viciousness. As for you, my poor Charles, it seems certain you will die on the guillotine! I hope that your last thought as the blade descends will be of me!'

Charles wasn't listening, he was panting warmly into her ear, holding her raincoat up round her waist with one hand, while he pushed his foot between her ankles and made her spread her legs apart. He held his uprearing part in the other hand to guide it between her thighs and up to where he wanted to put it.

'I must have you,' he breathed, 'you deceived me before – you made a fool of me. But not this time!'

With a strong push he went deep into her.

'I loathe and despise you,' she said calmly.

'Do you remember that day at Morillon's house at Poissy?' he sighed as he thrust insistently into her. 'Lunch in the garden we were discussing Barthes' methodology in *Le Degré Zéro*. Jules Ferraud was insufferable – he was drunk. You and I slipped away from them and into the house. We wanted to make love, we burned with desire for each other. We dared not go upstairs to look for a bed, not in Morillon's house.'

If, in other circumstances, it had been Suzette he was making love to, these reminiscences at so a tender a moment would have astounded her. She would have thought he'd gone completely mad, to think about abstract nonsense when the treasures of her body were at his disposal. And certainly she would have taken it as a lack of interest in the delightful task in hand. Discourtesy on that scale would have been unforgivable!

But Pauline was of the same brand of advanced intellectualism as her estranged husband, though it was tempered in her case by a certain female good sense.

'I remember,' she said softly.

'We went into his sitting-room,' said Charles, 'the shutters were closed and it was hot and stuffy. You put your hands on a bookcase and leaned over ... I pulled your knickers down ...'

Pauline could hear the swiftly rising excitement in his voice at the recollection of old times. He was ramming insistently at her, his arms tight around her and his hands on her breasts. In the rush of his sexual frenzy her long

146

dangling string of green jade had become caught under his hand and he was pressing the beads into her warm flesh, but he didn't notice that. His belly bumped against her bare cheeks to the rhythm of his thrust into her.

'The old cat is still staring at us,' she announced. She slid her feet further apart on the kitchen floor.

'I don't care,' he gasped, 'I love you, Pauline – even though I hate you.'

'Good!' she said. She swung her bottom back at him to meet his thrusts, 'then you must suffer as I have suffered.'

It is doubtful if he heard her words. His crisis had come and he was babbling her name. And as before she was ready for him. At the very instant his passion spurted she stood up straight – and the sudden movement slid her off his embedded stiffness, which sprang up like a steel spring suddenly released and spattered his desire over the cheeks of her bottom.

'No!' he shrieked, his belly shaking to the spasms of futile release. 'I don't believe it!'

'But you hate me and despise me,' she said, a malicious note in her voice. 'Be logical, Charles, my body is not yours to use as you decide. You told me I am no longer your wife, why should you expect me to give you pleasure? For an intelligent man you make very stupid and false assumptions.'

Charles was speechless at having been deceived a second time. His hands fell laxly from her breasts and his wet male part began to droop sadly. Pauline eased herself out from between him and the window sill and pulled her red knickers up over her bottom, where his thwarted passion trickled down.

While she was buttoning the coat and buckling the belt

tight around her waist, he tried – idiot to the last – to explain his feelings to her.

'It is I who am in chains, Pauline,' he said. 'I am held fast in bonds of emotion and sensation – you have done this to me on purpose, to amuse yourself with my enslaved condition. You have a cruel nature.'

'What nonsense!' she said, a gleam in her large brown eyes, her thin-pencilled eyebrows rising up her luminous forehead. 'I fear you are dramatising yourself, my poor Charles. But you are not so interesting a person, do not be deceived.'

'It is the truth,' he said soberly, hiding his limp part away in his trousers as if ashamed of its folly. 'I begin at last to understand an account a colleague gave me recently. At the time I thought it grotesque.'

'What was that?' Pauline asked. She was arranging her pretty Hermes scarf over her short hair before going out into the rain and she didn't sound at all interested in what he was saying – but at least she listened.

'It was the case history of a married couple who had allowed themselves to fall into an obsession with sexual bondage,' said he. 'The woman would strip naked and permit the man to tie her up with cords whenever he wanted to make love to her.'

Charles was not telling the truth, of course. It was Suzette, not a colleague, who told him this, and it was about her friend Gaby and a former boyfriend of hers named Claude, not a married couple. But what of it? Charles was constructing a version of truth which he believed would serve his purpose better.

'He trussed the woman up,' he continued. 'He arranged her in different positions and handled her. This would last for hours he'd place her upside down, face up with her ankles tied to her wrists – in every grotesque position that came into his head.'

'And?' said Pauline, ready to depart. 'What is the point of this story?'

'This is what you are doing to me,' he said with a sigh, 'but the bonds are not cords and chains, they are the subtler bonds of the mind. The patient in the case history was motivated less by sexual desire than by a need to control and humiliate – just as you are. You hate me and you are determined to humiliate me for a bizarre revenge.'

'That's very romantic, Charles,' said Pauline. 'I didn't know you were capable of such profoundly banal sentimentality.'

While he stood debating with himself what to say next to hold her interest, she reached under her close-fitting raincoat and dragged her little red knickers down her long legs. She stepped out of them and pushed them into his hand.

'I want you to have them, *chéri*,' she said with a broad grin. 'There's a damp patch at the back, but you understand why – you are responsible for it.'

'But, but . . .' he stammered, staring at the red satin.

'You can play with them in bed,' she told him with a sly grin on her face. '*Au revoir*, Charles, you may hate me and detest me but you haven't seen the last of me.'

'Don't go!' he said quickly. 'Stay with me, Pauline – I love you! I want you to come back to me.'

'You say that? With a picture of your girlfriend on the desk in front of you, practically stark naked? *Oh la la!*'

With a graceful wave of her hand, she turned on her heel and walked quickly out of the kitchen. After a moment

Charles heard the apartment door slam as she left and he remembered only then she hadn't given him the key back – that was deliberate, he was certain. She would return to torment him when he least expected it, she would arouse him and disappoint him, then she would take her revenge by making him feel guilty and stupid.

Would she ever decide enough is enough and return to him? He wanted her, yet he didn't want her . . . He leaned his forehead on the cold glass of the window where raindrops slid down outside. Across the courtyard, Madame Loussier still peered at him round her curtain.

As Pauline left the building, there was a taxi being paid off at the kerb. She hurried across the pavement – and stopped. She recognised the woman paying the fare. It was Suzette Bernard in a primrose yellow silk suit, a little umbrella in her hand.

At the same time Suzette recognised the woman she had seen at Charles' party – a bizarrely beautiful woman with short-cropped brown hair. At the party she had worn a turquoise-blue knitted frock that fitted closely to her slender figure. Now she was in a tight-belted grey raincoat, with a silk scarf round her head.

'Madame Desjardins?' said Suzette carefully.

'Mademoiselle Bernard,' said Pauline.

To Suzette's female eye it was evident Pauline Desjardins had nothing on under the raincoat. And she had visited Charles like that – in the middle of the day. The circumstances told a story that needed little interpretation. Suzette shrugged.

'I'll take the taxi now you've arrived,' said Pauline, a note of triumph discernible in her voice.

'I've changed my mind,' said Suzette.

She furled her umbrella and got back into the cab.

'I won't bother to go up,' she said with a tight little smile on her beautiful face. 'It would be a pity to disturb Charles at his work. Perhaps I can give you a lift, madame?'

Nicole plays games

It was the middle of the morning, not the most usual time for a bedroom encounter, perhaps. Afternoons and evenings, these are the times lovers choose most often. And the night, needless to say. But it is impossible to make hard-and-fast rules for these matters – when did the human heart ever wait on clocks?

Nicole Gruchy had persuaded her little friend Lucile to spend the night with her. By ten they were in bed together and they made love to each other for hours, kissing and touching and pressing their hot bodies together, breasts and bellies and thighs. Each gave the other many little climaxes of delight, then later they gave each other huge and soul-stirring climaxes of ecstasy.

Eventually they fell asleep with their arms about each other, heads close upon the soft pillows, mouths almost kissing, their thighs entwined moistly. They slept sweetly, only stirring now and then to turn, breasts against a back, to sigh faintly or to slip a hand between soft thighs.

They woke up after nine in broad daylight and kissed and wished each other *bonjour*. Nicole rang for the maid to bring in their breakfast on a tray, *café-au-lait* poured from a silver coffee pot, freshly baked croissants on thin china, a conserve of wild strawberries. Afterwards they lay side by side in the grand old bed, talking and holding hands.

To Lucile this was a dream come true, lazing away a morning in bed, chatting idly, content, unconstrained and naked – this she felt to be the very peak of happiness. She knew that Nicole would want to make love to her again before they got up for the day, it would be marvellous. There was no hurry about it, there was no clock in Nicole's bedroom ticking off minutes and hours. The love-making would happen when it happened.

It was a luxurious bedroom, decorated and furnished as if by a professional designer, everything in the height of good taste – the long curtains and thick carpets, the impressively large bed, the armchairs, the elegant dressing-table with a porcelain vase holding a spray of pink lilies. And next to it a framed picture of Nicole, a portrait photograph by Pierre-Raymond Becquet that made her look ten years younger and twice as desirable.

Meanwhile Nicole was telling her about a visit to Rome in the summer before. Lucile was lying back comfortably and listening with half-closed eyes, hands behind her head on the pillow. The bedsheet had slipped halfway down while they were sipping their coffee, the room was warm and Lucile was uncovered down to her slender waist. Her breasts were small and pert, she was content to leave them revealed because she knew it pleased Nicole. Now and then, while she was talking about Rome, Nicole reached with a lazy hand to cup Lucile's breasts and touch their pink buds for just a moment.

Into this blissful scene there came an intruder – at the very moment when Nicole was evidently starting to think about making love to Lucile. She was rehearsing her memories of Rome and the aristocratic young Roman who tried to put his hand up her skirt in the Vatican gardens.

'Imagine, *chérie*, it was so hot I left off my knickers when I dressed that morning! If he had succeeded in this disgraceful ambition, his fingers would have been on my *bijou*!'

'*Ah non!*' said Lucile. 'Just imagine that!'

'*Mon Dieu*, who knows what might have happened if his hand had touched me!' Nicole exclaimed, rolling her eyes in comic dread at the prospect. 'It was a hot and sunny day! And he was very, very handsome – he had curly black hair under his white panama hat, charming little curls over his ears. And the biggest bulge you ever saw up the front of his trousers!'

'But you don't like men!' Lucile exclaimed. 'That's why I'm here in bed with you! Why were you looking at his trousers?

'You know how inquisitive I am, *chérie*. If I have a failing – which I doubt – it is curiosity. I can never resist finding out about people and what excites them. Why should you be surprised by that? Isn't it the reason we met and became lovers?'

'But this bulge that interested you – surely you didn't want to find out any more about it? Or perhaps you did? Tell me.'

'There is little more to tell – it was out of the question to indulge my natural curiosity behind a tree trunk in the Vatican gardens – I would have been committing a sin almost beneath the eyes of the Holy Father himself!'

'*Bon Dieu!*' said Lucile, 'so you sent this pretty young man about his business, did you? With words of reproach burning in his ears for the lack of respect when he tried to put his hand up your skirt?'

'Well, to be truthful . . .' Nicole hesitated, with a sly little smile on her lips, 'not precisely words of reproach . . . The back of my hand brushed by mere chance against that tremendous bulge of his and he blushed a furious red. I informed him very coolly that what he had in mind was disgraceful. He babbled something. I didn't understand what he said but it sounded respectful and off he went toward the shrubbery by the garden wall. He had his hand over his bulge, evidently he meant to expose his stiffness and relieve his passion by hand, out of sight in the bushes.'

She laughed when she said it and Lucile came to realise an inconvenient truth about her dear friend Nicole – she delighted in asserting her power over others. It was easy to see she had led the young man on, perhaps permitted his hand to slide right up her bare thigh and discover she had no knickers on. And only at that critical moment had she stopped him.

Or had she stopped him in the nick of time? She hadn't made it clear – and even if she had, there was only her word for it. Lucile already suspected her dear friend Nicole of ignoring the truth when it suited her. She pretended to hate and despise all men, but it was possible she had let this unknown young man put his hand right up her skirt to caress her. And with no knickers on!

Nicole would do this, not because she wanted him, but to lead him on so she could make a fool of him by refusing at the final moment. And with his fingers on her warm and sticky *belle chose* on a hot summer day in Rome, his nature would be too aroused to control himself – Italians were not renowned for will-power and restraint.

It was probable, Lucile thought, that Nicole herself made the suggestion he went into the bushes to handle his stiff flesh to a desperate release. A cruel little smile would be on her face while she watched his retreating back – Lucile found it was not hard to visualise the scene, now she understood Nicole a little better than she used to.

'He didn't know I was going to wait there on the path for him to return,' said Nicole with a giggle, 'but I wanted to see his face afterwards. He was quick – it took two or three minutes at most to unburden himself of his desire. There must have been a long white splash up the garden wall, two metres at least above the ground.'

'How could you embarrass him like that?' Lucile exclaimed in astonishment. 'When he returned to the path and saw you waiting he must have been horribly mortified!'

'He blushed scarlet, *chérie*, his mouth fell open and his eyes were so vague and misty I thought he would burst into tears! A moment to remember and cherish! His male jauntiness was gone, he had a hang-dog look about him. I could hardly prevent myself laughing at him but I made a great effort and I was absolutely charming to him. I took his arm as if we were close friends and made him walk with me – he had no will of his own just then.'

'Nicole! You are terrible!'

'Not a bit of it – I adore pretty people, I am always curious about them. When he was calmer I pulled him behind a tree and I felt his bulge, or where his bulge had been before he went into the shrubbery. His *thing* was small and soft. He babbled away in Italian – I didn't understand him, but I imagine he was blaming me for stealing his manhood – some such idiocy, no doubt.'

'But you had, Nicole!'

'What a fuss over a few spurts! Anyway, after a while I felt him starting to stiffen up again. I had his trousers open for a look – and to keep him guessing! Before I came to a decision what to do with him, I spotted two Cardinals in purple, walking in our direction. I gave Mario – that was his name, he said – a quick kiss on the cheek and abandoned him to his own devices.'

'No!'

'He called after me as I headed for the way out. He said, "*Signora*", two times, but I didn't look back.'

Before Lucile could ask any more questions about that episode Nicole related another tale of her visit to Rome – of meeting a student by the Spanish Steps – an enchanting Italian girl, only eighteen years old. The dark-haired charmer took Nicole to the little *pensione* where she was staying.

'Not a very comfortable place, you understand,' said Nicole. 'It would have been much better at my hotel. But she had fallen in love with me at first sight. Just as you did, *chérie*, and she wanted to share all she had with me, however little. It was so charming a gesture I was unable to refuse.'

In the student's *pensione* they lay naked together on a narrow iron-framed bed and pleasured each other all evening and night and all the next day. And all the next night too.

'Her thighs were strong,' Nicole breathed. 'A little too much so for perfect style but no matter – between them she had this most awe-inspiring bush of jet-black hair! At first I was sure it was a wig – it was too thick and profuse to be natural! Did you know there are little wigs to wear between the legs?'

'Surely not!' Lucile said, giggling at the thought.

'But there are, I can assure you! Women who lose their hair through illness often wear them, not wishing to look like young untried girls when a lover takes their knickers down. There are other reasons too. I know a middle-aged woman who has a cabinet full of these little adornments. She shaves herself between the legs and then chooses a colour to suit her mood – sometimes she is blonde, sometimes a redhead, sometimes brunette. And she has a silver one, for very special occasions, with tiny seed pearls woven into it, and polished jet beads.'

'And your girl student in Rome,' said Lucile, her thoughts in a whirl at what she had heard, 'was it a wig between her legs?'

'Lorenza – she was called. The curls were entirely her own. I established that by tugging at them until she was in tears. And then I kissed her better. Such a thicket she had – it concealed her girlish *trésor*, nothing could be seen but thick black curls bushing out three or four centimetres!'

'*Oh la la!*' said Lucile. 'How very *sauvage*!'

'When she became aroused, which was the instant I kissed her, she showed me how she parted her curly bush to reveal her *belle chose*. She opened herself wide and pressed her finger in to let me see how she amused herself when she was alone.'

'No!' said Lucile breathlessly. 'She did that for you?'

'But of course – and so will you when I ask you, *chérie*. So I lay there on her hard little bed and stroked her belly while she took herself to a climax. And how she cried out and writhed in her spasms of pleasure, it was delicious!'

'And then?' said Lucile, her hand caressing Nicole's thigh, her blood stirring within her. 'What then?'

'Then I did it to her, of course, several times. And then she did it to me – what else? And so we continued, by night and by day, until we could no more.'

'Why do you tell me this?' Lucile sighed, jealousy rising in her heart.

'Because it amuses me. When I left Lorenza I demanded a lock of that shiny black hair as a keepsake. And by then she was in love with me, deeply and devotedly in love, she could refuse me nothing. She took her little manicure scissors and clipped her beautiful bush right down to the skin! Then she took the razor she used for her legs and she shaved her *joujou* as naked as the palm of my hand.'

'You let her do this?' Lucile gasped.

'She put her lovely black curls in a little pink handkerchief and folded it up and gave it to me. I kissed her and told her I would remember her forever.'

'You are cruel – to permit such an act of sacrifice,' Lucile sighed, her hand stroking the inside of Nicole's thigh.

'Her sacrifice was an act of beauty,' said Nicole. 'It was to prove she loved me. We sat on her bed side by side, looking at her bare *joujou* and achieving an understanding of what she had done for love. The sight was so exquisitely arousing we fell on each other, *soixante-neuf*, heads between thighs, and we did it once more, exhausted though we were!'

'There is something pitiless in your nature that terrifies me and at the same time attracts me,' Lucile said softly, a finger gliding over the soft lips between Nicole's thighs.

'Because I took little Lorenza's beautiful black curls? What nonsense – the very next day I took her to a little shop where they specialise in aids to beauty of all kinds and bought her a charming little wig. She swore never to let her own curls grow again, but to wear the wig forever to remember me by. And so we each had a keepsake of the other. Isn't that charming?'

'There will come a time when you are cruel to me, I know it,' said Lucile, her voice tremulous. 'I fear it, yet I long for it even while I shiver in fear . . .'

Nicole laughed a little and arched her back to make her small pointed breasts stand out further.

'Yes, you ought to tremble,' she said. 'You have good reason, my love is ruthless, it will devour you completely.'

'If you hurt me, you will make me hate you,' Lucile said.

'No, you will love me all the more. You will never be able to hate me, whatever I do to you, *chérie*. You will see.'

Lucile didn't understand, but she was content to leave it for the present, perhaps it would never happen. And other thoughts pressed into her mind, caressing Nicole had aroused new ardour. Nicole had an arm round her and was kissing her breasts. Fresh ecstasies of sensation beckoned, a vista of delight was opening ahead of them.

It was at this tender moment that the bedroom door swung back silently. In came the person Lucile least wished to see out of all the millions of people in Paris.

It was Didier Gruchy, Nicole's husband. Naturally, Lucile had never been introduced to him. She had seen him at a distance on several occasions, but that was all.

He had a perfect right to enter his wife's bedroom at eleven in the morning, that went without saying, though it was clearly understood he never slept there at night, never! He was a tall good-looking man in his forties, shiny dark hair smoothed back without a parting, a thin straight nose and a cleft chin.

He was dressed in a knee-length white silk dressing-gown over scarlet silk pyjamas – that much Lucile noted before she dived down under the sheets in pink-cheeked embarrassment. To be seen naked in bed with Monsieur Gruchy's wife – it was too much!

Lucile alone was shame-stricken, for neither Nicole nor the intruder seemed to be affected. It was true that Nicole made an offhand sort of complaint at being *interrupted* – but only after she had said, *Bonjour, chéri* in reply to Didier's greeting and her hand was kissed and also her cheek.

Then Didier seated himself on the side of the bed by Nicole, facing her and within easy touching distance. And he apologised nicely for startling her little friend.

'Come out, Lucile,' said Nicole with a chuckle, 'I wish you to meet my husband.'

Lucile emerged timidly, head above the sheet she was holding tightly to her body. She was, after all, stark naked in bed and everyone knew how men react to a woman in that condition. If he became aroused at the sight of Lucile's bare breasts, how very embarrassing for her that would be in front of Nicole!

With this in mind, Lucile wiggled herself carefully upward to half-sit with her back to the headboard, the sheet held closely to her breasts and only her pretty shoulders on show.

Nicole was unconcerned. She sat upright, with legs crossed in what appeared almost to be a yoga position. She was displaying herself completely to anyone who cared to look – small pointed breasts, her belly, the brown-haired *joujou* between her splayed thighs – she was fully exposed down to her painted toenails!

Didier was holding her hand and chatting away as if they were fully dressed and in a restaurant together – not on a bed with a naked nineteen-year-old staring at him wide-eyed.

'I congratulate you, Nicole,' he said pleasantly, 'I see that your little friend is very pretty – at least, what I am allowed to see of her is pretty. Knowing your excellent taste, I assume with confidence that the rest of her is just as delicious. You have the most enviable talent for discovering these enchanting creatures, Nicole – I am lost in admiration!'

Lucile stared round-eyed and open-mouthed when Didier put out his hand casually and fondled the inside of Nicole's thigh. And Nicole made no objection, though she had informed Lucile many a time that she found her husband's caresses insufferable. But no flicker of distaste or concern passed over Nicole's face, not a slight shadow even, when Didier reversed his hand, palm upward and clasped her between the legs.

'I'm sure Lucile gave you enormous pleasure last night,' said he, nonchalantly.

'But of course,' Nicole answered. 'Twelve times, *chéri*, if it interests you. She pleasured me twelve times.'

'You were counting?' Didier said, one eyebrow rising in mild surprise.

Lucile was astonished by the conversation. The night had been a long act of love, hour after hour of kisses and caresses, but she had certainly not counted the orgasms, neither Nicole's nor her own. In retrospect, the number was probably nearer six or seven she thought, not the dozen Nicole claimed.

There was much she didn't know about Nicole. She was learning more this morning than in the past months of their friendship. Presumably this false overstatement of what took place in the night was a manifestation of Nicole's desire to exercise power. It was obvious she was deliberately putting her husband down.

'Ah, how marvellous!' he said, not in the least discouraged, 'I admire you, Nicole! I am terribly envious of this fantastic ability you women have to achieve a sexual climax so many, many times with scarcely a pause to draw breath! We poor men cannot keep pace with you, we are finished after two or perhaps three times. It was always a source of great disappointment to me not to be able to exhaust you to a standstill with love-making.'

'That has happened only twice in my life,' said Nicole with a superior smile on her face. 'Both times with women, of course.'

'But of course,' said Didier, also smiling. 'May I be allowed to know who these formidable lovers were? Do I have the honour of their acquaintance?'

'Do not pretend you are unaware of my profound friendship for Germaine Brantome,' Nicole said. 'It began years ago before you and I were married.'

Didier nodded and asked her to explain further.

'What? You wish to play at true confessions here in front of Lucile?' Nicole exclaimed, raising a pencil-thin eyebrow. 'But why not? I am proud of my lovers. Germaine is much older than me, of course. We knew each other socially after she married my father's cousin, Georges. I was only twenty, when we became lovers – not a virgin, of course, but with no experience of love-making with other women.'

'She was the first?' said Didier. 'That makes her special.'

'She took me shopping with her one day – she and Georges were off on vacation to Cannes a few days later.

When we returned to their apartment, we went into the bedroom so she could show me one of the swimsuits she had bought. She undressed completely, hiding nothing, and posed in the swimsuit. It was white, as I recall – I think we had bought it at Chanel – and very close-fitting. As you know, Germaine is a Valkyrie of a woman, tall and sturdy, large-breasted, big hipped.'

Lucile was listening spellbound. She found it impossible even to understand how Nicole could speak of these private affairs to a man – and especially not to her husband. But Nicole showed no sign of embarrassment and Didier showed no sign of resentment – it was strange, Lucile thought, but it was almost as if there was a secret understanding between the pair of them.

'Germaine admired herself in the mirror,' Nicole went on. 'It was a cheval-glass, a magnificent Louis XVI antique. She stood with a hand on her hip, turning this way and that to see herself in the swimsuit from all angles. I told her she looked superb and she was pleased. She stroked my hand and took the swimsuit off. She stood naked, looking at herself in the mirror, asking if I thought her breasts were too big – and I realised she was tempting me. She saw I was uncertain how to respond and put her arms round me and kissed me full on the lips, pressing her warm naked body to me.'

But Nicole told me she adores little pointed breasts, Lucile was thinking as she listened, *pretty little breasts like mine – and like her own . . . now we are hearing a different tale!*

'After that kiss, there was no more uncertainty,' Nicole went on with a smile. 'Germaine sat on the edge of the bed, her legs spread wide, I fell on my knees and put my hands on her breasts and then between her legs. It took only a minute at most – she was already open and wet. I slipped my fingers into her and her orgasm came almost at once.'

'Excellent!' said Didier, he was gently stroking the inside of Nicole's thigh, 'I adore spontaneity. I find it so difficult to achieve myself.'

'A moment later she tore my clothes off and had me on the bed with my legs forced wide apart. Her hands were all over me, and her tongue. In two hours she forced me to more climaxes than I had ever believed possible – and at the end of it, I was destroyed, hardly able to raise my head from the pillow. How marvellous it was, that first time with Germaine.'

'This is fascinating!' said Didier, his palm sliding lightly up and down the inside of her thigh, just brushing lightly over the soft brown hair that adorned her *joujou*. 'I guessed long ago that you and she had been lovers, but I did not realise she was the first woman to make love to you. When she and Georges next come to dinner I shall regard her with a new respect.'

'Sadly, she has become too old to attract pretty young girls. She goes three or four times a week to a *café-dansant*, near the Place de la Bastille,' said Nicole.

'Ah, the notorious rue de Lappe!' said Didier. 'A street of thugs and streetwalkers, accordion-players and pick-pockets.'

'Perhaps so,' said Nicole with a shrug, 'but there is also a particular *café-dansant* frequented by young women of a certain type. Germaine selects one of them and buys her a drink or two, then takes her home and rewards her with a sum of money.'

'How interesting!' Didier said. 'She has always seemed to me a woman of enterprise and determination – I am delighted to hear she continues with her pleasures. And what of the other lover who could exhaust you, *chérie*? Who is she?'

'Someone you do not know,' said Nicole. 'Vivienne Lenoir, she is a divorced woman of twenty-seven. She has a small shop in the Palais Royale arcade. I met her by chance two years ago and we were drawn together at once. We were in bed an hour after we met – and she too is devastating in her love-making.'

The anxieties Lucile experienced when Didier Gruchy came into Nicole's bedroom had been much relieved by the amiable conversation between husband and wife. Her impression had been wildly wrong – she had imagined that because Nicole loved women and made no secret of it, relations between her and Didier must necessarily be strained and distant. Perhaps even antagonistic.

But it was evidently not so. And Lucile was reassured. Didier observed this and thought the moment right to hold out his hand to Lucile, the hand that a moment before had been fondling Nicole between her legs. Lucile let him take her hand and kiss it formally.

'You are very attractive, mademoiselle,' said he with a smile of candour and admiration. 'The colour of your hair is perfect, it is the colour of fine sandalwood. And I find your breasts to be exquisite – I have all my life been fascinated by delicate and pointed breasts. No doubt you guessed that from Nicole's?'

Lucile blushed a pretty pink and hardly knew what to say.

'There is no occasion to blush,' he said in reassurance. 'You have probably kissed Nicole's pretty breasts as many times as I have in six years of marriage. They are delightfully soft to the lips, yes? And when you flick the tip of your tongue very fast over the buds, she becomes very, very aroused – you have surely discovered this for yourself by now?'

Lucile stared at him, lost for words.

'Has she told you yet she can be made to climax in this way – just by her breasts being sucked?' Didier asked. 'And if I may offer another tiny piece of useful advice – darling Nicole can be kept in a state of orgasm for ten minutes without a pause, by continuing to suck her breasts hard.'

'No!' Lucile breathed.

'She makes a charming little moaning sound during an extended orgasm – surely you have noticed? Do you make a similar sound yourself, mademoiselle?'

From pretty pink, Lucile's cheeks turned to deepest crimson – then Nicole came to her rescue by rearranging her slender naked body on the bed and diverting everyone's attention to herself. While Didier had been talking to Lucile his hand had strayed back to Nicole's naked thighs.

Perhaps she didn't want him to touch her between the legs. Or perhaps the yoga position became a little uncomfortable. Or maybe she wished to remind Didier that this was *her* bedroom, not *his*, and the choice of conversation was hers. Or perhaps she thought he had paid enough attention to her little friend and wanted to turn his interest back to herself. Darling Nicole had a complicated personality – who could ever be sure what her motives were?

Whatever the reason, she uncurled those long slender legs and stretched them out fully, in a straight line from smooth thighs to scarlet-painted toenails. Her knees rested together and, her *belle chose* was hidden. Didier raised an eyebrow, then tried to open her legs gently with his hands. She tensed her muscles and kept her legs closed. A tiny frown appeared on his handsome face.

He gave up this futile struggle and put his hands over her bare breasts and Nicole did nothing at all to stop him. In fact, to Lucile's astonished eyes it seemed Nicole was deriving a certain satisfaction from being felt by a man – much as if it had been a woman's hands on her breasts. And this was so out of keeping with what Lucile had imagined about her friend that she could only stare and wonder.

A disconcerting thought flashed through her mind – was Didier about to demonstrate the usefulness of the advice he had given her? Surely he would not put his mouth to Nicole's breast and stimulate her to a long moaning climax in front of her? *Bon Dieu, non!*

But no, he only fondled Nicole's breasts with his hands. This provoked words from Nicole. The words were a rebuke, as was to be expected – but they were spoken in a tone which simply added to Lucile's confusion of mind.

'Beast!' Nicole said to Didier, her tone teasing rather than hostile. 'What do you suppose you are doing? Surely you do not for a moment imagine I will let you violate me in the presence of my dear friend Lucile? Really, Didier, are there no bounds to your selfishness and depravity?'

'Perhaps there are not,' he answered. The smile on his face seemed to Lucile as sly and cruel as the smile she had seen earlier on Nicole's face when she had talked about the frustrated man in the Vatican gardens, abandoned under a tree, with trousers open and his stiff part sticking out.

'We both know, *chérie*,' Didier continued, 'that depravity has its own subtle and perverse pleasures. To come to the point, my darling, there are certain understandings between us. In brief, my beautiful wife, I must have what is rightfully mine!'

Without waiting for an answer he had both knees up on the bed and was astride Nicole's legs, his hands on her bare shoulders. His elegant white silk dressing-gown hung open and his stiff male part was sticking up out of his scarlet pyjama trousers. Nicole seemed not to notice it, though she had often claimed to Lucile that it was an object of repulsion and horror for her.

Lucile was staring at Didier's stiffness with a certain naïve fascination. It seemed to her strong and well-shaped – more so than the only other one she had ever observed closely, that of her former fiancé, Tristan.

Didier inserted his knee between Nicole's thighs and forced them apart. Nicole stared into his face as if defying him to do his worst. As for Lucile, watching this by-play between the two of them, she was at the same time dismayed and aroused – surely this interfering man could not really intend to brutalise those soft lips between Nicole's parted thighs! Not in the presence of the woman who had caressed and kissed that delicious *joujou* through the night! It was impossible to believe Nicole would let him outrage Lucile's feelings by surrendering to him!

'No, no, no,' Nicole was insisting, but not very firmly.

She rolled her body from side to side, as if to escape from the touch of Didier's hands – but her movements served only to make him stroke her belly more thoroughly. And then his fingers were prying between her legs! She struggled feebly against him and her head turned away. Not in disgust, but only because she was looking closely at Lucile, to see the effect on her.

Lucile moved away from the struggling pair, sliding over

the sheet to the very edge of the bed. She was shocked, scandalised, repelled by what was being enacted – and she was fascinated enough to remain in the bed and observe. She saw Didier bending down to nibble at Nicole's breasts, she saw him sliding down to kiss her between the thighs.

He knelt upright to take off the splendid white silk dressing-gown and his scarlet pyjamas. Lucile saw the dark hair upon his chest and the dark hair between his legs, where his long thick part jutted up so demandingly. She blushed pink to realise that she wanted to have it in her hand to know what it felt like, to have it in her mouth and submit to its virile strength! But it was shameful, this desire she felt to handle Didier!

'What you are doing to me is disgusting!' Nicole said to her husband, her legs sliding wider apart, her loins rising up from the bed to permit his deeper penetration.

'Yes, Nicole,' he breathed, 'it is utterly despicable . . .'

He was pushing into her and she was yielding and open to him, as open as any woman could ever be. Her head rotated slowly on the pillow to turn her face fully toward Lucile, that face with the long thin nose and the olive-tinted complexion. Her shining dark-brown eyes stared at Lucile. There was a knowing smile on Nicole's face.

It was as if she was saying without words, *Look at me! Didier is making love to me – are you jealous?*

Lucile stared with wild eyes at the unbelievable scene before her, a knuckle in her mouth – she was biting it to stop herself crying out, *I hate you, Nicole, I hate you – no, no, I love you, why are you doing this, why do you want to make me suffer?*

Nicole's eyes were hooded by half-closed eyelids, what Didier was doing to her had aroused her furiously.

Whether she loathed the feel of hard male flesh inside her, as she said, or whether that was a pose – the plain truth was that Nicole was approaching an immense sexual climax.

'Lucile . . .' she gasped. 'Kiss me, *chérie*, come to me . . .'

'I hate you!' Lucile moaned.

But her hatred did not stop her from grasping the trembling hand Nicole held out across the sheet to her. She clasped it in both her own hands and showered hot kisses on it, on the soft little palm, on the tips of the long thin fingers and on the smooth back. She took the scarlet-nailed thumb into her mouth and sucked it. She wished it was the tip of Nicole's breast in her mouth . . . or Didier's stiff part . . . or either . . . or both. In truth, Lucile was so excited she no longer knew what she wanted.

Nicole was moaning now as Didier plunged up and down strongly on her, his lips against her flushed cheek and his eyes closed. Nicole's long legs were off the bed and round his waist, while she tugged at Lucile's hand to drag her closer. And Lucile went with the pull, easing herself closer to the entwined pair until she was close enough to hook a leg over Didier's outsplayed leg and feel how it quivered to his rhythmic pounding.

Nicole slid Lucile's hand in between her body and Didier's so it was trapped between her breast and his heaving chest. Lucile felt the harsh rub of hair over the back of her captured hand, and soft flesh under her palm. Her other hand was down between her own thighs – parting the wet lips to probe inside with her middle finger.

She knew Nicole was about to reach her climax – she wanted to feel the same ecstasy herself, at the same moment. She desired to enjoy Nicole in her mind, although someone else was enjoying Nicole's long naked body.

The slide of Didier's hard flesh inside Nicole drove her into a sexual frenzy. Her fingers were clenched tight about Lucile's hand, squeezing it tightly against her breast. Her orgasm came in quick little spasms and her back arched up under Didier. Lucile too cried out in delight, ravishing herself with her fingers to climactic thrills. They stared into each other's eyes, the two women, heads on the pillow, panting mouths almost touching. And neither paid the least attention to Didier as he squirmed about on Nicole's belly.

After a short period of repose, Didier made it clear that he wanted to enjoy Lucile. He lay between the women, his hot mouth on Lucile's pointed little breasts, his hand between her thighs and his fingers slid into her slippery wetness. Lucile lay with her eyes closed, content to let him do as he wished. She wanted him to make her feel what he had made her darling friend Nicole feel.

'Ah . . .' she sighed faintly, wondering if he meant to find out if she too could be hurled into orgasm by means of sucking her breasts, just like Nicole.

Nicole was lying on her side, with her eyes shut and her long legs modestly together. She came fully awake when Lucile began to sigh under Didier's attentions. She opened her eyes and sat up to see what he was doing to her dear friend.

'Ah yes, you beast,' she said softly to him. 'She has such a darling little *jouet*, so pretty pink and girlish. Last night I did marvellous things to it, until she collapsed completely. But you haven't the skill for that, Didier, you are just a brutal and insensitive man with only a single crude idea of how to make love – I see you are going hard again.'

And though she had told Lucile many a time that she detested the very sight of a male part, hard or soft, she moved close to Didier's back – and she reached over his hip to clasp his throbbing flesh in her long-fingered hand.

Lucile very nearly reached a climax at once, at the sight of Nicole's scarlet-nailed fingers sliding up and down that length of stiff male flesh, teasing it to full stretch.

But there was a limit – and it was reached when Didier rolled on to Lucile and laid his belly on hers, to slide his stiffness up into her. Nicole stopped him immediately by thrusting a knee into his side to push him away fiercely.

'You are here for what is rightfully yours,' she said. 'Well, you've had what you are entitled to. Be content – Lucille is not yours, she is mine! I will not let you have her!'

By the time Didier recovered from the surprise attack, Nicole was on her knees between Lucille's open legs, her head between the splayed thighs. Her mouth pressed to the darling object she had described a few moments before as *pretty pink and girlish*.

Her mouth took complete possession of it, as if by her action she asserted her right, her ownership of it. Her tongue slipped inside, conveying the very clear message, *this is mine, you are forbidden to do any more to it, Didier!*

Nicole was on her knees, head down between Lucile's legs, and her beautiful bottom up in the air. Didier was not to be fobbed off easily – he was behind her on his knees at once – his stiff flesh clasped in his pumping hand. By then both women were far too engrossed in their own sensations to give any attention to him. Otherwise they might have seen the look of faint amusement on his face.

'But if Lucile wants me?' he said to Nicole. 'Why not? She is not your slave, *chérie*, you have not paid for her. I am sure she would like the feel of me up inside her.'

'She doesn't want you,' Nicole insisted.

Her voice was a little muffled because her mouth was occupied between Lucile's thighs. Lucile was staring up beyond Nicole to see what Didier would do – would he seize his wife and hurl her away? Push her off the bed altogether? Fling himself down on Lucile's belly and ravish her? These thoughts whirled through her head, arousing her to a frenzy.

· But no, Didier knew another, easier way of getting his own back when his darling wife tried to thwart his pleasure. He abandoned all thought of having Lucile for now and pushed his hard jutting flesh into Nicole from behind, a long fast thrust that took full possession of her. She gasped at the penetration – Lucile felt her hot breath down between her thighs.

'You are right *chérie*, as always,' Didier said mockingly. 'If the girl is yours, let me see what you can do with that pretty pink plaything of hers – while I pay my compliments to what is indisputably mine.'

Lucile was much too involved with her sensations to take heed of what Didier was doing. The flickering of Nicole's tongue was sending tremors so adorable through her belly that nothing else existed for her. She shrieked a little and raised shaking hands to her own breasts, plucking at their pink buds.

Nicole's scarlet-nailed fingers caressed Lucile's groins, her tongue forced its way into the open lips.

Nicole was furiously aroused, though she would not admit it, by Didier's hardness probing strongly into her, sliding and rubbing against her secret bud, compelling her to become so wet that she knew the insides of her thighs gleamed.

She would have adored to see that. She had always found

175

the sight of her own body extremely exciting, especially when she was already aroused – inside thighs slippery-shiny, the lips of her *joujou* forced open by hard flesh . . . ah yes, yes! Nicole's orgasm was seconds away. She didn't care if Didier reached his pleasure or not, but she wanted to make Lucile experience hers before her own arrived.

She was very close to it, dearest little Lucile, tremors were fluttering through her belly. She gasped and squirmed and shook at the very point of collapsing into ecstasy.

'*Je t'aime*, Nicole,' she was moaning. 'I love you, love you – I hate you . . .'

And Nicole herself was a heartbeat away from her climax. She clawed her nails down the soft insides of Lucile's thighs, she lashed with her tongue at her bud, she *willed* her to respond – and she was rewarded by the sudden frantic jerking of Lucile's body as her orgasm seized her.

An instant later Didier wailed like a woman. Nicole felt the spurt of his sticky desire inside her belly. His hands held her narrow hips in an unbreakable grip as he bucked and thrust to the furious pumping of his sexual release.

Nicole had gained a victory over him, as she had over Lucile. This was vitally important to her, to use lovers and have power over them, to compel them to do what she wanted.

In this moment of pride she felt her own orgasm sweep through her. It was so sweet and strong that she cried and fell forward on to Lucile's twitching body. This collapsing descent slid her off Didier's impaling flesh, she had finished with him. And she had finished with Lucile. She yawned and smiled to herself. She was finished with both of them. For now.

In a little while, when she was recovered and in control

once more, she would send Didier away. She would sit up straight and cross her legs to hide herself from his prying eyes – she would put her hands over her breasts and inform him he'd had all the pleasure he was going to get from her that day. She would send him away, his male flesh drooping inside his scarlet pyjamas.

When she was alone with Lucile, she would stretch out on her back again, with her legs apart. And tell Lucile to caress her and feel the slippery wetness of Didier's desire inside her. An exquisite thought came into her mind, perhaps Lucile would weep because she'd seen someone else making love to Nicole! She had been made to watch while another, and a man at that, enjoyed to the full the woman she adored . . .

The tears would be very exciting. Nicole would taste them on Lucile's cheeks with the tip of her tongue, to savour the salty sorrow of love outraged. Then she would tell Lucile to wipe her wet cheeks with her own hand and transfer this evidence of love betrayed to Nicole's brown-haired *joujou*, to let it mingle with the evidence of Didier's love. And she would demand that Lucile ravish her to the brink of insanity as proof of her love.

Meanwhile, Didier lay across the bed, his head pillowed upon Nicole's bottom, well satisfied with his achievement. One hand lay flat between her sticky thighs and in his other he held his dwindling male part in an affectionate clasp. Nicole's head was on Lucile's perspiring belly. Lucile quivered now and then, her body shaken by nervous little tremors at the memory of what had been done to her.

On Nicole's face was that sly cruel smile that her lovers dreaded – and adored.

Didier plays the grand monsieur

Naturally, because women are by far the most inquisitive of all creatures, Suzette's imagination was caught by the words Nicole Gruchy spoke to her at Charles's party. The words were sardonic, of course, and spoken only to let Suzette know she was a person of no importance in the elegant world of Madame Gruchy.

If you want my husband, have him. But it would be courteous to return him in good condition when you've finished with him. That was what Madame had said, though it was not what she meant, of course. Perhaps it would have been better to ignore her and her husband completely, but the words seemed almost to dare Suzette to stray at her peril into territory Madame Gruchy regarded as her own.

Didier Gruchy was suave and good-looking, and he looked as if he had a close acquaintance with the arts and pleasures of the bedroom – he gave every impression of being the sort of man who knew one end of a woman from the other. Nevertheless, he had no no great fascination for Suzette and she had told his wife plainly she had no interest in him. She'd described him as *one of those sad creatures who lurk at stage-doors*.

This was true. And yet when all was said, there was a

certain satisfaction to be enjoyed in spiting the disdainful Nicole. it was difficult to imagine so very superior a person naked on her back with her legs apart and a man on her thin belly making her sob in ecstasy. So difficult as to be almost impossible. It was not a question of sexual jealousy, warning Suzette off Didier – it was a matter of ownership and property rights.

The *affaire* with Charles Desjardins had come to a very abrupt ending. In an awkward and embarrassed telephone conversation he had conveyed to Suzette that he thought it best if they did not meet again. He admired and esteemed her, he said, but naturally it must be accepted as axiomatic that we do not become what we want to become, and we do not become anything at all without an exercise of will.

When Suzette asked him to explain, he rambled on in a similar style, never reaching a point of any significance. And finally, listening to what he was *not* saying instead of his vague words, she came to the conclusion that his wife was back with him. She had a clear recollection of a comic moment in the bedroom when she had found the scarlet satin knickers and Charles had snatched up a pillow and buried his face in it. To identify the perfume, that was his excuse, but it seemed to Suzette that if he had been on his own he would have plunged his face into the knickers.

The conversation with Charles ended and he promised to send her a copy of the magazine with his article when it was published. No doubt he intended this as a consolation, but Suzette did not take it in the same spirit.

She was wrong in her conclusion about Charles's wife. At least she was partly wrong – Pauline had not gone back permanently to the apartment in the Place Furstenberg. But Suzette's instinct was right, Charles was no longer available, Pauline was deliberately draining him of his emotions and his self-regard and all of his will-power, by her unexpected visits.

In the unusual circumstances and for an inappropriate reason, Suzette decided to try out Didier Gruchy as a lover. If Nicole got to hear of it, so much the better!

Simone the dresser, who knew everything there was to be known about Suzette and fussed over her day and night like a hen with only one chick, pursed her lips and shook her head when she overheard Suzette agree to meet Didier next day. But the signs of evident disapproval were ignored by Suzette, who smiled in slightly infuriating manner and said nothing.

They met for lunch. That is to say, they met at a café first to share a drink and decide where to go for lunch. The Gruchys lived in style in the Avenue Victor Hugo, not very far from the Boulevard Lannes and Suzette's elegant apartment. They arranged to meet at Fouquet's in the Champs-Elysées, convenient for both of them, and there at 12.45 Suzette found Didier at a table on terrace, sipping a glass of kir and watching the passers-by.

He was wearing an impeccable silver-grey summer suit with a bright blue neck-tie. This was the first time Suzette had seen him in anything other than dinner jacket and watered-silk bow-tie, and she was pleasantly impressed. Needless to say, she had chosen her frock with great care that morning, though if anyone asked she would say casually that she had put on the first thing that came to hand.

In effect, she wore a couturier coat-frock in apple green

and gold stripes, with big buttons down the front and a gold buckle at the waist. The hairdresser had been ordered that morning to pay special regard – the raven-black coiffure gleamed with good grooming and health and the fringe was crisply cut. The shoes were of black alligator and so too was the elegant handbag from the Faubourg St Honoré.

Didier Gruchy rose and kissed her hand gracefully, his brown eyes shining with admiration. Indeed, Suzette was not merely admirable, she was lusciously desirable. The eyes of every man sitting on the terrace were upon her as she stood by Didier's table having her hand kissed – even the foreign tourists who didn't know who she was stared at her and envied Didier his luck.

Naturally, many of those on Fouquet's terrace recognised her – she was a celebrated singer, her picture was on posters all over Paris advertising the Casino. It could be seen displayed in the windows of record shops, in newspapers and in magazines. Suzette Bernard was of the first importance. A murmur of muted and discreet admiration could be heard across the terrace, then the pre-lunch drinkers returned to their own conversations.

Didier was a charming companion and an accomplished talker – that goes without saying. And though Suzette's motives for this tête-à-tête were somewhat devious, she enjoyed his company and found his wit amusing. Where to have lunch was a question that required some discussion. It was Didier's wish to make the best possible impression at this first encounter *à deux*.

For this reason he suggested various restaurants of imposing reputation, beginning with the *Grand Vefour* and, observing how Suzette's nose wrinkled prettily to indicate non-acceptance, he made his way through a list as if he were a restaurant guide – *Chez Drouant? Chez Prunier? La Tour d'Argent?* None of these found favour.

Suzette was playing a game with him. She suggested *Mon Bar*, a cheap bistro near Les Halles market where sausage and mustard was the most popular dish served. She laughed to see how Didier looked askance at the idea and she suggested an alternative on the Left Bank, the *Tire-Bouchon* – a small and unstylish bistro where hard-up students went to eat cheese fondue.

Eventually, because it was so fine and sunny a day and Didier saw the joke and laughed, she let him persuade her to go to the Bois de Boulogne. He paid the bill, tipped the waiter lavishly and found a taxi. The driver took them roaring at high speed up the Champs-Elysées and round the Arc de Triomphe, cutting a way through the lunch-time traffic as if driving a bumper car at a fair.

'Did you know,' said Didier, holding Suzette's hand lightly, 'in Paris one driver in every twelve has killed a man? This is an official statistic, but naturally it is kept a close secret. If it were generally known, there would be demands for action. Government ministers do not respect demands for action if there is nothing in it for themselves.'

'Ha!' said Suzette, an exclamation meaning that she was not in the least surprised to hear this sorry news.

'The only persons who have an interest in slowing the traffic are the families of victims,' Didier continued. 'The widows and orphans and the maimed survivors of accidents. But they do not have money to bribe a minister. For this reason the running down of pedestrians will continue as a Paris sport – almost as amusing as adultery and far more interesting than bicycle racing.'

They drove through the Bois de Boulogne to the *Grand*

Cascade restaurant. They had a table in the garden, within sound of the waterfall, where they ate and drank and talked and laughed for two hours. The moment of truth was at hand. It was necessary to decide now, while Didier was settling the bill, whether to take him back to the apartment or whether to say *au revoir*. It was a decision soon made – he had shown himself to be interesting and amusing, he deserved an opportunity to demonstrate how exciting he could be.

From the restaurant in the Bois to the Boulevard Lannes was a very short taxi drive. Even so, his kisses and his hand on her thigh had aroused her by the time they arrived – if the journey had been any longer she was sure his hand would have been right up between her legs. He kissed her again in the lift as they went up to her floor, his hands flat on her bottom to hold her belly tight to his.

Once inside the apartment, she took him to be bedroom directly, there was no point in wasting time. He closed the bedroom door behind him, gathered her up in his arms and carried her to the bed. His strength surprised her a little, he was a slender man and he was at least forty. But he swung her off her feet with no sign of strain and carried her easily across the room. Somewhere in between door and bed she let go of her elegant handbag.

He laid her gently on her back upon the black fur bed-spread. It was the widest bed he had ever seen, there was room for four people to make love there, in separate pairs or in a foursome. Sleeping on that bed was an incidental, it was a star's bed and designed for capitulation on a grand scale.

Didier was very much the grand seigneur, the man in charge of events. He moved decisively, he was used to having his own way, that was the impression he made in those first three important minutes. He took off the jacket of his impossibly elegant suit and pulled off his tie as he seated himself on the side of the bed. He bent over Suzette, kissing her passionately, while his hand rummaged under her clothes.

He surprised her at this tender moment by admiring the apple-green and gold striped coat-frock she was wearing. He was a man who knew a lot about clothes and couturiers, naturally, though this seemed an inconvenient moment for that. Suzette responded by informing him that the gold buttons down the front could be undone – she suggested he might like to undress her.

'Oh yes, but not yet,' he answered with a brief smile. 'I find you enchanting as you are, beautifully clothed but accessible – it is an intriguing situation. Do you not find it so? It is a development of the old question as to which is more arousing, a completely naked woman or a woman wearing only silk stockings.'

But a moment later his questing hand encountered an obstacle in the way of his easy exploration of Suzette's charms. She was wearing a tiny pair of black silk knickers, hardly more than a flimsy triangle. Didier stroked her through the thin silk, then flipped her frock up and took her knickers down.

She laughed as he pulled them down her legs – she was on fire already, her sexual emotions aroused by his direct approach to what he wanted. She put her hand between his thighs, where the fine cloth of his trousers was stretched over a long bulge. It looked large and useful, it throbbed to her touch. She squeezed it through the cloth.

Didier had her knickers off and her frock unbuttoned as

high as her waist and the gold-buckled belt. He had his first sight of the naked lips between her thighs – she was as smooth and bare as a billiard-ball. His eyes gleamed and a faint flush came to his cheeks. With a sudden movement his face was between her thighs to press a kiss of salutation on her *belle-chose*.

He did not continue, as men usually did when they kissed her there. He sat up again and leaned over her, his fingers roaming everywhere, into her mouth, into her ears – into the bare lips he had kissed and between the cheeks of her bottom. And he touched her with such deftness and finesse that soon she was sighing and the crisis was rushing toward her.

At the instant when she felt the orgasm must begin, her mouth open to scream in ecstasy and her legs straining apart – Didier took his hands off her and sat still, watching her, silent and brooding. She shrieked in disbelief and her body shook in violent frustration.

She stared up at him, her eyes wide with incomprehension. He had an ironic smile on his face. He was handsome in a saturnine way and, even in her emotional torment, she was vividly aware of his physical charm. His shiny dark hair was perfectly combed and undisturbed, his cleft chin was smooth and imperturbable.

'Be calm,' he murmured, stroking her forehead, it was just a little wet with perspiration, disarraying her black fringe. 'I promise you the most exciting experience of your life – as long as you put yourself entirely in my hands.'

'Like that?' she asked, wondering what he meant.

'We build up the tension,' he said easily, 'we nearly let you arrive at your release, then we make you pause. And then again. And eventually you will reach a state of tension you have never known before and the release will be utterly fantastic, believe me! Commit yourself to me, Suzette, I will show you what I can do for you.'

'Why not?' she said, sitting up to take off her frock. If he saw her beautiful body completely naked, this might inspire him to hurl himself on her to make love more normally. She stripped herself naked – except for the diamond bracelet on her wrist.

Didier too undressed, now that matters were reaching a point of seriousness. Suzette looked at him, his body was well formed and in good athletic shape. There were smooth muscles under his lightly tanned skin – muscles on his flat belly and long thighs that rippled to his movements. Not that she knew it, but he was a keen tennis player, playing a hard and expert game three or four times a week against the best opponents he could find.

Even more impressive was the stiff male part standing proudly out from his belly. It was not particularly long perhaps but it was more than usually thick. It was going to be very exciting, Suzette thought as she eyed it, to feel its hard strength inside her. But events did not conform to expectation, she did not know how strange a man she was dealing with.

What occurs between a man and a woman when they remove their clothes, important though it is to them, must always appear to be a comedy to others. Suzette lay back at ease while Didier studied her as intently as if he was learning by heart all the curves of her beautiful body. She was enormously proud when she was admired and through half-closed eyes she watched the changing expressions on his face as the impact of her beauty struck him.

His hand touched her shoulder. She gave a pleased little sigh and opened her legs a hand's-breadth – displaying to advantage the smooth petals of her *joujou*. Didier's hand travelled slowly over her breasts, shaping their magnificence by touch, printing a memory of their perfection in his memory. Then his hand found its way between those marvellous thighs and he caressed the smooth pink lips, probing them with a knowing finger.

Soon he heard the little moan which heralded the approach of her orgasm – her back arched and rose up off the black fur, her legs were shaking.

'Not yet, *ma belle*,' he whispered. Then his hand was gone and she was moaning in anguished disappointment, her heels drumming on the bed. It was impossible that the nervous system could tolerate these tremendous shocks, this was the thought in her mind when she calmed a little. One more disappointment on a similar scale would drive her insane, she was certain of it.

Didier was observing the progress of her sensations with care and skill. His hand passed lightly over her forehead, smoothing away the droplets of perspiration, easing away the little frown of concentration. And when he judged it prudent to continue, he surprised her by changing position to lie between her legs.

Oh! she exclaimed softly, feeling his mouth nuzzling at her. His warm soft tongue penetrated her, touching, caressing, until it was at her secret bud. The thrill of that caress sent spasms of delight through her body, and she sighed and trembled in languid abandon to the delicious ravishing.

She believed he was taking her all the way now and her belly pulsed in response. Yet even after so many shocks to her nerves by his sudden stopping, she was torn between two impulses: she wanted to experience an annihilating release from the tension Didier had created – and at the same time she wanted the growing ecstasy to last longer.

She drew her knees up and splayed them outwards, offering him her body fully. He raised his head for a moment to stare along her belly and up at her face. When she saw the commanding smile upon his face, she knew at that moment he was a sadist. The idea was so exciting her body shook. A sadist, a man to bully her and to abuse her body!

'Open your legs wider,' said Didier.

She obeyed him by forcing her knees further apart. He put his tongue into her again, and used it relentlessly on her bud – her passion soared to a fever. Her bare bottom was jerking upon the fur, she was rotating her hips as the wet tongue stimulated her to a frenzy. This was the critical moment – her loins shook and bucked in her headlong rush toward her climax.

Without warning, the flicking tongue was instantly withdrawn. For a moment Suzette could not believe what had happened. A cry of frustration and rage burst from her, a wail of despair. Her hands flew toward her open and slippery *joujou* to give the last three strokes that would take her over the edge into release.

Before she could touch herself, Didier seized her wrists. He was strong, he pulled her arms to her sides and held them down hard on the bed. She screamed and bucked, trying vainly to make her crisis come, but she could achieve nothing.

'No more . . . I'm dying. . .' she moaned piteously.

'I will not let you die, Suzette,' he said with a brief smile that held no amusement. 'You shall have what you want.'

All the same, he kept a tight grip of her wrists until he

was certain she had calmed a little and that there was no immediate prospect of her reaching a climax. When he thought it the right moment, he let go of her wrists and raised himself to his knees between her outspread legs. She stared with hungry eyes at the stiff male part standing proud from his belly, she yearned with all her being to feel its hard strength inside her, to feel the push of Didier's hard flesh, the fullness of its thickness in her belly.

His hands were under her, gripping the cheeks of her bottom. He sank down on her, his lean belly on hers, and he pushed home the hard flesh she had waited so long for. As soon as she felt him well inside she lifted her legs, hooked them over his back, and clamped him tightly to her. Didier did nothing after that long smooth insertion – he lay still and let her do as she pleased.

She rubbed her loins against him, undulating her belly on his, swinging her bottom from side to side. And soon she could feel the first warning of the approaching crisis – a spasmodic quivering of her thighs. Didier was still squeezing the cheeks of her bottom and now he began at last to ride up and down on her, his thrusts slow and deliberate.

'Now, now, now!' she moaned. 'Please, Didier. . .'

'Now?' he said calmly. 'As you wish.'

In a moment that rigid flesh was plunging in and out in a mad dance. *Ah, ah, ah!* she gasped – she was driven frantic by the feel of his thickness stretching her wide open. It was ramming in shorter harder strokes – she sobbed in joy to feel the start of her crisis, the delicious prelude in which body and soul are trembling on the brink of ecstasy, the moments when the senses seem to hesitate for a heartbeat before the breathless plunge.

At that critical moment, the throbbing part which was

working such havoc on Suzette's body suddenly ceased all movement. With her mouth open in a shriek, she stared up at the face above her and saw the sardonic smile.

'It is I who control your orgasm, Suzette,' he told her in a cold voice. 'I am the master of it – you will not be allowed to attain release until I decide you shall. Do you understand?'

Vaguely, through the overwhelming sensations surging through her, she understood that he had stopped his movements with the intention of forestalling her climax at the last moment. But he had left it an instant too long, the tide of passion had risen too high in her to recede now.

For two moments there was a hesitation, her body trembling as the in-rolling wave hung poised before it broke. *I decide when, not you*, Didier repeated. Then with a long shriek, Suzette bucked her belly upwards to drive his stiffness deep into her as the tide of passion swept irresistibly onward, carrying her with it on its crest. The wave broke. The orgasm burst in her. She gasped and and writhed in ecstatic release – and she was also laughing in the joy of her achievement!

It was a long hard orgasm, as he had predicted, though it was not of his doing – or with his permission. He was rigidly still throughout her pleasure, observing it but taking no part in it. When Suzette came to her senses again, she found him stretched out on her belly, his male part deep in her, as stiff as it had been at first.

'Why did you stop?' she asked weakly. 'Don't you want to?'

'Yes, but when I am ready, not because you want to,' he said.

She would have asked him about this, trying to understand his complex nature, but the opportunity was abruptly snatched away. The bedroom door was flung open and in rushed Simone, agitated and alarmed. She halted just inside the door, staring in wild surmise at the scene on the huge bed. There was Suzette, naked and on her back on the black fur, her legs wide apart – and on top of her was Didier Gruchy, equally naked, his stiff part evidently embedded in Suzette's *belle-chose*.

'What are you doing to her!' she cried in distress. 'Are you all right, madame? You shrieked so dreadfully I heard it right at the far end of the apartment! Such a scream – I thought you were being murdered!'

'Everything is all right,' Suzette assured the dresser with a giggle, 'I was carried away.'

It did not embarrass her to be seen naked with a man mounted on her. She giggled because she believed Didier might not be so insouciant at being discovered in his present position. And she guessed from the way he was hiding his face that he was anxious for Simone to leave them alone. She decided it would be amusing to prolong his mortification.

'Have you noticed Monsieur Gruchy's bottom, Simone? It is so very neat and trim, one of the nicest I've ever seen.'

'Very creditable,' Simone agreed, giving no more than a quick glance at the bottom concerned. 'Well, if you're sure everything is all right. . .'

Simone seemed reluctant to go, she was not entirely convinced that all was well.

'Perfectly sure,' said Suzette, giggling again, and there was nothing for Simone but to leave the bedroom and close the door.

When she was gone, Didier rolled off Suzette and lay looking at her strangely, as if unable to believe the interruption had taken place. He was still stiff and ready, but Suzette decided to keep him waiting a while before resuming his curious games.

'What you did to me,' she said, attacking before he had time to gather his wits, 'is that what you do to your wife?'

She couldn't imagine the slender and elegant Nicole Gruchy on her back, manipulated by Didier and begging for release. But it was idiotic to decide what people did together in the bedroom – Suzette's experience assured her the most improbable people did the most improbable things to each other.

'My wife adores me,' Didier said. 'There is nothing she does not do for me – and she insists I do everything to her. We have explored the limits of the possible – we understand each other extremely well.'

'Ah, you're not the only man to mention these frontiers of the possible,' said Suzette, 'but his interest was in crossing them, whatever that may mean.'

'Charles Desjardins,' Didier said at once. 'He has a theory! I am not certain I understand it completely.'

'At his party your wife suggested that you and she may not be so closely in harmony as you suggest.'

'No? What did she say about me?'

'Not that I believed her, of course, and why she confided in me I cannot guess. But she told me she finds you as predictable as all men.'

'Her experience of men is not so enormous she can generalise on the subject,' said Didier curtly. 'The truth is that she has a liking for young girls. I am a broad-minded man and I have no objection to that, and she has none to my adventures with other women. But *predictable* – no, I will not accept that!'

Suzette put her hands under her head and crossed her ankles.

'She also complained that all you ever think about is getting her on her back to pant and moan on top of her. She finds that very far from stylish, not at all *comme-il-faut.*'

Didier laughed and slid his hand up Suzette's thigh to stroke the smooth pink petals between them.

'What's more,' Suzette added to see how he took it, 'she warned me you are shameless and absurd.'

'Her favourite words!' said he with a smile. 'I know you're quoting her and not making it up when you use those words. Am I shameless? Yes, I admit it and take pride in it. Am I absurd? No other woman has ever said so.'

Suzette would have continued this conversation but Didier had other plans. He sat up and grasped her thighs. The strength of his hands thrilled her as he parted her legs.

'It is time for me to take control of your orgasm once more!' he informed her – and he mounted her with effortless dexterity. She felt her muscles opening to let him penetrate her with the steady pressure of his stiff male part. He lay on her belly and his hands roamed over her, caressing her full breasts and their coral-pink buds.

He intended to torment her to madness again. Suzette clenched her teeth to stop her urgent desire to cry out as sensations of urgent delight surged through her body. Her muscles clasped his hare flesh tightly – she wanted it to thrust in and out of her, to raise her to the peak of ecstatic feeling. But he lay quiet on her belly, his clever hands stroking her breasts. Inside her a tumult was rising fast – she started to buck her hips up and down in an effort to stir Didier.

'Ah, so soon?' he murmured.

He responded to her movements, thrusting strongly into her, his hands sliding down to grasp her bare bottom. *Oh!* she said, as she felt her passions surge torrentially. Her belly tensed in the first spasm of her climax – and Didier was gone!

She lay absolutely still, though the effort was terrible. She refused this time to let him have the sadistic satisfaction of hearing her cry out. She waited, it seemed an eternity, then he was back inside her, thrusting fast and ruthlessly. And now she sobbed with relief as her intolerable agony of pleasure raced toward its culmination.

He pulled out of her before she reached her climax. Her heels drummed on the bed, her body writhed – and Didier was straddled over her, a knee on either side. His hands were under her head, lifting it up from the black fur bed-cover, and she stared in incomprehension at his stiff part, throbbing so very close to her face. His knees gripped her sides tight and he raised her head higher. The unhooded purple tip of his proud part was touching her lips.

'Open your mouth, Suzette,' he said softly.

'No!' she gasped – and that was enough for him to push in at once. He pushed in deeper and she felt the big plum-shaped head slide along her tongue. Her mouth was full of warm hard flesh.

Didier jerked his hips in a short in-and-out rhythm, his hard knees gripped her sides. Now he, who had been so controlled and cool while he was playing with her, was panting and half frantic. How long could he last at this pace? Suzette wondered.

Her silent question was answered at once – by a hot spurting in her mouth. Now it was his turn to wail and gasp and arch his back in unendurable delight as his pent-up passion sprang from him. Suzette pressed her tongue close to his leaping flesh and felt his warm outpouring flow from between her lips and trickle down her cheek and over her chin.

He pulled quickly away from her again and he put his hands under her hips. The strength of his arms thrilled her when he raised her and turned her over on her face. He lifted her bottom up in the air and in an instant he had her on her hands and knees.

'I have absolute control over your orgasm,' he said. He panted and his body was trembling as he pressed himself to the soft cheeks of her bottom. She moaned and quivered to feel his still-stiff part pushing into her. In the fraught state of her emotions the penetration was enough – she dragged a long breath in, she gave a half-sob, half moan, heavy shudders passed through her superb body as she found her orgasmic release at last.

Afterwards, when they were calm again, she asked if he could explain why his wife had deliberately misinformed her.

'What do you mean?' he said. 'What did she say?'

'I've already told you – she said all you ever did was try to get her on her back and lie moaning and panting on her. But not with me, it seems – that was very far from your mind. The truth is you have strong sadistic leanings. Your wife surely knows it – you must have made her play your games often enough. There is a decadent side to your nature, Didier.'

'Oh, there is!' he agreed cheerfully. 'I nurture it tenderly and do all I can to develop it further. To be decadent in these modern times is not easy – so little is forbidden that it needs a strong effort of the will and imagination to achieve anything of note.'

'You would have preferred to live in an earlier time?'

'It was so much simpler to be decadent in the 1880s and 1890s – there were so many ways to shock others, so many things to do to shock oneself. The mark of the true decadent is simply that, to perform acts of pleasure which shock himself – which produce a guilty thrill, a tickle of outraged conscience . . . but this is becoming more difficult all the time!'

'A problem,' said Suzette. There seemed to her no reason why Didier wanted to shock himself but she was well aware that men were absurd creatures, never content with what they had, always striving for something else, usually something inappropriate.

'What was your last adventure in decadence?' she asked. 'Did you commit an unspeakable crime or a hideous perversity?'

'To the decadent, everything is possible,' said Didier with a wave of his hand indicating he would ignore her frivolity, 'and he does what interests him.'

'I understand the theory,' said Suzette, determined to remain frivolous in the face of his remarkable solemnity, 'but what in practice do you do?'

'I adore fairs,' he said. 'A few weeks ago I was at a fair in the Flea Market. I find a childish thrill in the contemplation of the steam engines and bumper cars, the noise and the blaring music. And the sideshows! One had a sign outside that captured my imagination, it said *La Jeune Fille Colosse*. I paid the few francs to go in and view this huge young creature. The glib and dishonest-looking man in charge claimed she was sixteen years old – but there is no way to tell. She was enormous beyond my belief a mountain of living flesh on a steel-reinforced chair. Her weight was two hundred and thirty kilos, according to her keeper, and I do not think he exaggerated much.'

'*Mon Dieu!*' said Suzette, who weighed only a quarter of that and thought herself in need of dieting. 'What an elephant – was she able to stand up on her legs?'

'Her legs were like tree trunks of flesh. She wore a cheap white imitation satin frock, the skirt very short to display her massive thighs. The barker reeled off her measurements and to amuse myself I said I didn't believe him. He evidently was used to being doubted, he handed me a tape-measure and invited me to check for myself.'

'This sixteen-year-old, was she attractive in any way?' Suzette asked, wondering what the point of Didier's story was.

'Her body was shapeless, her face was very round and full but there seemed to me an underlying prettiness,' he said. 'At this point she heaved herself cumbrously up to her feet, puffing and panting. She grinned at me and lifted her short skirt to let me measure round her thigh.'

'Ah, she flirted with you – she showed you her underwear.'

'Of the same cheap shiny white material as the frock,' Didier said. 'I measured round her thigh up near the join – and it was over a metre, one hundred and five centimetres to be exact, rather more than my waist – I was astonished and delighted!'

'Poor child,' said Suzette, shaking her head.

'Perhaps,' said Didier, 'but she was extraordinarily cheerful and naturally I gave her a few francs. At that I caught a gleam in the eye of the man in charge of the show and I spoke to him privately when the other sightseers had departed. To be brief I was able to persuade him to accept cash from me in return for an hour's freedom of the charms of *La Jeune Fille Colosse*. Her name was Marie, by the way, and the man informed me she was his niece, but you can never believe these people.'

'*Oh la la!*' Suzette exclaimed. 'but this is grotesque!'

'Perfectly grotesque,' said he, 'therefore irresistible! The line of demarcation between what is forbidden and what is not – such a line cannot be drawn because it does not exist, except for the common herd. To the true decadent nothing can be alien. What can be said to divide the most ordinary pleasure from the most outrageous perversity? Only the imagination.'

'That's enough of this second-class philosophising!' Suzette said. 'What did you do?'

'After the fair had closed for the night and all was silent, I went back. The showman and his niece lived in a decrepit motor caravan. He let me in, took the money I had promised and off he went to the nearest bar for the hour we'd agreed. It was badly lit, this caravan, confined and stuffy, which added to my sense of the deliciously sinister.'

'Were you drunk?' Suzette asked.

'No, no, that would have blunted my senses and spoiled a keen appreciation of the scene. Marie the colossal was ready for me, sprawling on a built-in bed. She had taken off the short white frock she wore for the exhibition and was swathed in a dressing gown of sorts – a vast and baggy garment tied round her waist – or where her waist would have been if she had one.'

'But two hundred and thirty kilos!' said Suzette. 'It is monstrous!'

'Oh yes,' said Didier with enthusiasm, 'utterly monstrous! I got her out of her wrapping and arranged her on the edge of the bed while I sat on a stool to study her young body. Her breasts were huge and shapeless – the biggest I've ever seen or ever hope to see! We call big breasts *melons*, but these made melons look like oranges. Her impossibly wide fat belly – so lascivious! I asked her to open those immensely plump thighs and permit me to see her patch of hair. And here I made a strange discovery.'

Suzette was thinking that Didier might be deranged. There was sometimes a streak of mild lunacy in old families. It resulted, they said, from marrying their own cousins for twenty generations.

'Marie had very dark hair,' he said, 'and naturally I expected to find a patch of dark brown curls between her thighs. But not so – the curious and interesting fact was that my young giantess had no body hair worth mentioning, neither between her legs nor under her arms.'

'Just as well,' Suzette said acidly. 'Otherwise the poor dear might grow up to become the Bearded Lady in the fair.'

'Between her legs she was as smooth as you,' Didier said, his fingers straying to the appropriate area of Suzette's body, 'but by nature, with no need to pluck the hair, as you do. I stroked her, she giggled and tried to open her legs further, but it was not possible. I pulled the stool close to the bed to stroke her all over – her flesh was pale and smooth and loose everywhere – like a boiled egg when you peel the shell away. Needless to say, I was as stiff as an iron bar, there was no question of not having her.'

'She was not a virgin, I suppose,' Suzette said. 'When a

girl has a so-called uncle who takes money for her, it is not likely she is untouched.'

Didier ignored the comment, reliving his moments of glory in the caravan.

'I rubbed her to a giggling orgasm,' he said. 'Those enormous legs kicked at me in her throes – if a foot had landed it would surely have disabled me permanently! How grotesquely beautiful she was at that moment – her thighs straining apart, her moist *joujou* stretched open to the limit!'

If that was what he found beautiful, Suzette thought, she had wasted her own superb body on him! How uncomplimentary he was, to tell her this sordid adventure! And he had refused her body – he'd done it in her mouth! It seemed this decadence he found so enthralling involved the deliberate humiliation of women. It was intolerable – he must be made to regret that!

'It was impossible to restrain myself,' said Didier, 'I swung her legs up on the bed – the effort of lifting that vast weight alone called for all my strength. Then I was on top of her, as if she were a bolster stuffed with cheap flock! I was clothed, only my trousers were undone enough for my purpose. I lay upon her vast flabby dome of a belly, I penetrated her with a single push, she was so wet and open.'

'This is too bizarre!' said Suzette.

'Yes, and it became even more bizarre. She was impervious to my thrusting. As you have seen, I am of ordinary proportions in this respect, but I made no impression on Marie's bulk. She lay silent and unmoving beneath me, though I had a massive breast in each hand and thrust brutally hard.'

'I find it impossible to imagine what was in your mind,' said Suzette in a tone of disapproval. 'The scene you have described is ugly, Didier.'

'I shall never be able to make you understand,' he said, 'you are too normal. What was in my mind? Ah, in those moments as I lay on that big round belly of *La Jeune Fille Colosse*, pushing into her soft hugeness, I felt superhuman. That she lay unmoved and silent increased my sensation of divinity – she was a thing of flesh to be used for my personal pleasure. The thought flung me into the most ravening sensations. My passion spurted up in her gross body, my loins thrusting in a frenzy I could not stop or control. It was beyond all belief!'

'Evidently,' said Suzette, fairly sure now he was deranged in some way.

'I detect a displeasure in your voice,' he said with a smile, 'I told you that you could never understand.'

'Perhaps,' she said, 'but I may yet surprise you. Let me show you a different decadent pleasure. Sit on the side of the bed.'

He gave her a quizzical look, as if to say *if you think there is anything you can teach me, you are mistaken*. But he did what she suggested, sitting with his back turned to her. She mounted herself on his shoulders, her hands clasping his forehead, her naked thighs pressing his cheeks closely.

'Carry me round the room,' she said. He knew it was a game of some sort, though he failed to see how it could be interesting. All the same, he stood up carefully, got his balance and strode round the bedroom with her perched on him like a jockey upon a racehorse, her bare feet tucked back under his armpits.

'Good horse,' she said. 'Once more round – faster!'

He walked faster, across the room to the door and back again, almost reeling.

'There, on the armchair,' Suzette said, 'sit down slowly.'

There were two pink-satin armchairs in the room, Didier chose the nearest. He turned slowly and lowered himself into it – his hands gripping the arms to steady himself. At the final moment Suzette leaned back to make him lose his balance – he fell down into the chair, his legs shooting out in front of him. She was still perched on his shoulders, her bottom resting now upon the chair back.

Didier sat panting, his head clamped between her thighs. Then her heels drummed against his chest, hard little blows to make him gasp. He was wondering what was the point of her game when she slid forward on his shoulders as far as she could, the back of his head pressed against her belly. She stretched her superb long legs down, her heels were beating a rhythm on his belly.

'Oh, yes!' he said. 'That's very exciting – do it a faster, and a little harder...'

Suzette could see the effect, hands clasping his forehead she glanced down the front of his body, down past her drumming feet to where his limp male part was stiffening again. She did as he asked, smiling thinly to herself.

'Oh, oh!' Didier gasped, almost breathless. 'You are driving me mad with the strangest sensations...'

Her heels drummed a savage tattoo below his ribs, kicking him as hard as she could. She was steadily driving the breath right out of him and he hadn't yet realised it, though his mouth was gaping wide and he was struggling to draw breath. When finally he understood and grasped at her ankles to make her stop it, he had left it too late.

'Yes?' she said mockingly. 'You are enjoying this? A little harder still for you?'

The continued oxygen shortage had weakened him, his movements were feeble and unco-ordinated. His mouth stretched wider open, he was trying as if his life depended on it to gulp in air – as indeed his life *did* depend on it.

The heavy beat of her heels had paralysed him. He gurgled and his perspiring body strained upwards in the armchair to throw her off his shoulders. But she was too firmly seated and he was too far gone to free himself. He convulsed and passed out.

When he regained consciousness he was lying on the floor upon his back. Suzette was sitting astride his belly and using both hands to massage his chest, to help him breath normally.

'I thought I was dying. . .' he sighed.

She quoted his own words back at him with a smile that boded no good, 'I won't let you die, Didier,' and then she added, 'not yet. You must suffer much more first.'

His arms were twisted awkwardly under him. He rolled his body as far to each side as her weight on him allowed, but he could not free his arms. While he was briefly unconscious his wrists had been tied firmly together with a silk stocking – one of the pair he had stripped himself from her legs – and with the other stocking she had tied his ankles.

'What are you doing. . ." he sighed, his voice weak.

'Surely you recognise the decadence you search out?' she said, sliding herself up his chest, 'the pleasure that shocks.'

'But this is. . .' he sighed, and became silent as the elegant smooth pink lips between her parted legs came nearer and nearer to his face. And then she was poised over him, her *belle-chose* no more than two centimetres above his mouth.

'It is a pity I cannot be a mountain of flesh,' she told him, 'that would add to your pleasure, no doubt. On the other hand if I weighed two hundred and thirty kilos, you would die under me too quickly. Yet on behalf of the fat girl, I am about to show you just what she would have done to you, if she'd been able.'

With that she lowered herself to sit over his face, her soft smooth flesh covering his mouth and nose so completely that his breathing was severely hampered. In a moment he began to panic, he twisted his body from side to side and thumped his tied feet on the floor.

'They say that the approach of death by suffocation causes an extraordinary sexual arousal in the victim,' he heard Suzette's voice say in the distance. 'A girl I used to know in Belleville told me she had a man friend who liked being hanged with a silk scarf. He'd string himself up to a hook with his trousers open and his *Julot* sticking out – and step off a chair – she kept an eye on him while he hung kicking and pushed the chair under his feet again at the last moment...'

Didier couldn't hear what Suzette was saying, his breath was cut off and there was a thumping in his chest.

'She said he'd gush like a fireman's hose-pipe before he lost consciousness,' Suzette was saying. 'Sometimes it flew three or four metres across the room. Imagine! I thought she was making it up, but we'll soon find out now.'

Didier was groaning dully in his throat, in desperation as he felt his senses slipping away from him in a red blur. His eyes were bulging from his head, but he saw nothing.

'You didn't want my pretty *joujou* before,' said Suzette

as she smiled down at his purple face, 'now you've no choice.'

His body jerked convulsively.

'Is it true then?' she asked. 'Was that it, Didier? Did you spurt behind my back?'

She eased herself back from his face, to sit on his chest and watch his eyelids fluttering feebly.

'You must have a little rest, *chéri*,' she said sweetly, 'come back to your senses, wake up and find out what is happening to you. Then we do it again. And then again. And again. A little lesson in humility for you, Didier, three or four times more.'

Pierre-Raymond is disconcerted

The celebrated photographer Pierre-Raymond Becquet had a studio on the Left Bank, naturally. It was to be found on the Quai St-Michel, overlooking the river Seine. It was to this first-floor studio that half the society ladies and actresses of Paris made their way to have their photograph taken. In effect, a portrait with *Becquet* scribbled in the bottom corner was the equivalent of a work of art.

The studio itself, where the pictures were taken, was without windows, Pierre-Raymond regarded natural light be disposed of. The windows in the studio had been filled in by a carpenter and his permanent screening painted over in white. But the adjoining room, furnished most elegantly, where Pierre-Raymond greeted his clients, had windows through which could be seen the tall towers of Notre-Dame cathedral upon the island in the Seine.

Nearer, down below on this side of the river, where the traffic never seemed to stop night or day, could be seen the stalls of the second-hand booksellers on the pavement along the Quai. They dealt in more than books, of course – they also sold old prints and more recent publications. An occasional stall even had a copy or two of the illustrated publication that gave an account of Suzette Bernard's life.

The pictures showed her more or less naked, being old Folies Bergère publicity photographs. But there was a studio portrait by Pierre-Raymond of Suzette in black velvet, looking impossibly beautiful and desirable, the famous diamond bracelet sparkling on her wrist. The day she arrived at Pierre-Raymond's studio to have that picture taken was a momentous occasion for him, a day he could never forget – it was the day he became infatuated.

It would be kinder to describe it as the day he fell in love but Pierre-Raymond was no longer an inexperienced young man to lose his heart to a beautiful face. He was halfway through his thirties, he had been married, separated and divorced. And there was no shortage of women interested in him as a lover. They pursued him relentlessly – including the highest and richest who sat for his camera.

In truth, sometimes he almost came to believe that the richer and better born and more elegant they were, the more eager they were to take their knickers down for him and spread their legs. But then, in justice, it must be said that Pierre-Raymond was a man of commanding appearance: tall, broad-shouldered, quick and neat in his movements. He dressed well and he looked like a member of the leisured class, even when he was working.

Most important of all was his reputation for being a fantastic lover, the type women dream about. How he had acquired this, he was not certain, but the truth was that women chattered to each other about these things on café terraces and at receptions and parties. Pierre-Raymond's name was high up the list of men who were known to be satisfactory lovers.

In consequence, he had new clients phoning all the time for a convenient appointment to have their picture taken. They wanted to see him, having heard from a friend of his other abilities. Most of these ladies were married, many of them middle-aged but still very *chic*. By and large the actresses were unmarried – or between marriages. They too were usually over thirty, but it is not always possible to determine the age of an actress – many untruths are told about this delicate topic.

When the camera shutter had clicked enough times to make sure there would be pictures available, it would be indicated – subtly or openly, depending on the sitter herself and her usual way of doing things – that a closer and more profound acquaintance with the celebrated portrait-photographer would be welcomed. Pierre-Raymond had come to expect these approaches, they were part of his profession, so to speak. How very disappointing it would be if a sitter displayed no interest in him at all! He would have feared he was getting old and unattractive. As much out of conceit as anything else, Pierre-Raymond very rarely declined an offer.

Even for a Frenchman, he had made love to an unusually large number of women – elegant women in their thirties, interested in experiencing his alleged unusual abilities; elegant women in their forties who were beginning to find it difficult to attract young lovers; elegant women in their fifties, now a little desperate to find a man to strip them naked and make them thrill to the climactic pleasures they had become accustomed to when they were younger . . .

Pierre-Raymond certainly knew how to please. He was bold and strong he could make any woman, twenty-eight or fifty-eight, sob with delight and throw her legs round his back while he thrust into her. And not just once – he had the stamina to continue for hours – half a day or half a night, whichever was more convenient. One lady in particular, the wife of a very wealthy industrialist, swore solemnly to all her friends that Pierre-Raymond had made love to her five times in the course of an evening – and was still stiff when the time came for her to put her clothes on and leave.

It goes without saying that his reputation grew and his business was a success. When he found himself immensely attracted to the *chanteuse* who came to have her picture taken, he anticipated no problem at all in getting her into bed. But in this he was over-confident, Suzette seemed immune to his charm. The position was totally reversed – instead of a sitter offering herself to him, it was necessary for him to make advances to her!

Was it because Suzette was younger than his usual sitters? he asked himself. He put her at twenty-two or twenty-three, which was nearly correct, but even so, it seemed hardly enough to account for her lack of response to him.

Was she a lesbian, he asked himself? Did she respond only to women? But the newspapers had a story about her being in love with Antoine Ducasse, a rising young French film star. Although Pierre-Raymond could not know it, the story was made up by the show-business journalist Jean Dalmas and was not remotely true.

When Suzette opened at the Casino de Paris, there was no more devoted a fan than Pierre-Raymond Becquet. He made every use of his celebrity and his slender acquaintance with Suzette to get into her dressing-room and present himself – every evening when he was not making a client rapturously happy. Suzette liked him. He was an amusing companion, he knew everyone of significance and told scandalous stories about them.

But as for becoming more intimate with him – that idea seemed never to enter Suzette's head, even when he tried repeatedly to put it there. True, she treated him with increasing familiarity which was encouraging. So he thought at first but he was not pleased when he came to see she was treating him almost like an employee – a confidential employee, no doubt, like her dresser – but that was not how he regarded himself.

Take, for example, the little incident in her dressing-room – it had delighted him at the time. But later it took on another significance. After the performance one evening someone knocked at the door, there was always someone knocking at her door. It was astonishing that Pierre-Raymond was the only admirer there that evening – until the knock at the door!

Before Simone the dresser went to see who it was, Suzette told her to wait *while she put her knickers on*! And Simone waited, hand on the door – while Suzette opened a drawer of her make-up table and found a pair of knickers. Pierre-Raymond was sitting astride a chair, his arms on the back of it, like a cowboy in a Hollywood movie. It goes without saying he was fascinated – and amazed that Suzette paid him no attention to him while she put on her underwear. It was as if he was her assistant dresser!

As she had come off stage only minutes before, it was evident that she had performed bare-bottomed under her charming evening frock. Why she chose to do that, Pierre-Raymond couldn't guess, perhaps it was a type of theatrical superstition. Since then he had enquired of the dresser, but Simone was very close-mouthed, even when given money. If she knew Suzette's secrets she kept them to herself.

But the reason for her bare-bottomed condition was forgotten in the excitement of seeing her *joujou* – she had made no attempt to conceal herself while she pulled the knickers up her long legs. Pierre-Raymond's male part stood stiff in his trousers when he saw the smooth bare lips between Suzette's thighs. She had been a show-girl at the Folies Bergère and wore a tiny *cache-sexe* on stage – he guessed that was the reason why she removed the hair from her *belle-chose*.

He glimpsed it for only an instant while she was pulling her knickers up her elegant black silk stockinged legs – but it was long enough to confound him completely. Her bare *joujou* was so stunningly beautiful that if he were not already infatuated, he would have been from that moment on. Then while his heart was turning somersaults in his chest, Suzette had settled the tiny triangle of her silk knickers over her *belle-chose* and smoothed her skirt down.

Pierre-Raymond felt he was very privileged, as perhaps he was, but then the moment was gone. Simone opened the door for the visitor – an idiot named Dorville, evidently an acquaintance of Suzette's from the past. To Pierre-Raymond's analytical eye it was clear this Robert Dorville had been Suzette's lover and was still in love with her to some extent. The talk soon turned to the old days, when Suzette had been a show-girl, and soon after that Pierre-Raymond was gently dismissed.

But it was impossible to put out of his mind what he had been allowed to glimpse. To sleep was out of the question, he walked aimlessly from the Casino to the Boulevard de Clichy, trying to lose himself in the night crowd of pleasure-seekers. Along the Boulevard the shops stayed open all night – bakers selling long loaves, sausage shops, pharmacies with remedies for everything except what was ailing Pierre-Raymond at that moment, neon-lit bars, stalls selling *frites*, kiosks and restaurants.

He strolled, he looked, he sat in a bar and ordered a cognac. At about one in the morning he was hungry and found himself in the Steak Service – an all-night eating-place somewhere between the Place Pigalle and the Place Blanche. He ate a lightly done rump steak with *pommes-frites* and washed it down with a few glasses of Beaujolais.

The food settled his thoughts – after all, he was a Frenchman and therefore a member of the most logical nation on earth. His long-term problem was to gain the affections of Suzette – it was surely not beyond a person of his immense success with women to attain his heart's desire. The immediate problem was simply resolved, his blood was boiling because he had seen Suzette's *joujou* – he could cool it for the present by making use of another woman's.

Between one and two in the morning was an absurd time to call any of the hundreds of amiable ladies he knew on the telephone. Many of them had husbands. And why should he put himself to the trouble of explaining his sudden urge when hundreds of women were available outside on the pavement for his selection? Only a few years ago, in this state of mind he could have gone to a superior *maison de tolérance*, but a prudish post-War government had closed them down and put the girls out on the streets.

He found what he was looking for on the corner – a red-headed woman in a fake leopard-skin jacket and stretch trousers above high heels. The two policemen standing nearby looked away while he quickly agreed a price with her. She led him into one of the narrow streets off the Boulevard running up the Montmartre hill and into a small hotel.

It was all reasonably satisfactory. The red-headed woman undressed – she was plump of belly and thigh and starting to sag elsewhere – but it was of no consequence. He was not here for an aesthetic experience. She climbed naked onto the narrow bed and spread her legs for him. He knelt between her thighs to look at her mop of dark-ginger curls and the plump lips they covered. A cold fascination seized him – he had been impelled here to this dingy little hotel by a chance glimpse of a woman's *joujou*.

The situation was not rational – he had seen so many of them he could persuade dozens of women to take off their clothes and let him touch them between the legs! Why was he so affected by a momentary glimpse of a singer's? What could be so different about it, to cast him into this absurd obsession? Leave aside considerations of bare or hairy – in what possible way could it differ from the one now offered by its red-headed owner for his amusement?

He found no answer to his question, though he felt the fleshy lips at his disposal and parted them to see inside. He was lost in his thoughts until the redhead enquired in a slightly bored tone if he meant to do anything or not? He arranged himself on her plump belly and rode her hard and fast, his eyes closed and his thoughts elsewhere.

214

The redhead kept her legs as wide apart as she could, to let him thrust in as deep as he wished. He had his hands underneath her and was half lifting her heavy bottom off the bed to ravage her depths. The weary old bed rattled to the rhythm of his lunging as Pierre-Raymond uttered a loud puzzled moan and spurted his obsession into her.

Afterwards, when he was dressed, he gave her a few francs extra, as a tip for her co-operation. She thanked him grinning and said she could be found on the same corner every evening after six. Pierre-Raymond took a taxi to his apartment.

He had calmed his body and escaped from his obsession. He was in his bed by two-thirty, pleasantly tired and he fell asleep easily. But in truth he had achieved nothing but a brief respite. The image in his mind was another matter and it could not be erased by a redhead spreading her legs in a cheap hotel bedroom.

Pierre-Raymond began to dream of Suzette. Again he was in her dressing-room and she raised her evening frock to let him see she had no knickers. Her *joujou* was smooth and bare and beautiful – the most desirable he had ever seen, this lover of hundreds of elegant women. Or so it seemed to him in his dream.

'*Je t'aime*, Suzette,' he shouted. He ripped open his trousers to show her his stiff part, it throbbed furiously in his hand. *That won't do at all*, she said, *not for me. But you must!* cried he in dismay. She shook her head and dropped her skirt to hide what he wanted. Then they were not in the Casino de Paris but, in the mysterious way of dreams, the scene transformed itself to Suzette's apartment in the Boulevard Lannes. He had been there once, months ago, when a magazine editor sent him to take some pictures of Suzette at home, for an article.

In the dream he was perched on one of the white leather sofas in the sitting-room, Suzette was sitting on the low table with the etched-glass top. She had her skirt up round her waist. His trousers were wide open and his long hard part reared upward.

Ça ne va pas, Suzette said again – with hardly a glance at his pride. He went on hands and knees across a white goat-skin rug between him and the low table – and crawled under it. He lay on his back on the black-tiled floor to stare up through the glass at her bare bottom and the smooth petals between her thighs.

He was so aroused he knew he was going to spurt his desire in two more seconds. Ah, but there was a barrier of glass between his jerking part and Suzette's *joujou* – a sheet of glass etched with long-stemmed Lalique flowers.

If he had not calmed himself earlier with the redhead in the fake leopard-skin, his desire would perhaps have spurted during his dream into his pink silk pyjamas. But all that happened was he woke up, stiff and thwarted. Two more seconds, he thought to himself in dismay, only two seconds more sleep, that was all it required – he would have seen his spurt on the glass. How very inconsiderate dreams were, how unrewarding!

Poor Pierre-Raymond, obsessed by what he desired with all his heart and strength – like a chevalier in the ancient legend who rode by night and day in search of the Grail, his long lance at the ready! And there was a worse trial to come – less than two weeks after his ecstatic glimpse of the heavenly vision, he was tested to the full, pitted in combat against his own obsession.

This was when Suzette came to his studio to have photographs taken for a new promotion by the record company. It was in the afternoon, she refused to go anywhere before lunch any day. She sat on a gilt and tapestry armchair in the ante-room to Pierre-Raymond's studio and smiled and drank a little glass of cognac while he talked to her. He did this with all his clients to put them at ease before they went before the lights and camera. Not that Suzette needed any reassuring but Pierre-Raymond did – he was afraid his hands would be shaking too much from emotion for him to take her picture.

Finally they went into the studio, the big bare room with no windows, where spotlights stood on tall metal legs or hung from the ceiling. A large stand held long rolls of tinted paper that could be pulled down to make a background for the sitter, white reflectors stood ready on tripods and an assistant was at hand to change the plates in the camera as they were used.

Simone the dresser had accompanied Suzette to the studio with several frocks in wrappings draped over her arm. Evening frocks of course, that was how Suzette presented herself to the public – black velvet, bare shoulders, high heels, a diamond bracelet. But horror! Simone had neglected to bring the particular shoes Suzette intended to wear with one of the frocks! She was sent off by taxi immediately to the Boulevard Lannes to fetch them.

'We won't wait for her,' Suzette said, 'we can start with the chiffon and the black patent leather shoes. Help me out of this – it buttons at the back.'

Pierre-Raymond was enraptured by the suggestion he

might help to remove her clothes! He stood behind her, his hands trembled while he unbuttoned the sage-green taffeta frock she had arrived in. It undid from the neck to the waist, then he carefully lifted it over her head. His assistant – a nineteen-year-old learner named Alain stared open-mouthed as the frock moved upwards to reveal Suzette's long thighs, then her tiny black lace-edged knickers. Standing close behind her, Pierre-Raymond's view was restricted but he could observe her superb bottom in the black silk and he could guess what his assistant was looking at.

'Alain, go and help Patrice in the dark-room,' he said, 'I'll let you know when I need you.'

The assistant scowled at him and left the studio reluctantly. Pierre-Raymond hung the taffeta frock over a chair back, it was the chair he had selected for Suzette to sit upon while he took photographs. He moved round in front of her, his male part hard as iron and twitching in his trousers. His eager glance took in her beautiful breasts in a black lace brassiere. He sighed and stared at the lace-edged silk knickers and wished he could see through to her smooth-lipped *joujou* . . .

Suzette seemed not to notice his interest – performing at the Folies Bergère for a year had accustomed her to being stared at by hot-eyed men with long bulges in their trousers. She sat on the chair and crossed her knees.

'Bring me a pair of black stockings,' she said nonchalantly, 'there's several pairs in that bag, if Simone didn't forget to bring them too!'

Pierre-Raymond found them and brought a pair to her, thinking she would have removed the ones she was wearing by then, but no, she was waiting for him, looking impossibly desirable in just her underwear.

'You may take my stockings off,' she said, smiling at him. 'Do you know how? A man of your reputation ought to know.'

It required all Pierre-Raymond's resolution to stop himself babbling in mindless wonder as he knelt at her feet to take off her stockings. He reminded himself he was no inexperienced boy with his first woman – no, he was Pierre-Raymond Becquet, lover of many, many elegant ladies, a devil of a fellow with a way of reducing females to sobbing ecstasy.

Kneeling so close to her, her perfume was entrancing – he could not be sure if it was Lanvin or Chanel. He took a deep and shuddering breath, his hands trembled only a little as he unfastened her suspenders and smoothed the first silk stocking down her leg. A sigh escaped him when his fingertips brushed along her thigh – this was unavoidable.

Then the second stocking, after she uncrossed her legs and he thought his heart would stop beating. He put on the first black stocking, guiding her foot into it, easing it up her smooth leg to the knee and then up her thigh. *Bon Dieu*, he could hardly catch his breath while his fingers brushed her skin – while his eyes stared at the silk concealing her *belle-chose*!

Eventually it was done and the black silk stockings were attached to her suspenders. She held her legs out in front of her while she examined the stockings for wrinkles, runs or any other blemish, then she dropped her feet to the floor and smiled her ravishing smile at Pierre-Raymond. His heart was leaping inside his chest and he could hardly speak but he controlled himself.

'You said a man of my reputation,' he said, trying not to be too serious. 'What do you mean by that?'

'Women talk about you, Pierre-Raymond,' said Suzette, 'as you well know. They say you make advances to every woman who enters your studio and refuse to let them leave before you have them. They nickname you *Monsieur Ten-Times*, but that's only a joke, I imagine. It is true you know how to take stockings off.'

Pierre-Raymond was still on his knees on the floor. She stood up and he rose with her.

'I can't wear a bra under the chiffon frock,' she said with a tiny frown. 'It's cut too low for that.'

'But of course!' he answered – he had only just realised she was playing a game with him. Her casual manner and the showing of her body was a deliberate tease – to see how much of it he could tolerate. She knew he was as stiff as an iron bar inside his trousers, she could see the faint flush of emotion on his face, she was amusing herself at his expense!

'Undo my bra then,' she said, turning her back toward him. He thought he might lose his mind, his emotions were so tremendous when he undid it. She shrugged her perfect shoulders out of it and let it fall, Pierre-Raymond's male part jerked so furiously that he believed his passion was about to spurt! And he was so far gone he welcomed the thought!

Naturally, it didn't happen. Just as in his dream, the night when his obsession began, the process halted itself two seconds before completion. Or so it felt to Pierre-Raymond. Even though Suzette had turned to face him, her full round breasts openly displayed. They were beautiful beyond words, he wanted to kiss them. But that was only a diversion, what he desired most of all in the world was to take her little knickers down and touch and kiss the smooth pink petals between her legs . . .

'You're staring at me as if you'd never seen me naked before, Pierre-Raymond,' she said with a smile.

'But I haven't,' he answered, puzzled by her words.

'What, you were never at the Folies Bergère in all the time I was on stage there!'

'Ah that! Yes, of course I was! But that doesn't count, you were one of many beautiful naked young women. I didn't know you then, Suzette. Now that I do, I am enchanted, I adore you.'

'Naturally,' she said with a little shrug, keeping a straight face. 'Every man who wants to make love to me adores me. Bring me the black chiffon frock and you can start to take pictures.'

'I would prefer to take pictures of you as you are now,' said he, greatly daring and still hopeful.

'I'm sure you would,' and she touched his cheek for a moment. 'In black silk stockings, with no bra. And perhaps you'd prefer it more if I took my knickers off as well!'

'Ah yes,' he murmured, his face dark red with emotion and his stiff part bounding in his underwear. Before his delighted eyes Suzette shrugged and hooked her thumbs in the sides of her tiny black lace-edged knickers. She bent forward, her breasts swayed freely in a manner to arouse a saint, and she slipped the knickers down her legs and stepped out of them.

Pierre-Raymond stared at the smooth petals between her thighs and almost stopped breathing. His knees felt weak, his head was spinning – but only for a moment and then his normal reactions asserted themselves. He took a step forward, arms outstretched to embrace her. He intended to kiss her and carry her into the ante-room, where he could lay her on the brocaded chaise-longue and throw himself on her. There was no time for anything else – the confounded dresser must be already on her way back by now!

Nothing of the sort happened. Suzette took a step back as he stepped forward.

'No nude photographs,' she said, shaking her head – as if she didn't know what was in his mind and it wasn't photography. He moved toward her once more and she turned aside from him as if she hadn't noticed his lunge at her. He stood still, wondering, and meanwhile she had found the chiffon frock among the others and slipped it over her head. She sat down on the little gilt chair and crossed her legs with easy elegance.

'Is my hair all right?' she asked. 'Is the fringe ruffled? No? Then I'm ready – you can start photographing.'

Pierre-Raymond stared in bewilderment. This could not be true, this farce! It was not possible that he, Pierre-Raymond, lover of so many women – *Monsieur Ten-Times* – could be eluded in this manner by the only woman he had ever truly adored!

But there she sat, looking demure and tranquil and desirable, wearing only a thin chiffon evening frock and silk stockings! Her superb breasts were hardly concealed by the low-cut frock, and between her gracefully crossed legs, she had no knickers to cover the divine *joujou* he was burning so fiercely for. Without knowing it, his hand was on the hard bulge in his trousers to contain its wild jerking.

Suzette pouted at him, then gave him her ravishing smile.

'I'm ready,' she said. 'Start taking pictures.'

Two days later he put five black-and-white prints on the wall – Suzette head and shoulders, Suzette half length, Suzette full-length, Suzette half-profile, Suzette looking sideways into the camera. Not on the walls of the ante-room, of course – that was furnished as a sitting-room with very stylish furniture and two water-colours by Bernard Buffet. No, he attached his life-sized glossy prints to the walls of the studio – to see them while he was working.

There they were seen by Madame Picard when she came to have a portrait of herself taken for some worthy charity or other that she sponsored. Madame Picard's husband was a prominent and rich manufacturer of glassware, not exactly the beautifully designed pieces that sell for high prices and are for display only – but the type most people buy and use. Cheap wine glasses for bars, carafes for bistros – the sales were excessively large and the profits very acceptable. While he expanded his business further and further, Madame Picard had little to do but visit shops and attend dress shows by important couturiers, chat in cafés and sit on committees for the relief of various unpleasant maladies in Guadeloupe or other overseas territories of France.

Giselle Picard was forty-one – a tall thin dark-haired woman of impossible elegance. Monsieur Picard was fifty and extremely busy. They spent little time together and Giselle turned naturally to other and more attentive men for the affection necessary to her well-being. When she had heard of Pierre-Raymond from a friend, who praised his abilities with warm enthusiasm, Giselle had made an early appointment to have her photograph taken.

The first session was remarkably satisfactory. An affinity quickly developed between sitter and photographer during the shooting – an understanding, it would not be an exaggeration to say. After the last picture was taken and Alain despatched with the plates to the dark room, Pierre-Raymond escorted Giselle back into the ante-room for a glass of fine champagne – so necessary after the fatigue of sitting in a chair and looking elegant while her picture was being taken. `

They sat and chatted and drank their champagne. Giselle asked for a second glass! Twenty minutes later Pierre-Raymond turned the key in the door to the studio, preventing Alain from coming back that way. And he locked the door to the stairs, barring it to further clients – in truth, he had no other appointments for that afternoon but Madame Picard could not know that.

He removed her expensive silk summer frock with her willing assistance. He laid her down in her expensive silk underwear on the green brocade chaise-longue. He knelt beside her to remove her brassiere and kiss her soft little breasts. Naturally, this was precisely how he expected things to go, this was how it had gone before with so many women. It was the honour due to him as a superior lover, this baring of their bodies to permit him to exercise his skill!

As for Giselle, she closed her big brown eyes and lay at ease on his chaise-longue to let him demonstrate his highly praised ability at love-making. She raised her knees and parted them to draw him on, she felt his hands stroke the inside of her thighs and she smiled a secret smile.

It cannot be hidden that this was an area of human endeavour in which Giselle had considerable experience with numerous men. Ever since Monsieur Picard developed in his middle years a marked appetite for young women – preferably eighteen or nineteen years old Giselle had directed her attention to other men. Younger men, active men, men of prowess. Many of her women friends were of a like disposition, feeling they were neglected at home. Giselle was very favourably impressed by Pierre-Raymond.

After that first encounter, they became lovers on a frequent if irregular basis. Giselle looked in at the studio when there were no other demands on her time, committee meetings or dress shows. When Monsieur Picard was away from Paris she stayed all night at Pierre-Raymond's apartment. He did not know it, but it was Giselle who had nicknamed him *Monsieur Ten-Times* when she spoke about him to her women friends. Perhaps it would be more exact to say when she *boasted* about him to her women friends, to make them envy her.

It goes without saying that when she arrived one day to find life-sized portraits of Suzette Bernard on the studio walls, it was a formidable shock to her. She knew perfectly well he was a lover of many women and not only herself – for example, he was the lover of five of her friends. And those were the ones she knew about – not everyone discussed their *amours* so frankly. As for the rest, Giselle assumed he made love to every woman who came to his studio and perhaps many who didn't.

All that was well understood. But this – pictures of a woman on the wall, this was something different! He had never before displayed pictures of any of his conquests, it would have been in doubtful taste. But this open display for all to see! Could it be possible *Monsieur Ten-Times* had fallen in love? The idea was absurd. And yet . . .

She said nothing while he arranged lights and reflectors and fiddled about, as photographers always do. He took three plates and sent his assistant with them to the dark room. Giselle went with him into the ante-room, seated herself and took the glass of champagne he always offered.

'Those pictures on the studio walls,' she said, with studied insouciance, she was looking down her long thin nose at him. 'I know that face, I've seen it on posters.'

Pierre-Raymond perched on the edge of the chaise-longue close to her and he was equally casual when he answered.

'Yes, it's Suzette Bernard, the singer,' he said. 'She's on at the Casino de Paris. She came in for some photographs the other day – I think they're for publicity.'

'How very interesting,' said Giselle, not sounding the least interested. She craned her long neck to look down while she set her glass on the floor and suggested he lock the door. He did so without a word and sat down again near her. She put her hand on his thigh at once.

'But why pin the photographs up on the wall?' she enquired.

He shrugged and said there was no special reason. Perhaps for publicity for the studio – Mademoiselle Bernard was well-known. Giselle had his trousers undone and open, his lengthening part between her long thin fingers. She stroked up and down quickly with a nervous little movement.

'You had her on this chaise-longue, I suppose,' she said very casually, her fingertips sliding on the smooth skin of

226

his long hard part, then up over the purple head as it became distended. 'How was she with her legs open, Pierre-Raymond, amusing?'

'Ah no,' he breathed, squirming from embarrassment, 'I assure you I have not made love to her, Giselle.'

He was telling the truth, not that Giselle believed him for a moment. She gave an artificial little laugh and closed her hand tight round his upright part.

'There is no need to deny it,' she said, 'we have no secrets. I know you make love to every woman who lets you, young, old or in-between.'

'No, no!' he protested. 'This is very unjust, Giselle!'

'Pah! Why make ridiculous excuses? I know for a fact you've had five of my dearest friends – Marguerite, Fleur, Marie-Anne, Nicole, Lucienne. I suspect you've had Marie-Laure, Nadine and Therese as well. All on this chaise-longue!'

To that he said nothing, he shrugged slightly and waited. She was correct about all of them except Marie-Laure Le Cateau, who had burst into tears of remorse when he took her knickers down. He had kissed her and sent her home untouched. *Almost* untouched – he had been unable to resist giving her pretty blonde *joujou* a quick caress before pulling her knickers up again.

'These are ladies of a certain standing,' Giselle continued. 'They belong to families of significance. Until now you've been aroused by that, to be admitted into the intimate affections of superior ladies. But now you abandon us for an entertainer, it seems.'

Pierre-Raymond put a hand on her wrist to stop her movement – his stiffness was so hard-swollen and jerking it would take not much more to make him spurt in her hand.

'Giselle, believe me,' he said earnestly, 'you are mistaken – I have not made love to Suzette Bernard. I swear it!'

Not for want of trying, he thought dismally, *but it is clear she has no wish to let me. Though she tantalised me till I almost went insane with desire – she stripped naked and let me look at her – but when I would have taken her in my arms she laughed at me and slid out of reach!* Naturally, he made no mention of this disappointment to Giselle Picard.

Giselle chuckled to feel how strong and taut the flesh in her hand had grown. As for Pierre-Raymond's protestations, what was she to think? She stared into his face, seeking the truth. His eyes were clear and frank, his brow furrowed and his expression absurdly solemn. She decided he was telling her the truth – for some inexplicable reason he had not had this dark-haired singer on her back when she came to be photographed.

But because she believed him, that was no reason to let him think he was forgiven. Let him suffer a little, it was good when men suffered – it deflated their ridiculous self-esteem for a while at least.

'As you wish,' she said with a shrug, disbelief in her tone. 'You are a strange man, my poor Pierre-Raymond – we know you so well, those of us who are your good friends and have entrusted our happiness and reputation into your hands.'

Truth to tell, the situation was the reverse of what she said – Pierre-Raymond's immediate happiness was in *her* hand. He had let go of her wrist, being a little calmer, and she had resumed her nervous stroking.

'You must trust me,' she said, 'I have your interests much

at heart. Are you in love with this cabaret-artist? Be honest now – I am very understanding, you know that.'

She smiled into his eyes with great candour – she was waiting for him to make a fool of himself. And that he did. He solemnly assured her again that he had not had Suzette on her back, that he was very mindful of the happiness and reputation of his dear friend Giselle – and much more meaningless protestation of this type, all of which served to make her smile cynically.

But while Pierre-Raymond was as complete an idiot about women as every other man, there was one simple thing he understood. A direct appeal to their emotions, bypassing reason and logic, is usually the best way to proceed. This glimmer of comprehension had rescued him many a time from awkward situations. He put it into effect now. While he rambled on about trust and reputation and other imponderables, he slipped his hand up Giselle's grey-and-pink frock and into her expensive silk knickers.

With the skill of years of making love to a variety of women, he caressed between her thighs, his fingertips roamed over soft warm flesh and through thick curls. His hand moved slowly – he wanted to make her feel he understood her superiority and that he appreciated the value of her warm affections. And of course, that he was overwhelmed by her desirability. These things need not be said in words, they can better be expressed in the touch of a hand between woman's legs.

'Ah *chéri*,' Giselle sighed, opening her legs to let his hand caress her more easily. She was an intelligent woman, she knew he was merely changing the subject by this caress – she had him at a disadvantage and he was taking this way out to escape. Men were absurdly simple, she told herself.

On the other hand, what he was doing to her felt so delicious that she had no intention of stopping him. The discussion could resume later, when other pleasures had been enjoyed.

'Do you adore me, Pierre-Raymond?' she said with a malicious little smile.

'Oh yes!' he sighed. 'Yes, Giselle . . .'

His caress had made her moist, he felt it on his fingers when he pressed in between her soft petals. In a moment he was on his knees beside the chaise-longue, turning her frock up and sliding her knickers down her legs. They were of ivory silk, he noted with total lack of surprise, Giselle never wore any other colour or style – she must have dozens of identical pairs!

He put his hands on her parted thighs and leaned over her to stare closely at her *joujou*. Like all the rest of her, the lips were long and thin and set in thick dark-brown curls. Truth to tell, since that evening at the Casino de Paris when obsession seized him at a chance glimpse of Suzette without her knickers, he had made love to nine women – some on several occasions – and he had subjected each of them to this keen scrutiny.

Needless to say, the one he sought between so many thighs, he did not find – but that did not impede him from making a proper use of the ones put at his disposal. A man may be obsessed, but he is not required to forego the normal pleasures of life. When he had stared in puzzled melancholy between the legs spread for him at the moment – when he had regarded the brown curls or the blonde curls or the reddish curls or the mouse-coloured curls – he penetrated the owner's warm belly and rode her to ecstasy – whoever she was.

'Do you like what you see?' Giselle murmured as she opened her legs a little wider.

'You are beautiful,' he said, 'beautiful . . .'

His thoughts were elsewhere. He presented his stiff flesh to the subject of his inspection and pushed in deep. To Giselle's long thin face came a satisfied smile, it was for this she came to Pierre-Raymond's studio, nothing else. He was a good-looking man, and courteous, but his main attraction – perhaps his only real attraction – was his stamina and strength in love-making.

That was what Giselle and her circle of friends enjoyed – and discussed in detail when they compared notes – and came back to enjoy again and again, whenever they could escape from family duties and other social routines. They adored to be devastated to destruction by Pierre-Raymond's solid length of stiff flesh.

Pierre-Raymond gasped as he thrust in and out. In his mind he was doing it to Suzette – it was her long beautiful legs curled round his waist to hold him tight, not Giselle's long thin legs. It was into Suzette's belly he was sliding, not Giselle's. He gasped again to feel his moment of crisis approaching rapidly, he leaned forward to press his lips to Giselle's in a long kiss – and he made himself believe it was Suzette's tongue touching his tongue.

Giselle was enjoying all this immensely, her body shook with tremors of pleasure as Pierre-Raymond performed in his vigorous and usual way. She vibrated her tongue in his mouth and locked her legs over his back, holding him very close. She made up her mind to devote the rest of the day to him – Monsieur Picard had gone to Brussels for some business reason or other. Perhaps he had a young girlfriend there. Who could say?

Yes, she would devote the day to Pierre-Raymond and to love. Or, to be more precise, she would persuade him to devote the day to love-making and her. *Oh yes!* she thought, overjoyed to feel the orgasm starting to flicker in her belly – it would burst in two more seconds – today she would make him so excited that his nickname would be true and exact: *Monsieur Ten-Times!*

When she was not making her friends envious, Giselle was well aware that he'd never gone beyond five times with her. And that was a special occasion. Perhaps it was his limit, perhaps even Pierre-Raymond was incapable of ten times. But it would be very amusing to find out!

And if he could? It was impossible to imagine how the tenth time would be, the orgasm would surely be formidable! Giselle tried to picture herself after a tenth time, her body bathed in perspiration, legs sprawled weakly apart, her breath fluttering in her chest as she hovered at the point of unconsciousness... How delicious, she thought wildly – he must do it for me!

As for Pierre-Raymond, sliding in and out with easy strength, he was lost in his dream of doing it to Suzette. He gave a long sigh, spurting his passion into Giselle, and she bucked under him as she was gripped by a fierce little orgasm. *One down and nine to come*, she cried exultantly in her mind. Perhaps.

Simone makes her arrangements

After her prolonged act of retaliation against Didier Gruchy the bedroom, Suzette did not expect to see him again. Ten days passed and he did not show up backstage at the Casino de Paris. She had almost forgotten him and then there he was one evening after the show, waiting for her. Fortunately, there were others in the dressing-room, one of them the journalist Dalmas, ready with notebook in pocket for any trifle of gossip he could use.

Didier brought flowers, an impressive and expensive basket-arrangement. Suzette thanked him briefly and told Simone to find a place for them.

'I have been away,' Didier said, as if they had parted on the best of terms the last time they met. He smiled and seemed very pleased to see her again. 'May I call upon you in the Boulevard Lannes tomorrow?'

Their parting had not been friendly and certainly not tender. Suzette had held him prisoner on the bedroom carpet, his wrists and ankles tied with a pair of silk stockings behind his back. She had drummed the breath out of his body with her heels until he passed out three times. And three times he came to after a few seconds, weak and dazed.

After that she had thought it wise to stop. She had left him tied and helpless on the floor while she pulled on a sweater and slacks. She bent over him to say *goodbye*, a malicious grin on her face, and touch her fingers to her lips and then to his in mockery of a kiss. Then she was gone.

Evidently she had left instructions. Five minutes passed and the Simone the dresser came into the bedroom. She said very little, the expression on her face was impassive, though perhaps in her secret heart she was laughing at him. She rolled him over like a sack of flour and untied his wrists and ankles. And, seeing he was confused and enfeebled, she cradled his head in her arm to support it while he sipped from a glass of cognac she fetched him.

When he could stand up, still unsteady, she helped him into his clothes. If she was impressed by his naked body she gave him no indication of it – she treated him almost as if he were a small boy, pulling his silk undershorts up his legs and tucking his limp male part back inside when it flopped out through the slit in the front. She pulled his socks on for him, tied his shoe laces, and tucked his shirt down inside his trousers.

Eventually she took him down in the lift and outside to where a taxi was waiting for him.

'*Au revoir*, Monsieur Gruchy,' she said as she closed the taxi door, and only then did he see the faintest sneer on her face. If ever a general had been defeated outright on a battlefield of his own choosing, it had been Didier.

Now, almost two weeks later, he presented himself at the door of Suzette's dressing-room at the Casino. And he had the aplomb to say *bonsoir, Simone* as if nothing had happened. As if there was no memory of him lying naked and moaning while she released him from his humiliating bonds! But he hadn't forgotten and he slipped a large bank note into her hand, murmuring a few words of gratitude for her assistance.

Suzette came off stage and her smile faded to see Didier waiting for her. Simone listened in astonishment to hear him making his excuses about being away from Paris for some days. She was more astonished still to hear him ask Suzette if he might call round at her apartment the next day.

This man is without self-respect, Simone thought – but no, it wasn't that, his sort always admired themselves warmly. He must be a little demented, as Suzette believed, old families usually were.

'No,' Suzette said to him. Not a sharp or an angry *no*, just a firm denial. Didier took it well, no one could find fault with his manners, he bowed and smiled very politely and off he went. *But we haven't seen the last of him*, Simone thought to herself though she said nothing to disturb Suzette.

She was right, of course. The next afternoon, a little before three, there he was at the apartment door, more flowers in his hand. Refusing him permission to call had had no effect whatsoever, it seemed. The maid who let him in informed Simone, those being her instructions, and the dresser went to speak to him.

'Mademoiselle Suzette is not here,' said Simone, 'and even she were, I don't believe she'd want to speak to you.'

'Really, Simone? How can you be so certain? Has she said so to you?' he asked, nonchalantly. He was most elegantly dressed for his visit in a silver-grey mohair suit, a borsalino hat and a pair of lemon-yellow kid gloves in his hand.

'There is something I must tell you, Monsieur Gruchy,' Simone said. 'Come with me.'

There was a faint but satisfied smirk to be seen on his face as he followed her, not to the sitting room and certainly not to Suzette's star bedroom, but through the ten-roomed apartment to where he had not been before. It was a small bedroom at the far end, with a window that looked out over a courtyard. It was Simone's own room, he guessed that at once. Why the secrecy? he was asking himself. What could she possibly have to say to him that required these precautions?

It was in his mind that his cash gift to her had secured her loyalty and she intended to make some revelation about Suzette which he could use to his advantage. The thought was reinforced by the care with which Simone shut the door and stood with her back to it. He glanced about the room, at the narrow bed and at the simple dressing-table, two chairs and the garish picture of St Sebastian on the wall.

It was the usual picture of the martyrdom, Sebastian had been tied against the trunk of a tree and shot full of arrows by his torturers. The feathered ends of shafts stuck out of his naked body and thighs like quills on a porcupine, but he looked alive and interested. The painter had made Sebastian's loincloth slip down to show the top of his dark curls – one arrow was sticking through the cloth close to where the Saint's male part might be expected to dangle.

If Didier had given the coloured print on the wall a moment's thought, it would have made much clear to him concerning Simone and her general attitude to male sexuality.

'What is it you have to tell me?' he asked. He stood with a manicured hand in his jacket-pocket, posing elegantly, almost a fashion plate.

'You are a dangerous man, Monsieur Gruchy,' Simone said. 'You were doing bad things to Mademoiselle Suzette the last time you were here. There's no point in denying it, we both know it's a fact. I heard her scream and I saw what you were doing to her.'

'What nonsense! You saw nothing out of the ordinary. You saw Mademoiselle Suzette on her back naked, and me on top of her. A perfectly normal arrangement. And in any case, what concern is it of yours?'

'It is very much my concern. It is important for Mademoiselle Suzette to have a lover to take her to bed and make her happy, because then she sings all the better. But you are not a proper lover, Monsieur Gruchy.'

'What!' he said. 'You accuse me of being dangerous and doing bad things to her. Yet I must remind you I am the one you found unconscious and bound on the floor. Bad things were done to me. I was in bed for days afterwards, with my doctor calling twice a day!'

'Perhaps,' said Simone, who seemed unconvinced, 'but the fact is, monsieur, I cannot permit you to harm her because you have abnormal ideas.'

A sudden thought occurred to him then – was Simone spying him through the bedroom door keyhole when he showed Suzette how he took control of her orgasm? Did she really know anything or was she only guessing?

'What abnormal ideas?' he asked, 'what do you mean?'

'I think you understand me perfectly well, monsieur, abnormal ideas about *this*!'

While speaking she had advanced slowly toward him,

small step by step, so when she said *this*, she was able to reach down with both hands and have his trousers open before he could stop her.

'What the devil are you doing!' he exclaimed as she rummaged around inside. He grabbed at her wrists, but by then she had jerked the front of his silk shirt out of the way. She had a firm hold on his male part and dragged it out none too gently through the slit of his underwear for scrutiny.

'Whatever you had in mind to do with it today, you may forget it now,' she said. 'Mademoiselle Suzette will have nothing more to do with it – I shall make sure of that.'

As is the way of men faced with disappointment, Didier jumped instantly to the most obvious conclusion. The wrong one.

'Ah, she has someone else! Who?'

Simone didn't trouble herself to reply, she knew exactly what she meant to do in order to discourage his unwelcome attentions to Suzette. She made a start by going down on her knees to take his half-limp part into her mouth. She knew how easy it was to arouse a man – ten flips of her tongue and he was stiffening in a most useful manner.

Didier stared down wide-eyed at the thick fleshy limb jutting out of his open trousers and into Simone's mouth. Until now he had never given a thought to her in terms of sexuality, she was an employee of an acquaintance. But what she was doing startled him into assessing her as a woman, as a sexual accomplice. She was thirty he guessed, or thereabouts, lean and small-breasted, but not bad-looking. Her hair was light brown, a mass of curls, she brushed out to make it look bushier.

Her eyes were half-closed as she attended to him. The

look on her face was sly and provocative – she would have
been grinning if her mouth was not otherwise occupied.
There was a small dark mole on her cheek to the left of her
mouth. While he was taking this in, she tilted her head back
and looked up at him, keeping hold of his length of stiff
flesh between finger and thumb.

Now he was certain she had been watching through the
keyhole where he forced himself into Suzette's mouth and
spurted his passion. Why else would she be doing this to
him now – unless to let him know she understood his
preferences and was herself in sympathy with them? Her
dark-drown eyes stared boldly at his face while she
massaged him, he believed he could read a message in
them.

'Well ... if Mademoiselle Suzette is not here ...' he
murmured, 'but this is ridiculous, you know ...'

Indeed it was. But while he was aware of it, Simone was
not – to her it was a matter of the utmost seriousness. She
intended to protect Suzette from this man. Still smiling at
him, she got up from her knees and raised the hem of her
frock to her waist. The gesture drew Didier's attention and
he realised she did not wear a servant's plain clothing. She
was in a pale brown frock, a *café-au-lait* colour, which
looked as if it might well be made of shantung.

Be that as it may, what he really stared at was Simone's
lean bare thighs between stocking-tops and knickers.
Although he did not fail to notice that the knickers were
good quality.

'But no,' he said, not sure what he wanted to say.
Perhaps in his mind there were forming haughty comments
about servants not knowing their place and taking it upon
themselves to behave in an insolent manner toward their

betters. Such comments might be expected from one of Monsieur Gruchy's background and position. Not that Simone Plon was a servant – she was Suzette's dresser – but to a *grand monsieur* every female employee is a servant.

Until now he had believed it understood between them that her mouth was the chosen receptacle of his passion. But lifting her skirt was an indication she expected him to make use of another and more banal orifice. And that was insolence on her part! If the comment was in his mind, it remained unspoken. After all, a passably good-looking woman showing an interest in a man's stiff part could no doubt be persuaded to let him insert it where he pleased. And if she couldn't be persuaded, she could be forced.

'But no what?' Simone asked with a grin. She slid the front of her cream-coloured knickers down to reveal her tuft of dark-brown curls.

Didier was in a highly aroused condition, but his senses were not yet entirely swamped. He made a last effort at commonsense.

'When do you expect Mademoiselle Suzette to return? An hour, two hours?'

'Not today at all,' said Simone, her fingers gliding over the thicket of curls between her legs, 'tomorrow midday, or the day after, perhaps – who can say?'

'Then there is someone else!' Didier said. 'She is with him – she is staying with him!'

Simone was pouting at him, her red-painted mouth seemed to be an invitation to him to make any use of it he pleased. While at the same time she parted the curls between her thighs to expose the long pink lips there. *This or that*, she seemed to be saying *take your pick, Monsieur, or both if you please – my body is at your disposal.*

Who could resist an invitation like that? All the world knows that when a man's proudest part stands up hard his intelligence drops down into it and he becomes capable of any idiocy. Didier took a short step forward and put his hand where Simone's hand lay, between her legs.

'Ah, you charming little slut,' he said, 'I shall take control of your orgasm.'

'That sounds dangerous,' she said, letting him stroke her. He was due for a surprise before long. Whatever he thought he was going to do to her, it was very clear in her mind that she was going to control him. That was the point of this comedy she had arranged.

Her knickers had descended to her knees. She took hold of his throbbing part and steered it in between her thighs – not where he wanted it to be, but close. She pressed her legs together to keep him in position and Didier let her have her way, sure he could reduce her to sobbing sexual frustration.

'Yes!' he exclaimed, he was thrusting gently in and out the soft flesh of her thighs as if properly in place. Simone's arms were round his waist tightly and she gripped his bottom through his trousers to keep him close.

'Are you so well disposed toward every visitor?' he gasped, his decadent imagination taking flight.

'No, only the interesting ones,' she said. 'Let's get on the bed.'

He thought she wanted to lie on her back for him and this was acceptable for the time being – when he had her in a frenzy he would lift her head from the pillow and slide his hardness into her mouth ... But he discovered he was wrong about her intentions. She pushed him down to sit on the side of her bed, then she sat beside and took his thick male part in her hand. He was sighing with pleasure, his eyes staring at how she massaged him firmly.

'I want you to understand, Monsieur Gruchy,' she said softly. 'You must not make love to Mademoiselle Suzette again. You must find another girlfriend to play your games with. I am serious.'

Didier stared blankly at Simone, his mouth open and his face flushed dark red. Her insolence angered him, he shook all over, his loins were jibbing forward.

'*Salope!*' he said furiously. 'How dare you speak to me like that!'

Simone took his hand and pushed it into the lace-edged leg of her cream-coloured knickers. While he was calling her bad names his open palm was rubbing trembling over her thatch of nut-brown hair and his fingers explored it thoroughly. So different from the smooth flesh he had stroked between her employer's thighs! He touched the soft lips concealed in Simone's fleece, he pressed a knowing finger inside, to take control of her orgasm.

He was furiously angry with her, he meant to make her pay for her insolence – he would take her to the brink of orgasm ten or twelve times and never let her achieve release. He intended to shatter her nerves, to reduce her to a sobbing wreck! When she lay sweating and shaking, finished and ruined, he would use her mouth – and if she could still struggle, so much the better!

His finger caressed her wet bud, raising her toward her first disappointment, or so he thought. But Simone judged it was time to administer the first shock. Her gripping hand rose and fell without mercy, And Didier wailed, in his anger he had permitted himself to become too excited to stop now.

His trembling hand reached for the nape of Simone's neck, he wanted to press her head down into his lap and thrust his stiff part into her mouth – but it was too late, he spurted furiously over his shirt-front and his blue silk tie.

'*Sacre nom!*' she said. 'Your lovely tie! Take it off quick and I'll wipe it before it is permanently stained.'

Without waiting for a response, she undid his tie and took it off. And his shirt, to wipe it dry – for that she had to remove his jacket. Didier sat on the bed slightly bemused, stripped to the waist, his trousers wide open. He was asking himself how it was possible for his scheme to assume control to go so wrong.

At the dressing-table Simone took a small handkerchief from a drawer to wipe his tie and shirt. She draped both over the back of a chair, her attentions casual, to say the least. Didier got to his feet and crossed the small room to look.

'Let me see,' he said, examining the blue tie. 'It is ruined; I cannot go through the streets wearing this.'

There was no reply from Simone. He turned in surprise, tie in hand, and saw she had returned to the bed. Not to lie on it, or to sit on it. She was kneeling at the bedside, lying forward on it. The skirt of her coffee-coloured frock was turned right up to her waist, she had pulled her knickers up and her bottom was on display to him, thin cream-coloured material stretched tight over the lean cheeks.

'You told me you were going to take control,' she said. 'What happened?'

Ah, if he knew the answer to that question! But it was of no consequence – she had offered herself again and this time there would be no mistake, he would control her until she shrieked!

He knelt behind her, grinning. He stroked the warm bare flesh above the tops of her stockings. With tantalising slowness, his fingers found their way into the loose legs of her knickers, to touch the short curls and fleshy petals between her thighs. The blood was pounding in his veins and his male part was swelling and stiffening by the second.

He held it in his hand and played while he observed Simone's bottom. She had pulled her knickers up so tight that the narrow strip of silk between her thighs was stuck in the cleft of her cheeks, thick brown curls visible on both sides of it.

'Now we are in a more appropriate position, Simone,' he said, 'it is pleasing to see you understand clearly we are master and servant.'

He rubbed his fingertips up and down the thin strip of silk between her legs to enjoy the warmth of her flesh through it. A few moments of that and she began to sigh faintly. He eased the knickers over her bottom and down her thighs. He put a hand in between her legs to stroke the hairy lips of her *joujou* – then his imagination produced an appropriately decadent idea for his urgent consideration.

'Ah yes,' he murmured, 'but of course!'

He parted the cheeks of her bottom and rubbed the ball of his thumb over the puckered little knot between them. She shuddered and stifled an exclamation, perhaps of horror, perhaps distaste – perhaps of excitement, who could say? At once Didier pressed his advantage.

'I am in control of your body, Simone,' he said, pressing the swollen head of his eager part between the lean bare cheeks and rubbing it up and down slowly. 'I control your orgasm.'

'*Ah non!*' she panted, her loins jerking up and down as if to escape his attentions.

He could not see her face, lying as she was away from him, he did not see her expression – much the same gloating triumph as the archer taking a careful aim at Sebastian's hidden part must have shown. She wriggled her hips again and uttered a gasp – it caused Didier to congratulate himself on being in total control of her at last.

Now was his moment to be super-decadent, to abuse this woman and debase her – to shock himself with a perverse pleasure! He leaned forward and pushed strongly, she shrieked, he pushed it again – and he entered her by the back door!

She was moaning faintly – he held her hips, steadied her and pushed until he sank the whole length of his stiff flesh in her and his belly was tight against her bare bottom. He plunged and gasped, his violence shook her body on the bed – and shook the bed itself! His hands were groping underneath her, between her thighs. He forced his fingers into her to ravage her secret bud – it was wet and slippery to his touch.

He had her at his mercy now – ten or more times he would take her right to the edge of ecstasy – then stop abruptly and smile to hear her cry of frustration. He would grate her nerves until she was frantic – until forced pleasure became unbearable pain. She could not escape him – the weight of his body held her down on the bed, his stiffness inside her pinned her to him – he was in control!

But alas for Didier, betrayed by his own decadent imagination in what ought to have been his triumph! Reason deserted him as he stabbed brutally into Simone's depths – without realising it he had gone too far to stop.

There was a moment of confused and violent ecstasy, then he was spurting into her. His head jerked back and it was he who wailed, not her!

Under his hectic strokes her body was bouncing on the bed and she was laughing quietly to herself, a knuckle in her mouth, as with her internal muscles she held Didier fast and drained him. In those moments of farce, he realised that she was controlling him. He collapsed feebly on her back, morally devastated.

When Simone had informed him earlier that Suzette was out, it was not the truth. She had been in the apartment ever since she woke up that morning about eleven, she was in her bedroom still – but not alone. With her on the star bed were Robert and Gaby and they were all three naked. Naturally, Simone would not let Didier – or anyone else – intrude on so delicate a scene.

Poor Robert had been driven to desperation by the need to pay back the large sum of money he had borrowed from his brother-in-law Daniel to settle matters with Marie-France's irate husband, the cyclist. Looking back, it was an act of idiocy to have asked Daniel to lend him the money, but all else had failed.

He had returned to Ariane Sassine, of course, and very nearly ruined his health forever in extended love-making all one day – even the insatiable Ariane was shattered! He made her happier than she had ever been in her life before – she told him that a thousand times, kissing his feet and his limp and dejected male part when it would no longer perform. He was a god, she adored him, all she had was his, even her life!

But when he asked for money, her enthusiasm rapidly dried up. And when he mentioned how much he needed, she burst into bitter laughter. She said she had deluded herself into the belief that he made love to her because he worshipped her. But no, she had been a sentimental fool! Now the truth was out – he did it for money, he was a gigolo like all the others.

So saying, she opened her handbag and counted out the fee she normally paid a gigolo for his services. She threw the money in Robert's face and stormed out of the suite sitting-room. He let the money lie where it had fallen, shrugged in resignation and left.

Ariane had been his last hope. Now Daniel was being awkward – the loan was for a month, he reminded Robert in his irritating accountant manner. The month was up. Robert was already overdue – Daniel did not want to say anything to embarrass him, but it was necessary for Robert to meet his obligations. Daniel didn't actually say *Or else*, but Robert could feel the words suspended over his head. Unless he repaid Daniel soon, Daniel would talk to Robert's father, with unfortunate effects on Robert's future prospects as a non-employed but overpaid director of the family business.

In this impossible position, Robert confided in Gaby. She was closest to Suzette, she could advise him what the outcome might be if he approached Suzette for the money. He was reluctant to explain the reason he had borrowed it from Daniel, but Gaby laughed and insisted on being told the truth, if he wanted her advice. He told her about Marie-France Lavalle, the insane cyclist and the sharp lawyer. To his chagrin, Gaby was helpless with mirth.

She advised him, when she could speak seriously again, not to mention Marie-France to Suzette, not if he hoped for money. She suggested he told her he had lost the money gambling – perhaps on the tables at Monte Carlo or Deauville. And she offered, for Gaby was good-hearted and she liked Robert, to be with him and give moral support when he told his sad story to Suzette.

He picked his moment well – so far as there is ever any good moment to ask a dear friend for money. He read in a newspaper a highly commendatory article about Suzette and her career – by a certain Jean Dalmas, of course – and in it was an item of exclusive inside information such as journalists live for and die for.

In a few more weeks at the end of Suzette's engagement at the Casino de Paris, Dalmas reported, the celebrated and beautiful and talented Mademoiselle Bernard planned to take her ease for a month on the Cote d'Azure before she opened at the internationally known Folies Bergère. Robert knew instantly why she had accepted that offer – she wanted to go back in triumph and sing fully clothed on the stage where she was once a bare-breasted show-girl.

Naturally, she would be in an excellent mood, he guessed. And he was right about that, but she didn't believe in his gambling tale for a moment. She knew Robert very well and was certain a woman was the cause of his problems. But she liked him, she had once been half in love with him, so she made no comment on his unconvincing excuse. She agreed to lend him the money – though she knew it was a gift, not a loan and that Robert would never be able to repay her.

Gaby fetched a bottle of champagne, although it was not clear what was being celebrated. They drank to each other, the three of them, and their mood lightened – they were again friends of long-standing. All this took place in Suzette's star bedroom at two o'clock as she had not yet risen for the day. Robert sat on one side of the huge bed, Gaby on the other side. They talked about former times, when Suzette was a show-girl at the Folies Bergère and Robert her lover. They talked about the little apartment in the rue de Rome which she and Gaby shared. And so on.

The spirit of friendship and harmony prevailed and a moment came when Suzette lightly flung aside the satin sheets and suggested they got into bed with her. She had been alone the night before and therefore was not naked, she was wearing a short white silk night-dress that hardly covered her breasts at all. But it soon came off when Robert and Gaby undressed and climbed into bed.

For Robert his dreams had come unbelievably true – the money was promised, he was free of Daniel, and he was in bed with the two most beautiful women in all Paris! It was like winning the national lottery and being handed millions and millions of francs by Brigitte Bardot!

Poor Robert – he had no suspicion he was being written off by Suzette, exactly as she had written off the money she had promised him. But Gaby understood, she understood her friend far better than Robert ever had. And seeing that Robert's dismissal was going to be an amusing event, she was eager to join in.

Ah, poor Robert, sitting naked on peach-satin sheets with his fifteen centimetres of stiff flesh on show – he had no idea what was really going on! The two women hurled themselves bodily at him and he went down laughing in a mêlée of arms and legs, breasts and bellies and bottoms.

Suzette and Gaby had him flat on his back. Their hands roamed all over him, their mouths touched him in quick little kisses, their teeth nipped at the flesh of his belly and thighs. Robert was aroused frantically, his hard male part bouncing up and down on his belly, as if with a life of its own. Gaby rolled over on to his chest and Suzette was across his thighs, between them he was helpless to move.

In a flurry of movement they changed their positions, Suzette sat astride his loins, his swollen part in her hand, while Gaby arranged herself behind him, sitting back on her heels with his head cradled on her lap. Robert was almost dizzy with pleasure as he stared up at Gaby's small pointed breasts, then at Suzette's full round breasts.

'The truth now,' Suzette said. 'Have you ever been had by two women at the same time, Robert?'

Her hand encircled his throbbing flesh with a knowing touch. His heart beat in his chest like a drum and his legs trembled. She stroked the taut flesh to make it grow harder and bigger.

She was so beautiful, he thought, her face without a trace of make-up, her raven-black hair shining, her fringe perfect ever, after the delicious little scuffle on the bed. On her wrist was her famous diamond bracelet, the stones glittering in the light as her fingertips tickled underneath his hairy pompoms.

'Never,' he murmured, fascinated to see how she opened the bare-shaven lips between her thighs with the purple-swollen head of his pride.

'Is that the truth?' she demanded, staring into his eyes while she impaling herself on him.

'I swear it, *chérie!*' Robert sighed.

It was not entirely the truth, there had been the affair some years ago with two pretty sisters he met on vacation at Cannes. He had wined and dined them on alternate evenings and took them to bed separately in his hotel room – after six days he had persuaded them to get into bed with him together. They fell out over who should be the first to open her legs for him and to resolve the problem he lay on the belly of the eldest and used his fingers to bring the other one to an orgasm at the same moment. Then vice-versa. Needless to say, only an idiot would mention that little episode in present circumstances.

'I adore you,' he sighed, 'and you too, Gaby.'

While Suzette rode slowly up and down on his embedded part, Gaby was running her hands over his chest. Her crimson-painted nails clawed at his skin and he watched as she sent shivers of pleasure through him by tickling his flat nipples.

'Gaby – look how far he goes into me!' Suzette sighed as her soft flesh slithered up and down Robert's stiff part.

'Ah yes, all the way!' Gaby murmured. 'Push harder, *chérie* – perhaps you can make him go in even further.'

From the tremor in Suzette's voice Robert could hear she was coming close to the crucial moment, although her sliding up and down on him had not become any faster or more forceful. And he was himself very near the crisis – his belly was trembling, his legs were shaking against the satin sheet. Soon – it was going to be soon!

'Oh yes, now Suzette!' he heard Gaby gasp, and Suzette's body convulsed.

'Yes!' Suzette cried out and Robert spurted up into her, his spasms shaking him and her too.

When Suzette's orgasm was finished, she raised herself slowly from him. He watched his wet part sliding out of her centimetre by centimetre. *Ah*, he heard Gaby sighing behind him. She, too, was fascinated by this gentle withdrawal.

The women lay on either side of him, Suzette with a hand

upon his thigh, Gaby with a hand on his belly, and both hands were suggestively close to the slack part that lay drooping.

'A little rest for you,' Gaby said, her lips touching his ear. 'Then Suzette and I change places and I have you. *Ca va*?'

'Oh yes,' said Robert, lost in a languorous dream of paradise on earth, two beautiful women taking turns to make love to him, a glass or two of fine champagne to revive him . . .

'He'll have you moaning in no time,' Suzette told Gaby. 'Once you feel that long thick thing inside you, you're done for.'

'Let's see if we can stiffen it up again,' said Gaby.

Robert wondered if Suzette knew that he had made love to Gaby before. It had been two years ago, on the day of Suzette's debut as a *chanteuse* at an exclusive night-club in the Avenue Montaigne. He had called at the apartment they shared in the rue de Rome. Gaby was alone and he was miserable because he knew his affair with Suzette was over.

Gaby felt sorry for him – and for herself. Her own boyfriend, the little pervert Lucien whom she adored, had skipped out of Paris to escape being arrested and she feared she might never see him again. She had comforted Robert, and let him comfort her while they sat on the sofa talking about Suzette. She had unbuttoned the silk shirt she was wearing, then she took his hand and slipped it inside to caress her bare breasts – she had no brassiere on.

We are betraying Suzette, Robert had objected sorrowfully, but his objections evaporated when Gaby kissed his mouth and opened his trousers to put her hand in. And he was very willing to go with her into her bedroom and remove her shirt and slacks – and her tiny knickers. His fingers stroked her silvery-blonde tuft of curls and he had kissed the smooth bare lips below.

Gaby was so beautiful, with a slender dancer's body, long blonde hair tied back in a ribbon, small round breasts, pale blue eyes and a taut-cheeked little bottom – she was so exciting to look at that Robert was half afraid he'd spurt in her hand long before she was ready to lie on her back and spread her legs wide for him. But in the end all went well. As if it was only two day's ago and not two years, he remembered how he had knelt upon her bed and lifted her loins up, her legs hooked over his arms. He had opened her petals with his thumbs and pushed his stiff part into her.

It was going to happen again now! Except this time Gaby was on her knees and he was on his back. And Suzette was behind him cradling his head in her lap and stroking his face and watching her dear friend do it to him. Did Suzette know this was not the first he had been inside Gaby's pretty *joujou*? Was it of any consequence, whether she knew or not?

'I like a man to have a long thick one,' said Gaby, teasing Robert's to full stretch by rubbing it on the soft lips between her spread thighs. 'Small ones are often disappointing. They're more trouble than they're worth.'

Elsewhere in the apartment, Simone had taken Didier Gruchy to one of the bathrooms. She made him sit naked on the bidet while she washed his dangling part in warm soapy water. She dried him with a fluffy white towel, monogrammed SB in a corner. From the shelf under the mirror she took a scent-spray, aimed the nozzle at his deflated pride and squeezed the rubber bulb half a dozen times to spread a mist of expensive cologne over it.

She expertly helped him into his clothes. That was, after

all, her employment. But his blue neck-tie had a large stain-mark on it and Didier said it was impossible to wear it in the street.

When she had dressed him in his elegant silver-grey suit, she shrugged and said he'd have to go home tie-less. Didier scowled in annoyance, but he couldn't expect her to find him a neck-tie in a woman's apartment. She escorted him through the apartment toward the door, where his elegant borsalino hat had been left on a small side-table, along with his lemon-yellow kid gloves.

Along the way they went past the closed doors to the sitting-room. Didier heard music playing inside, one of Suzette's songs that was enormously popular. It was called *Avenue Foch* and was about a beautiful woman, walking her fluffy little white dog on the Avenue. They pause for a moment under a tree, then walk on. A handsome young lover is eagerly waiting for her in an elegant apartment, he will enchant her with his love-making – she tells her little dog to hurry up with his *pipi* . . .

Didier had no time for the amiable sentiments of the song, he was angry and he glared at Simone.

'You have lied to me!' he said sharply. 'Suzette is at home – I've been tricked by the two of you!'

With that, he flung the sitting-room doors open and rushed in to remonstrate angrily with Suzette. She was not there – Didier stared about in confusion. The large radiogram was playing, and there was a stack of records on the auto-changer. On one of the white leather sofas a young man lay full-length, his shoes off his eyes closed and his hand inside his undone trousers.

He was a good-looking young man of twenty, or not much more – he was dark-haired and very slim, as if he didn't eat enough. When he heard Didier barge in, he opened his eyes – they were large and dark, set in a sensitive face.

'Who are you?' Didier demanded, all politeness forgotten.

The young man said nothing, his hand remained inside his open trousers and he stared past Didier to Simone, a look of silent appeal on his face.

'This is Monsieur Michel,' said Simone, her hand on Didier's arm to pull him away and out of the sitting-room. 'He is a poet and he composes the words for Mademoiselle Suzette to sing. And he lives here.'

'Lives here?' said Didier, sounding bewildered. 'But why?'

Naturally, Simone had no intention of confiding the household arrangements to an outsider. And it would not have been easy to explain Michel Radiguet's reasons for living there as a guest – *she* understood them because she understood Michel, but that was because she was a woman. Didier did not have that advantage.

Poor Michel, hopelessly in love with Suzette and unable to be apart from her. She adored him and she let him make love to her when she had time. Alas, adoring him was not the same as loving him. As for faithfulness, she did not offer it, or expect it.

He knew she was in her bedroom with Robert Dorville and Gaby and he knew they were there to make love. He was tempted to go and join them, Suzette would not mind, he believed. Nor would Gaby. He often went into Gaby's room when Suzette was too busy with her career to give him her time or attention.

But it would be unbearable to see someone else making

love to Suzette – and impossible to think of making love to her while another man watched. He wanted Suzette alone, he certainly did not want her to see him make love to another woman, as he would to Gaby if he went into the bedroom now. After he'd done it to Suzette, that is. No, what he wanted was for Suzette to demand he was faithful to her alone, as a proof of his true love!

Her insouciant attitude dismayed Michel, ardent worshipper as he was. Why couldn't she be jealous of him in the normal way? His worst fear was that her indifference to what he did when he was not with her indicated his love was of no great importance to her.

And so he lay alone on the white leather sofa and listened to the words of one of the love songs he had written for her and composed another in his head, stroking his sad part to console himself a little.

Simone dragged Didier, protesting, as far as the entrance hall of the apartment. She handed him his hat and gloves. But before she opened the door for him she had words to say. To make sure he didn't escape before hearing her out, she edged him close up to the wall, her hands holding his arms.

'Don't forget what I've told you, Monsieur Gruchy,' she said, 'you must stay away from Mademoiselle Suzette. You are very bad for her, we both know that.'

'I shall do as I please,' Didier retorted with a sudden show of spirit, his courage returning now he was almost free, 'there is nothing you can do, impertinent slut that you are. I mean to inform Mademoiselle Suzette of your insupportable behaviour and request that she dismiss you.'

'And I thought we had come to an understanding!' Simone said with a sigh of resignation.

Her fingers slid quickly down his arms, from the sleeves of his jacket to the uncovered skin of his wrists, where his pulse beat, encircling his wrists, holding him . . . the touch was light but strangely intimate. A shiver ran through Didier. This woman had insulted him intolerably, he had given her to understand he intended to control her orgasm – and she had thwarted him!

For that she ought to be punished – now he was dressed and on his feet he felt capable of asserting his superiority. He began by shaking off her hold and he thrust his hand roughly up her pale brown frock, straight up to the bare flesh above her stockings. He gripped her *belle-chose* cruelly through the thin material of her knickers, squeezing the fleshy lips hard between finger and thumb. Simone winced and wriggled uncomfortably.

She slipped out of his painful grip by sinking to her knees on the hallway floor and, while Didier sneered down at her, she was busy with his trousers, opening them and feeling in to take hold of his slack part. She stroked it up and down a few times, then ducked her head and took it in her mouth. This was what he had desired all along – to symbolise his control of her orgasm by taking charge of her mouth. He was overwhelmed by the sudden and unexpected prospect of his wish coming true.

'Yes,' he murmured, 'now you are begging my forgiveness – and perhaps you will be granted it, and perhaps not.'

He reached down to put his hands on her shoulders and support himself, his feet apart on the floor. His body was beginning to shake with delightful emotion, then he realised that he was not in control of her, not even of himself. In effect, Simone again had taken control of him!

With an exclamation of annoyance he put a hand on the back of her head and told her to hold still – and now at last he took control, sliding his stiff flesh in and out of her wet mouth.

What difference this change of active and passive made is not easy to determine, except to Didier. But the change aroused him out of all proportion to the actuality – his imagination became captivated and bound. There was no possible explanation for it, but sexual passions require no explanations! All that concerns those taking part is the continuation of what gives pleasure.

Not that any lengthy continuation was necessary in this case. Didier's crisis was at hand – his mind and body were responding ardently to his final victory over the woman who had humiliated him in her bedroom. He held her head fast and thrust rapidly in and out, his stiff maleness bigger and harder than he ever remembered.

It was impossibly big. Didier felt he had become superhuman – he was decadent beyond belief, a creature of the dark side of Nature, a worthy descendant of Baudelaire and of Huysmans – and still his proud part swelled thicker and stronger. But Simone did not remain entirely passive – her hands slipped into his trousers and underwear and began to claw at the bare cheeks of his bottom.

'No!' he gasped. 'Oh no!'

This *no* didn't mean he wouldn't spurt in her mouth in five more seconds and it didn't mean he wanted her to stop what she was doing. It meant, *no, this is so exciting I don't believe it!* And perhaps also it meant, *I can't bear this intense pleasure – I shall go mad!*

He said *no* once more when her sharp fingernails dug into the flesh of his bottom, this final *no* was more like a long squeal. Blind ecstasy gripped him, churning through his body until it turned his belly inside out. His stiffness strained upward like a steel ramrod – it felt half a metre long – and suddenly he spurted his frantic desire!

But not into Simone's mouth. At the final instant she had pulled her head away from his grasp, ripping a hand out of his trousers and seizing his jerking part. If he had been more determined, he would have held her head tightly to control her while he rammed into her mouth. But in this comic battle of wills he was again the loser and for a second time he was martyred – Simone pushed his spurting part up under his shirt, hand flicking up and down fiercely, spraying his belly with his sticky passion.

'You know Monsieur Dalmas,' she said cheerfully, handling him heavily through his crisis, 'the journalist who comes to drink in Mademoiselle Suzette's dressing-room most evenings. He hopes to pick up little items of gossip for his newspaper.'

Didier leaned weakly against the wall, his knees like jelly – he was only just taking in Simone's words.

'You'd be an interesting little gossip item for him, Monsieur Gruchy,' she said. 'A well-known and important person like you. A lover of the arts, a society figure. If Monsieur Dalmas found out you'd been turned down by Mademoiselle Suzette and instead made love to her dresser, he'd be very amused. Especially if he knew it had been a face-down back-door job . . . what a laugh!'

'You wouldn't dare tell him – he couldn't print it anyway!'

'If you ever turn up in Mademoiselle Suzette's dressing-room again,' said Simone, 'I shall tell him at once. That is a firm promise. As for printing it, a cunning man like him

259

would find a way to drop hints, no names, but everyone would guess.'

She opened the apartment door, took Didier's arm and steered him outside. His trousers hung wide open and his wet male part stuck out forlornly, its head starting to droop – like poor St Sebastian, his tormentor had finished with him.

Jules rides his racing bike

The newspaper story that encouraged Robert Dorville to approach Suzette for the money he so desperately needed was true in only one respect – after her engagement at the Casino de Paris ended she had contracted to appear at the Folies Bergère. So much was fact. But the part about a month's vacation on the Cote d'Azure – that was made up by Dalmas the journalist, to flatter her.

In effect, she had only a week between engagements to prepare for her grand opening at the celebrated Folies Bergère – there were too many demands on her time at this time of the year even to consider leaving going on vacation. Later on in August, when everyone departed for the coast or the country and only foreign tourists roamed Paris, that was when she planned to have a long rest in the sun.

As for Robert, he was immensely relieved Suzette had made him the *loan* to pay off his irritating brother-in-law at last – but he had to accept that his long intimate friendship with her had undergone a profound change. *What a pity*, he said to himself and shrugged tragically, *mais c'est la vie!*

The cause of all this, his on-and-off love affair with Marie-France was in the off mode at the time. Truth to tell, she left him so many times after quarrels that Robert was

261

often confused whether she was living with him or not, at any particular time. Why they quarrelled so frequently was also a mystery to him – he had very little understanding of women and their strange manner of looking at things. He could get their clothes off, that was never a problem, but he never knew what went on in their heads. Sometimes this worried him, more often not.

Where Marie-France disappeared to each time she stormed out of Robert's apartment in a rage, vowing never to speak to him again, this was yet another unanswered question in his mind. When she came back to him after a day or two, he never dared ask where she had been, for fear of enraging her yet again. For a woman so young, so delicious and so desirable, Marie-France in a temper was not to be lightly faced! Robert had learned to duck objects flung at his head and lock himself into the bathroom until he heard her leave the apartment.

She was of a large family. In addition to her parents she had four married brothers and sisters living in the Paris suburbs and Robert assumed she went to stay with one or other of them when she deserted him. At least he hoped so. But all the same, he had a disturbing, if vague, suspicion – perhaps Marie-France passed these absent nights at the apartment of her husband, the bicyclist.

Why Robert had this disconcerting thought, he was not able to explain to himself. There was nothing to suggest it was so – in fact the record of past events was against it. She left Lavalle when Robert's love-making had taught her what passion was. Till that moment she was almost a virgin – in a manner of speaking – although Jules Lavalle was in the habit of throwing her down on her back daily and riding her for ten seconds.

In the circumstances, Robert assured himself constantly, there was no logical reason to believe Marie-France would ever return to the apartment near the Bois de Vincennes. He was wrong about this, of course, for he made the usual mistake men make of assuming women's emotions are somehow subject to logic and reason – which is an absurdity.

If the entire truth is told, Marie-France had returned to the Avenue Daumesnil several times, sometimes when her husband was there and sometimes when he was away cycling up mountains. When he was there, he demanded his marital rights – after all, there had been no divorce as yet, and might never be. Lavalle was a good Catholic and regarded divorce as a worse offence than desertion of the marital bed. Marie-France might be living with another but, in the eyes of Jules Lavalle, she and he were still married and would always be so. From which it followed that he had certain rights of access. To say that he demanded these rights is misleading – he took them. It had been so since the day they were married. Nothing was now changed in that respect.

The first time Marie-France came back to the apartment after leaving, he stared at her in amazement for a second or two – then scooped her up in his muscular arms and ran into the bedroom with her. And so, fifteen seconds after she walked into the apartment, she was flat on her back on the bed, her skirt up round her middle, her knickers being wrenched off by a hairy-backed hand as big as a dinner plate. Jules was in his pyjamas – it was almost ten o'clock in the evening and he invariably went to bed very early so he could be up at dawn. His short thick *chose* stuck out stiffly through the slit of his pyjama trousers.

One second later it drove into Marie-France like a battering-ram smashing through a city gate in the good old days of walled cities and sieges. That was his way, there was no surprise, but as usual the sudden impact almost forced the breath from Marie-France's body. She lay limp and panting, her golden-blonde hair spilled out across a pillow and her legs spread apart. Her body jolted on the mattress under his violent thrusts. Eight furious stabs after his penetration – eight, nine, ten – he groaned loudly and spurted his passion.

While he was moaning and shaking, Marie-France glanced surreptitiously at her small gold wristwatch. She wondered if he had set a new world record. She had noted the time when she had let herself into the apartment with her key and shut the door behind her. Since that instant, twenty-two seconds had elapsed. Jules' performance was, to say the least of it, *formidable*!

The truth was that she was in some awe of Jules' athleticism – on mountain roads, in the velodrome, in the bedroom. It was not love she felt for him, and perhaps never had been, it was admiration of a sort. She took pleasure in seeing him naked, though he was not conventionally good-looking or attractive. He was not tall, being a little under average height; his thighs and calves massively developed by his profession, his shoulders equally muscular and impressive from weight-lifting. His belly was as flat and hard as wood, ridged with muscle.

Between those huge thighs his male part seemed inadequate and undersized, but that was an illusion of comparison – in reality it was of normal length and thicker than many. It seemed also, in Marie-France's experience, to be in constant training, ready night and day for the starter's gun. When he returned from his dawn cycling, for example, to find her still in bed and asleep with her nightdress up round her hips, he was on her instantly – and it was all over before her eyes were properly open.

If during the day he came upon her anywhere in the apartment, bending to pick something up, he would seize her by the hips without hesitation, flip her skirts up, snatch her knickers down – and be up her and spurting before her first surprised gasp! Even in the car when they were driving, should her skirt slide up to show her legs above the knee . . . the glimpse of a few centimetres of silk-stockinged thigh was enough to set him off.

He would turn under the next archway or into a courtyard or- sidestreet or an alley and slam on the brake while he dropped the seat-back down flat. He would be on her in a flash – trousers ripped open, a meaty hand dragging at her knickers . . . and ten seconds later he would be sitting up again with a broad grin on his face, driving away while Marie-France mopped herself between the legs with a handkerchief.

It was grotesque, she told herself, it was bestial. Jules was like a machine, you pressed a button and *blim-blam* – he'd done it! It was over like that – *fini!* – and she would be wet between the thighs and gasping, ready for the thrills of passion. But Jules would merely grin and ignore her – until the next time he was aroused. Robert's very different attitude to love-making was for her the discovery of a whole new world of exquisite thrills, of overwhelming passion!

When she knew this was how it could be, she became insatiable – Robert was required to demonstrate his total adoration of her every few hours. To give him his due, he was very enthusiastic about obliging her.

Having left Jules, she came to like him better. Now that he could no longer reach out and tip her on her back and ravish her as the mood took him, she started to think of him almost as a type of large and clumsy pet. Now it was for her to decide when he was permitted to display his inarticulate affection. She decided if and when she returned to the apartment.

She didn't go to him often – she was content with Robert. But sometimes she went to see Jules because she found an elemental thrill in being knocked over and ravaged by her big clumsy pet. It was a peculiar thrill – one she would never find in the many delightful hours when Robert kissed her breasts and stroked her thighs and made use of all his knowledge and skill and devotion to bring her to a series of excruciatingly marvellous orgasms.

On the day of Suzette's opening at the Folies-Bergère, Marie-France let herself into Robert's apartment at ten-thirty in the morning. He had tickets for the opening and had talked about for the past week. He had never hidden his long friendship with Suzette, though he pretended to Marie-France that it was only a light-hearted affair, long since over.

Women cannot be deceived in these matters unless they want to be deceived. Marie-France's instincts told her Robert was lying and a quarrel had followed – after which she had stormed out of the apartment. She passed the night with Jules. In her mind she was getting her own back in on Robert in advance, for making her to hear his ex-girlfriend sing.

On the Metro taking her across Paris to her former home Marie-France thought it would be a pity to do things by halves. Both men annoyed her at times in their different ways – so why not get her own back on both at the same time? It was an interesting idea. She decided she would put Jules to the test, as she had Robert more than once – she would find out how many times he could be tempted.

How far up the mountain could Jules pedal his bicycle before his stamina ran out and he fell off the saddle? There could be no possibility of getting right to the top – the point when she herself had enough. Not even a Tour de France winner could ever pedal that high. It would be entertaining to see how high Jules got before his muscles turned to jelly.

Needless to say, he had her the moment she walked through the apartment door, before any words of greeting were exchanged. He had her again half an hour later, after they had had a glass or two of Beaujolais. To spare her expensive underwear from his clumsy depradations, she removed her knickers on the stairs before she went into the apartment, and put them in her handbag.

At ten-thirty the next morning, she found Robert in dressing-gown and silk pyjamas, reading a newspaper and breakfasting on rolls and *café-au-lait*.

'*Bonjour, chérie,*' he said, glancing up at her with a shrug.

He still liked Marie-France and was pleased to see her – but her tantrums were beginning to bore him and he suspected he was sharing her with someone else, perhaps her husband, perhaps a stranger. He felt the affair between them would not last much longer. It was a pity, she was very pretty, so blonde and slim. And much more interested in making love than any woman he knew. But alas . . .

Robert was stretched out on the sofa in the sitting-room, his rolls and coffee on a tray beside him. Marie-France wished him good morning and sat on the pale green striped sofa by his bare feet. She took his cup from his hand and sipped a little coffee before handing it back – it had too much sugar for her taste.

'I suppose you stayed the night at one of your sisters?' he said not very interested in the answer, certain it would not be true. He had phoned Jules Lavalle's number the evening before; twice, at ten o'clock and at midnight, to see who answered. Both times it was the muscular cyclist himself, Robert put the phone down without speaking, none the wiser.

To be truthful Marie-France did not look as if she'd passed a hectic night with her former husband. Her long blonde hair was beautifully combed and shiny, her make-up perfect, even at this more or less early hour of the day. Her pale blue summer skirt and jacket were uncreased, her stockings unwrinkled and without runs. There were no dark shadows under her eyes.

All of which simply proves how deceptive nature can be when a pretty young woman has a secret to conceal. Jules had cycled a long way up the mountain last night but there were no signs of his achievement to be seen. Marie-France looked at Robert with her head held on one side, her floating blonde hair partly over her face. She had no intention of answering his question, she knew it was he who had rung Jules last evening and put the phone down.

'Were you at Diane's?' Robert asked. 'Or at Claudette's?'

She pouted beautifully at him, the sulky look that devastated him every time, and she slipped a hand into his silk dressing-gown, then into the slit of his pyjama trousers.

'I missed you, Robert,' she murmured, her fingers tickling the limp part lying between his thighs. It stirred at once and she ran her fingertips the full length of it, her painted nails trailing down the warm flesh.

'Did you?' he said, a little breathlessly. He could feel his male part stiffening fast to her tickling, 'Then why didn't you come back to me? I was here alone all night.'

She didn't trouble herself to continue what was essentially a meaningless conversation. She slipped off the sofa and knelt to open Robert's red silk dressing-gown. He was going to ask her again if she really missed him, when she bent her long neck and took his stiffening part into her mouth.

'*Chérie* . . .' he sighed, enchanted by how her long shiny blonde hair hung like a curtain to his bare belly, almost hiding what she was doing to him. He adored her, he knew that now, in spite of her childish tantrums and her overnight disappearances. She came back to him fresh and untouched each time, instantly ready to make love, to show him how much she adored him . . .

Poor Robert had never been very clever at the best of times – and when a pretty woman touched his stiff part his intelligence ceased to function completely. But what of that? He was happy in his way – he accepted what life offered and he did not worry about the future. For Robert, tomorrow was a foreign country. He would explore it when he got there.

Marie-France let go of his straining flesh and stood up – she was shrugging off her elegant little jacket and fumbling at the fastening at the side of her skirt. And there she stood in her blouse and her knickers and her silk stockings – there was no question of returning to Robert's apartment bare-bottomed, that would be as much as to confess she had let another man make love to her!

Robert was up on one elbow, his other arm round her waist to hold her close while he kissed her thighs above her stockings. She felt his lips pressed to her bare belly, then lower down to kiss her petals through the thin pink silk. She stared down at him, smiling a little at the expression of rapture on his face. She looked at his fifteen centimetres of hard flesh standing proudly up out of his pyjamas. She meant to have it – not just once but as often as Robert could do it that day.

He was sliding her knickers down her thighs, she shuffled her feet together on the carpet to make it easier. She balanced or one foot and lifted her leg and bent her knee so he could slide the knickers off. At once his face was between her thighs, his tongue flickering over the soft lips of her *joujou*. In her mind was the thought that Robert suspected she had been with Jules – and he was desperate to reassert his own rights of access.

And so he shall! she thought, pouting in secret amusement at the comic idea. Such absurd notions men had – they thought they could own her! In another moment she was straddling him on the sofa, her knickers hanging from an ankle. She had his stiffness in her clasped fist. She guided it up between her thighs at the appropriate angle for smooth entry – and before she could spike herself on it, Robert gave a fierce upward jerk of his hips and drove it into her belly.

She sat down on it to push it in further, her hands busy with blouse buttons and bra, until her pale breasts and their darker buds were displayed to Robert below her. *Je t'adore, chérie*, he cried out in delight, his stiff part jerking inside her.

'You'll make me do it,' she said, her voice shaky as

emotion rose from between her legs to her heart in spasms of delight, 'I know you, Robert – you always make me do it!'

She was riding him in nervous little movements, rising up and down to her gasps and sighs. Pleasure was throbbing through Robert's body as he stared down to see her splayed thighs rising and falling over his loins, her moist flesh clasping his hard pride and caressing it up and down – a quick light stroking that would surely drive him right out of his mind with delicious sensation.

Robert wanted to get hold of her and pull her down to cup her breasts in his shaking hands but she was leaning back and out of reach, her face raised upwards and her eyes closed while she rose and fell on him.

'You're so strong,' she murmured, as if to herself. 'A man is no use when he's small and weak . . . no use at all . . .'

It was fortunate for Robert he could not guess what was going on in Marie-France's mind. She was completing her programme of revenge most satisfactorily. During the hours she had been with Jules he had had her five times. The first was a reflex gesture, so to speak – he had heard her key in the lock, and came dashing out of the sitting-room. His thickset figure had loomed in front of her in the entrance hall, his trousers already wide open and his stiff part jutting out in front of him like the long bowsprit of an old-time sailing ship.

'Marie-France,' he had moaned hoarsely, '*je t'aime!*' and without another word he had slammed into her and driven her back against the wall – under a large framed photo of him receiving an award of some sort for a bicycle race!

He had her powder-blue skirt bunched up round her waist in an instant and if it surprised him to find she wore no knickers, he made no comment, not even a gasp of surprise. Words were *de trop* when he was occupied in stuffing his length of stiff flesh into her. In it went, in a single push – just like a guardsman in a plumed helmet on duty outside the Elysée Palace protecting the President of the Republic, a moustachioed guardsman sliding his ceremonial sabre into its sheath!

Marie-France had been ready for his furious attack. On the landing outside the apartment, where she paused to remove her knickers and put them in her shiny black handbag, she had leaned on the wall, her hand under her skirt to arouse herself. With a fingertip she had caressed the soft lips between blondish curls and pressed slowly inside to touch her secret bud.

She had leaned back on the landing wall for two or three minutes, stroking herself, her eyes closed, making herself slippery and ready for Jules. And all this time she was thinking of Robert – imagining it was his wet tongue gliding over her bud. This she took great pleasure in. Robert could make love to her as often as he liked, upwards, downwards, sideways, but she always persuaded him to do this to her as well, some days two or three times.

Needless to say, since the day Robert first aroused dormant emotions in her, Marie-France had become almost insatiable. Not for her the once-nightly of the respectable married woman, that was ridiculously insufficient for her. However often she spread her legs for Robert, she always moaned, *more, more, again, chéri – do it to me again!* When his strength failed, as even his did after a few times on top of her, he made use of his fingers and of his tongue. By these means he could reduce her finally to a calm sobbing and then to peaceful sleep.

Outside her former home, on the landing, Marie-France played skilfully with herself to prepare for Jules. She knew very well he would have her the moment she set foot in the apartment and she intended to take herself almost to orgasm before she went in to present herself to him. But, dreaming of Robert making love to her with his tongue, the little *frissons* of pleasure in her belly were so delicious that she didn't stop in time.

Her finger slid a little faster on her wet bud and her legs began to tremble beneath her – *oh!* she sighed as she shook in sudden orgasm. When it was over she rested a little while, her back to the landing wall, waiting for her breathing to slow down before she found her door key and went in. It didn't change anything, this fast little orgasm by herself, it was a personal pleasure. She was ready to do it again, ready for Jules.

And when he had her against the wall inside the apartment, he lasted only eight seconds. It was almost three weeks since she had been with him, evidently he ought not to be left alone for so long! Marie-France's pretty *joujou* had been so delicately sensitised by her little game alone on the landing that the fury of Jules' sexual assault swept her instantly into a second orgasm, harder and longer than the first.

She sobbed and cried, she beat at his head and shoulders with her small fists while she squirmed in ecstasy against the wall under the framed photograph. When she was quiet again he picked her up as if she weighed nothing at all and carried her to the sitting-room. He was grinning at her as he carried her, one big paw between her bare thighs and clamped over her wet and sticky *joujou*.

Half an hour later, while they were drinking a bottle of

273

wine in the sitting-room, she had provoked him by letting her skirt ride up, as if by accident, until he saw her thighs – just a glimpse of bare flesh above her stockings! For him even a glimpse was enough to set him going. He was off his chair so fast it was as if a strong spring had uncoiled! He hurled himself at her like a naval torpedo – ripping his trousers open in mid-stride!

The sudden impact of his burly body tipped the sofa over, and she went helplessly with it. There was a crash as it struck the floor, Marie-France's legs flew high in the air – Jules between them, his blunt-nosed stiffness stabbing as it sought a way in. She burst into laughter at the farce of it all – she was still laughing nine seconds later when Jules groaned and spurted his passion into her.

But now, while she rode Robert on his own sofa, it was to the fifth and final assault by Jules that her thoughts turned. This had been after the second anonymous phone-call, at about midnight. Anonymous to Jules, perhaps, but not to Marie-France, who knew it had to be Robert. So he was worried what she might be doing, was he? *Very well then, Robert, you shall have something to worry about*, she said to herself with a grin, *or you would if you knew about it*.

To be truthful, Jules was looking a little the worse for wear – his eyes were heavy and he was slumped in a chair, his sturdy legs sprawled out. Those massive-thighed legs that powered him up the winding mountain roads of the Massif Central – they were trembling slightly now, Marie-France noted. After his last dash up the slope of pleasure, he was too listless to remember to do up his trousers. His limp part dangled, exposed. It was small and had a defeated look about it.

Ha! Marie-France said to herself. He is proud of his

stamina and being an athlete – but look at him now! A little hour with me and he slumps there as weak as a kitten! This will not do, my dear Jules, you had your way with me as often as you liked when I lived here – now it's your turn to do something for me!

She had taken all her clothes off some time ago, to keep them from being creased or torn by Jules' sudden onslaughts. All she had on was a pink-and-white dressing-gown. When she had moved out she had left some clothes behind, things she rarely wore – they were useful on her occasional visits to Jules.

She undid the belt of the dressing-gown and sat herself upon Jules' lap. The dressing-gown hung open, revealing her breasts, her flat little belly with its round dimple and a glimpse of blondish curls below. But Jules seemed un-responsive, he put his huge hand over one perfect little breast, enclosing it entirely, but beyond that he did nothing. He was still wearing most of his clothes – it never occurred to him to undress before making love to her. No doubt he thought the effort not worth while for the length of the time involved.

Marie-France pulled his shirt up and put her hand between it and his chest to tickled him. For a dark-haired man he had very little hair on his chest, mostly it seemed to be on the back of his hands and round his male part. And down his massive thighs. Her tickling produced no effect, he remained lethargic, hardly conscious, it seemed. Unless she took stronger action, he would be asleep in two more minutes!

She climbed up on his lap to kneel on his huge thighs, hands on his shoulders to balance herself. She pressed her soft belly to his face. He hadn't shaved that day and the bristles on his face prickled her soft skin. It was an exciting sensation and she rubbed her belly up and down slowly to experience it again. Jules sighed, he still hadn't put his hands on her body, though she was giving him every opportunity.

When she realised he wasn't going to touch her, she slithered down his body slowly and the soft lips between her legs left a wet trail down his chest. She touched a forefinger to the moisture and pressed it to his lips. He stared at her without interest, then she was on her knees between his ankles, groping inside his trousers. He sighed and tried to sit up but her hand on his chest pushed him firmly back into the chair.

A spasm flicked through his body, he stared down and saw how she was jerking at his limp part. She held it tight in her hand and subjected it to a heavy beat to rouse it from its torpor.

'No,' he said, 'not again . . . I can't . . .'

He wanted to close his thighs and push her away. She resisted his enfeebled push, she was determined to stay there and tug at his tormented part.

'I want you stiff, Jules,' she said with a malicious smile on her pretty face.

'Stiff!' he said wildly. 'Impossible. I've been stiff enough times for you for one night. I'm done for, I'm going to bed to sleep.

'We'll see about that, *chéri*,' Marie-France said softly. She stood up and moved a few steps away from him. When she was out of arm's reach, she turned her back toward him. She let her dressing-gown slip off her shoulders and glide down her body to the floor.

'*Voilà!*' she exclaimed as she bent over to grasp her

ankles, presenting Jules with a perfect view of her round bare bottom – and because her legs were well apart, the blondish tuft between her parted thighs. Her head was down at knee level and she watched Jules through her legs.

For a moment he stayed in his armchair, staring at her pretty bottom as if he did not comprehend what she was suggesting. But his male part stirred, in spite of his earlier protestation. It raised its head and became longer. Marie-France giggled as she remembered a picture she'd seen in a school book years ago – it was of a North African snake-charmer in a *souk*. He sat in the dust cross-legged, a sort of home-made flute in his hands and before him a woven basket.

The snake was rising out of the basket to the tune, its broad head held up on a long sinuous body – just the way Jules' *chose* was rising out of his open trousers. She'd played the right tune at last! She could see it growing bigger and bigger – and harder. Jules was on his feet, he lumbered toward her till he could get hold of her bare hips. He gripped her tight and she felt him press against her, his upright part in the crease of her bottom.

In another moment he would be inside her. He'd have her bent over holding her ankles with her legs splayed as far apart as they would go, her bottom up in the air like a schoolgirl playing at leapfrog – just so he could get into her for his little explosion of desire! But it was not to be so easy for him this time. Marie-France giggled and straightened her back suddenly so her *joujou* was safe between her legs at the moment Jules tried to drive up into it!

She pulled away from his grip and skipped away. He roared his frustration and stumbled after her. She led him at a trot round the sofa, up on its feet again after its earlier accident when his over-enthusiastic approach upset it. She twisted and eluded his clutching hands. She was improvising, making Jules work for his pleasure or, more precisely, for her pleasure. She ran out of the sitting-room, hearing his heavy tread close behind.

He caught her in the kitchen. He trapped her against the table and would have bent her over it face down but she wriggled and turned to laugh at him. He gripped her waist and heaved her up and sat her on the table top, where a bowl of apples stood.

'Marie-France,' he moaned, staring at her bare thighs and her *joujou*, with its tuft of fair curls. The fleshy lips were loose and moist from his constant assaults that evening. He slid her forward to the edge of the table, still gripping her waist, and she put her legs round him and crossed her ankles behind his back. His thick and hard part nodded up and down between her thighs. She took it between fingers and thumb and steered it where they both wanted it to be – it was the first time she had ever done that for him!

This was his fifth lap of the velodrome and he wasn't so fast as before. His dark brown eyes stared into hers, bulging from his head with effort. Fifteen seconds and he was still jabbing into her determinedly. Twenty seconds! Then she felt his legs begin to shake under him – the winning-post was close and he had started his final pounding sprint! He slid his hands under her bottom and raised her – then with a long furious thrust crossed the finishing line and won his race!

And this tempestuous attack of his was in Marie-France's mind while she rode Robert on his elegant green-striped sofa, only a few hours later. When Robert's climax arrived

278

it would be just as frantic in its way as Jules' had been! His clenched fists would beat on the sofa, his head up off the cushion to stare at Marie-France above him, his mouth open. And she? She knew that she would shriek to feel her own orgasm seize her – just as she had shrieked as Jules did it to her on the kitchen table.

It was true that Robert was fortunate not to know what was in Marie-France's mind while she made love to him – and fortunate for her that she could not guess what was in his at that moment. For the awkward fact was that when she straddled him he remembered too vividly an encounter with Madame Sassine in her hotel suite – an occasion when she had ridden him as Marie-France was doing now. Not that final and terrible meeting when he had told her about his financial difficulties and asked her to lend him the money. That was when she had screamed at him and then counted out what she normally paid a gigolo for his services – and threw the money in Robert's face.

No, it was months before that, when they were on good terms – though she had been far from pleased that he did not visit her every day when she was staying in Paris. It was a rainy afternoon, he remembered that well because it was almost impossible to find a taxi and he was very late in arriving at the Hotel George Cinq. Ariane was fuming with impatience, she thought herself insulted by his lateness.

He was hardly inside the suite before Ariane had snatched his hat and flung it on a side-table in the hall – from which it rolled off to the floor. She had dragged him by the wrist into the sitting room, pulled his jacket off his shoulders and flipped his trousers open – before he had even had time to greet her. She pushed him hard and he found himself sprawled on an imitation Louis XV chair –

with Ariane on her knees and his stiffening male part in her mouth.

'Ariane,' he murmured, feeling almost overwhelmed by her show of impatience. He stroked her hair, fingers gliding over glossy dark waves. In seconds she made him hard enough for her desire. She jumped up and unbuttoned her skirt all down one side and it fell off. She was wearing shiny black satin knickers, her plump belly and bottom filling them out admirably. Off they came – she smiled at Robert and pressed the satin to his face. He breathed in deeply and recognised the Chanel 5 Ariane drenched her ample body with. He felt the warmth of her flesh in the satin.

She sat on his lap, legs astride his thighs, her back to him. He heard her shuddering gasp when she impaled herself upon him and he stabbed upwards into her slippery warmth.

'At last!' she cried. 'Robert, harder!'

But in truth it had not been necessary for him to do anything, her fiery nature did everything that was required. She writhed and she squirmed on him, she bounced and squealed, her body shaking to her own savage passions. Robert's own body responded eagerly to her, long throbs of pleasure made him gasp and tremble. Then her hand was between her spread thighs, her fingers grasping the base of his stiffness where it plunged up into her, and she stroked it firmly up and down . . .

'Ariane . . .' he sighed, 'not so fast!'

If she heard him, she gave no sign of it. The crisis took him quickly and his body jerked to the gush of his desire into her. She screamed shrilly and bounced up and down on his lap till he feared his thighs were bruised black and blue. It was Ariane's way – she took what she wanted, whether it was free or paid for, and gave no consideration to her partner or anything else, only to the satisfaction of her own desires.

But it was not Ariane astride him now, it was Marie-France, a very different person. Or so Robert believed. Marie-France did not try to rape him by force – she rode him in a gentle rhythm, a dreamy smile on her face, the cascade of her long blonde hair falling toward him. She adored what she was doing to him – with Jules it had never been possible, with Jules it was always like being hit by a fast-moving truck. But with Robert there was the opportunity to savour the pleasure and understand it.

How skilful he was as a sexual partner – and how perfectly he was matching her rhythm with his nervous little thrusting, not too hard and not too languorous. Each twitch of his loins sent a charming little stab of delight through her and helped her to advance another centimetre or two up the long wonderful path to ultimate ecstasy! Then he gasped, and his belly jerked upward, his moment of climax had arrived.

Marie-France was leaning forward, her hands on his shoulders, her eyes wide open to stare down at his handsome face and catch his expression at this instant of release. As she expected, his fists were clenched, beating on the sofa, and his head jerked up to stare at Marie-France above him. Her mouth opened in a long cry, it was the same as when Jules made her shriek on the kitchen table!

Her body shook in an extended orgasm to the spurt of Robert's desire in her belly. She was still picturing in her mind Jules fifth and final lap, though Robert had dismissed Ariane from his thoughts at this supreme moment. To have the image in his mind of Ariane's plump belly perched over his loins and draining him of his passion would be a betrayal of Marie-France, he thought feverishly – Marie-France who was proving she loved him!

'*Je t'adore*, Marie-France,' he murmured as he subsided into a condition of trembling content. But even as he spoke the words a picture of beautiful Suzette came unbidden into his thoughts. Robert was confused.

When he had woken that morning, alone in bed, he had forgotten the dreams of the night – but the moments of ecstasy Marie-France had just given him caused him to remember it and blush a little with guilt. He had dreamed of Suzette. No doubt her imminent appearance on stage at the Folies Bergère was the reason for it. This evening he would see her. He had bought tickets as soon as the date was announced in the press.

On stage she would be elegantly dressed for she was a celebrated singer now, not a show-girl. But in his dream he saw her as she was in the old days, her beautiful body naked, ostrich plumes a metre high on her head, studded with coloured glass gem-stones. Those superb breasts of hers were proudly displayed and between her thighs she wore a tiny gold-spangled *cache-sexe*.

The music was playing, the other show-girls moved sinuously back, to leave Suzette standing alone. They were all beautiful, naturally, but they were only a background to Suzette. She was incomparable, Robert looked at her and sighed. She seemed to be waiting for someone to come on stage, then she was beckoning to Robert in the audience.

He saw her smile while she took off her glittering *cache-sexe* and stood with feet apart, to show him her bare-shaven *joujou*. She was beckoning to him – she was inviting him to go up on the stage and make love to her. In front of the entire audience of the Folies Bergère! No, it was impossible – he couldn't – but he was moving to the stage, he was looking for steps, for a way up. Suzette advanced to the edge, she was almost above him, and when he looked up he could see the smooth pink lips between her thighs.

'*Je t'adore*, Marie-France,' he said again. He was trying hard to sound sincere.

Suzette at the Folies Bergère

While Robert and Marie-France lost themselves in pleasure upon his striped sofa on the morning of Suzette's grand opening at the Folies Bergère, the subjects of their fantasy were both asleep. In his apartment in south-east Paris, Jules Lavalle lay face down on his rumpled bed. He was snoring slightly, his male part shrivelled up between his legs. He ought to have been with his team, preparing for a bicycle race in four day's time, and the trainer had already phoned twice without getting an answer. Jules was too sound asleep to hear the phone ring – it had been the most exciting night of his entire life.

In her elegant apartment overlooking the Bois de Boulogne Suzette slept in her big star bed with the black fur cover. Her hand lay under her cheek on a peach-coloured satin pillow. She breathed lightly and slowly, one bare and shapely shoulder exposed.

By the time Suzette woke, not long after midday, Marie-France and Robert were in bed, continuing their pleasures. Jules was still snoring and the team manager was on his way by car to find him.

Suzette slid out of bed, stretched her arms and back, and put on a chiffon negligée. In the kitchen she found Gaby, drinking *café-au-lait* and nibbling a croissant spread thickly

285

with black cherry preserve. She wore a long scarlet silk dressing-gown and she too had only just got up.

'*Bonjour, chérie*,' said Suzette. She sat down at the kitchen table opposite Gaby and the maid brought her a large cup of coffee and a plate and knife.

'Tonight,' said Gaby with a grin, 'we'll be on stage together for the first time. And I'll be the one with my *nichons* hanging out. This will be an historic moment! How times change!'

Even when she had only just got out of bed Gaby could somehow look fresh and well-groomed. Her silvery-blonde hair looked as if it had been groomed for half an hour, although she'd done no more than drag a comb through it. Her blue eyes were bright and her complexion was flawless. There was not a trace of make-up to be seen on her face, but her cheeks were a delicate pink. How she performed this daily miracle was beyond Suzette to comprehend – it was the one thing about Gaby that made her jealous.

They talked for a while about Suzette's return to the Folies Bergère and they laughed. They were the best of friends and had been since the day they met. It went without saying that, being such good friends, their talk turned to men before long – as is usual when women are together.

'Last night,' said Gaby', after the show, you wouldn't believe what happened to me!'

'I can guess from the way you said it that it was outrageous whatever it was,' Suzette answered with a grin. 'You were very interested in one of the men dancers, the last time we talked. What was his name? I've forgotten.'

'Marc,' Gaby said, a gleam in her eyes. 'I pointed him out to you at rehearsal. Last night it all happened!'

AMOUR TOUJOURS

Suzette remembered him well, this Marc Martel – he was
one of three male dancers in an exotic number that seemed
part Mexican and part Hollywood fantasy. They were
much of a muchness – long lean bodies, a dancer's strong
legs, conventionally handsome faces. Marc was the one
with the intense look. She had paid no great attention to
him beyond that and did nothing to encourage Gaby's
interest in him for the reason that dancers of his sort were
very often left-landed. But apparently not, if as Gaby now
said, it had all happened last night.

The three men danced bare-foot and nude. They leaped
in the air like ballet dancers, they whirled about like
dervishes they posed like Greek statues. What had caught
Gaby's interest, Suzette knew, was Marc's prominent
cache-sexe and what might be concealed within it. Needless
to say that was what caught the attention of the women in
the Folies-Bergère audience – and was intended to!

*Zut alors! Perhaps I have permitted myself to become a
little too sceptical*, Suzette said to herself. *I assume they all
stuff a handful of cotton wool into the cache-sexe to make
bulge it out – but there must have been something in it to
make Gaby so pleased!*

On stage, all Marc, and the other two wore was a broad
belt of black leather, shiny and polished, gleaming with
chrome studs. It was cinched in very tightly and fastened
with a round chrome buckle designed to frame and expose
the belly button. It supported a gleaming white glacé
leather *cache-sexe* which was pulled back very tightly.
When they whirled round, it could be seen that the lean
cheeks of their bottoms were totally bare – the thong
holding the soft leather *cache-sexe* being pulled cruelly
tight between them.

'Evidently it was not a straightforward evening of *lie-down-and-open-your-legs-chérie-I-love you*,' said Suzette, a tiny smile on her face. 'I haven't seen you so interested since your little pervert Julien ran away from the police.'

'This one is also a pervert,' Gaby said happily, 'but not in the same way. No one could be like Julien.'

'You thought you had found a substitute for him when you met Loulou's brother,' Suzette reminded her.

'Marceline, my pretty transvestite,' said Gaby with a giggle 'the man who thinks he's a lesbian. It was amusing for a while, yes, but after two weeks it became less so. And then for me it became tedious, though poor Marcel went down on his knees and wept and implored when I told him it was the last time.'

'He was wearing lace knickers at the time, I suppose!'

'The truth is,' said Gaby with a sigh, 'I only really adore a man if he dominates me in bed. I do not wish to lie on top of a transvestite in women's underwear and convince him he is a she. I love it when a man holds me so tight I am helpless and tears my clothes off to run his hands over my naked body! To be held so tight I can't breath – to be suffocated with love – this is what happened last night with Marc!'

'So tell me what he did! Where did he take you?'

'It was the first time he'd asked me to go anywhere with him. I thought he never would! But after the show he waited for me outside and invited me to have a drink with him. Well, I jumped at the chance, of course. I've wanted to try him out for ages.'

'I'm sure he never guessed!' Suzette said with mild irony.

'When he dragged me halfway across Paris I could tell he was serious,' Gaby went on, after putting her tongue out at Suzette. 'Obviously he wanted to get me close to where he lives so it wouldn't be far to go when he had me in the mood.'

'Naturally,' Suzette murmured, still ironic.

'We went on the Metro,' Gaby explained, 'to the Place Denfert Rochereau, halfway to nowhere down the Boulevard Raspail. There is a café opposite the Lion of Belfort statue, not far from the entrance to the Catacombs. We sat talking at an outside table, and after a glass of wine we were very friendly. I could see he was keen on me, so I asked him the big question I'd been dying to ask since I first laid eyes on him . . .

'*Mais non!*' said Suzette, trying not to laugh. 'You had the nerve to ask him about his fancy *cache-sexe*?'

'Certainly. I told him I found it eye-catching, because it is so tight, and I asked if it became very uncomfortable, with so many beautiful naked woman on stage at the same time. It amused him and it flattered him. He held my hand and kissed my cheek. I put my hand on his thigh – only for a moment – I didn't want to attract attention.'

'But you wanted to know if he has anything worthwhile stuffed down his *cache-sexe* – yes?'

'Of course. I was astonished by what I found! I touched him only briefly and he was soft, but the size of what he had down there seemed very impressive! In fact, it felt like a handful of soft figs – a bit like squeezing the fruit on a market stall to see if it's ripe. When this goes stiff it must be enormous, I thought and I was moist between the legs.'

'Well, well!' said Suzette with a chuckle.

'He confided in me,' Gaby went on. 'He felt he could trust me because he saw I admired him.'

'Or part of him, at least,' Suzette contributed.

'For men that's the only part that ever really matters,'

Gaby said. 'Anyway, this will amuse you. He told me the sight of so many naked women on stage with him aroused him and made him stiff – and that's a catastrophe in the tight little glacé *cache-sexe*. So every evening, just before he leaves for the theatre, he opens his trousers and makes himself stiff by thinking about the girls, then he rubs himself to a climax and spurts into a handkerchief. After that he can stay soft right through the performance and is safe from embarrassment.'

Suzette shrugged, men did the strangest things.

'I told him I hoped the effect didn't last long,' said Gaby, 'and he assured me it didn't. I touched him again to make sure and he was stiff, so that was all right. Then the oddest thing happened – another man came to the table and sat down with us. Marc introduced him as a good friend. His name was André and he lived in the same building.'

'*Oh la la!*' Suzette said ominously.

'That's exactly what I thought, when they started to talk and I saw what close friends they were. "Just my luck!" I said to myself, "I've picked a left-handed one! That lovely big thing I touched is being wasted on another man"!'

'What a pity,' Suzette said sympathetically.

'No, it turned out all right. We drank another glass of wine, paid for by André, then Marc whispered that he couldn't wait any longer, he was dying to make love to me. So up we got and went to his apartment. André came along too – I told you he lives in the same building, a tumbledown old place in a side street not far from the café. Naturally, Marc lives on the top floor.'

'They always do,' said Suzette. 'They drag you up dirty stone staircases till you're gasping for breath – and then expect you to look glamorous.'

'We didn't get to the top,' said Gaby with a grin. 'There was no light at all on the staircase – the landlord is far too mean to pay for new light bulbs when they wear out. We stood in the hall groping about for the stairs and Marc and André put their arm round me to guide me and we started up in pitch darkness. After the first flight it got even darker, I was putting one foot in front of the other and hoping there were no broken steps.'

'*Mon Dieu* – where is the romance!' said Suzette.

'The staircase was narrow – one of the men was in ahead of me and the other a step behind. I was so confused by then I didn't know which was which any more – not that it mattered because at that moment they both took advantage of me.'

'On the stairs?' said Suzette, her eyebrows rising. 'How?'

Gaby laughed and explained. The man ahead of her stopped, she thought it was Marc but couldn't be certain. She bumped against him in the darkness and the man following her bumped into her And there they were, stationary, on a dark staircase, a knot of warm bodies. The man on the step below her reached down to take hold of her ankle, the man in front, Marc perhaps, felt for her skirt and pulled it up above her knees.

Gaby gasped in surprise, wondering what they meant to do. She felt a hand slide up from her ankle to the knee, but whose hand she could not tell. It slid further up her stocking, it stroked the bare flesh between stocking-top and knickers. A second hand – perhaps André – touched the back of her thigh – and then went higher to caress the cheeks of her bottom through her knickers. *But this is ridiculous*, she said, *why stop here on the stairs? Is there no bed in your room, Marc?*

Neither man answered her. The hand caressing her thigh moved higher and slipped into the lace-trimmed leg of her knickers. Fingers were touching the smooth petals between her thighs in a slow and lascivious exploration, although it was evident to her that nothing beyond caresses would occur here on the staircase. Her legs were awkwardly apart, one foot on a step higher than the other, so it was impossible for her knickers to be removed. The most she expected was this feeling of unseen fingers in the dark, edging her gently towards a climax.

She felt warm breath on the inside of her thigh. She guessed that André on the step below her – if it was André and not Marc – was kneeling to put his head between her legs. *Ah!* she murmured, her body trembling as the warmth of his breathing sent tremors of pleasure through her.

She twisted at the hips and reached down with both hands. She touched a man's head, his hair was thick and wavy – like Marc's hair. With her fingers she traced the contours of his forehead and nose, but it did not feel exactly as she remembered Marc's. Perhaps it was André after all. Whoever it was, his eyes were closed. Her fingers traced lightly over the eyelids.

The hand on her bottom became bolder. It slipped down inside her knickers from the back to caress the smooth bare cheeks. And then between them, fingertips exploring slowly and very thoroughly. The warm breathing on her inside thigh intensified and she felt the warmth of it moving over her flesh to where her legs joined.

It was Marc, surely – or perhaps his friend André. Who could tell? Whoever, his mouth lay over the thin silk between her thighs and his hot breath reached her *joujou* through it. *Oh, oh!* she gasped. She swayed and steadied herself by putting a hand flat against the cracked plaster of the stairwell wall. She was twisted half round still, her other hand on the head of the man behind her. She turned back and hooked her hand firmly into the belt of the man above, hanging on to him to keep her balance.

Holding on to his belt made her realise she could find out if it was Marc in front by feeling the stiff part in his trousers. If it was enormous, it was Marc – if not, then it was André. But the pleasure the two men were giving her made her light-headed and she dare not let go her grip on the belt.

And between them they had made her highly aroused, there was no doubt of that! The hot breath through thin silk, the finger that probed the little knot between her cheeks, the hand inside her knickers rubbing her belly in a slow circular motion – how bizarre it was, this staircase seduction *à trois!* And all in total silence and in the dark!

Gaby moaned as she reached her climax. Her belly clenched and her knees wobbled and collapsed under her. Strong hands caught her and held her under the arms and by the hips, bearing her up while she sighed and shook in spasms of ecstasy.

'*Cieux!*' Suzette exclaimed. 'Standing on a staircase, I don't believe it – it's too comic for words! Did you ever get to see Marc's room?'

'Oh yes,' said Gaby, pouting at her friend. 'After I'd got my breath back they helped me up the rest of the stairs, right up to the top of the building. We went into Marc's room, the three of us. Nothing had been said but it was very clear I was going to be shared between them. The idea struck me as perverse and I was very excited by it.'

'You said this Marc was another pervert,' said Suzette,

'that is no longer in question. So after the prelude on the staircase – what form did the main drama take? High-heeled shoes, whips, handcuffs?'

'Nothing like that,' Gaby protested. 'The trouble is, *chérie*, you don't appreciate perverts.'

'Then make me understand.'

Gaby did her best to explain what happened when the three of them reached Marc's room. She tried to make Suzette understand it was not only a matter of naked bodies together, there was an extraordinary atmosphere that beguiled the mind and the senses, that transformed what might have been a banal rubbing of skin against skin into an experience almost out of this world.

She went with the two men into Marc's room under the roof and he locked the door. He did not turn on the light and the window must have been heavily curtained, for there was no gleam from outside. Marc knew his way around the room in the dark. He took Gaby and André by the hand and led them carefully across to the bed. Gaby only knew it was the bed when her legs touched it and she felt down and recognised what it was.

In seconds they were all stripped, their clothes scattered in the dark about the floor. They lay on the bed together, side by side, hands touching, Gaby in the middle. She was sorry for a instant or two about the dark because it made it impossible for the men to see how beautiful she looked naked. The silvery-blonde tuft of curls above her *joujou* that sent most men into rhapsodies was concealed!

But she revised her opinion after a minute of lying there in complete darkness. The atmosphere of the room was close and intimate. And tranquil, late-night traffic on the boulevard was only a distant soothing rumble. The three of them lay still for some time, Gaby stretched out between the men, enveloped in their sensuality and her own.

At last she felt hands take her pointed little breasts – she neither knew nor cared whose hands they were. The hand caressed and played, then warm lips touched the buds. She felt a finger touch her *joujou* and stroke the lips. It probed softly to find her secret bud and tease it. In each hand she felt a stiff male part, squeezing and stroking. And they seemed to her to be much the same size – there was no way to determine which was Marc's.

Sighs and murmurs filled the dark room while hands moved, slow and lazy, over Gaby's long and beautiful body. It was strangely exciting that there was no sense of hurry or urgency, just long hours of pleasure stretching ahead. Gaby surrendered herself to it entirely – and three or four times her back arched off the bed in orgasm, her gasps of release cutting through the sensual sighing.

At that sound the hands would pause in their play for a while – a palm lay over her breast but it remained motionless, a hand between her thighs ceased to caress her, the mouth on her belly was still, the tongue withdrawing slowly. But not for long, only until she had stopped panting and her body ceased to shake in delight – then the hands would begin again, stroking and arousing, the mouths would return, their tongues seeking. And each time a new arousal would begin . . .

After what seemed hours of ecstasy one of the men rolled over and put his belly on hers. Her long dancer's legs lay wide open and he was between them, his hot hard part sliding into her wet *joujou*. His mouth was on her mouth, his hands gripped her shoulders tight, but other hands played over her neck and in her long silver-blonde hair. It was in her mind that she had never been made love to so slowly and deliberately – a long and deep thrust in, a long slow pull out, teasing her nerves to breaking point.

When at last he spurted his desire, Gaby's orgasm was so very fierce she screamed loud enough to wake everyone in the entire building. She heard the man lying on her belly chuckle at that and she decided from the sound of the chuckle it was Marc. And then he was off her and gone. In the dark another body was pressing her down into the mattress and another long hard part was sliding into her slipperiness. Her next climax came quickly, before his, but he paused for a little while and resumed his slow thrust, and she slid into ecstasy with him when he spurted. André – it must have been André that time was the thought in her mind when she could think rationally again – but was it?

'You were right,' Suzette said. 'It all happened to you last night – it wasn't what you expected to happen, but who cares so long as you enjoyed it.'

'Oh, I did, I did!' said Gaby with an impudent grin. 'It was marvellous. They had me twice each with hardly a pause between. One of them, I don't know if it was Marc or André, had a third ride, marvellously long and gentle. When I woke up this morning between the two of them I felt on top of the world. I eased out of bed without disturbing either of them too much and whispered *au revoir* to Marc while I was fumbling about for my clothes. By seven I was back here and went straight to bed.'

'You intend to continue this friendship *à trois*, I suppose?'

'Every night after the show, till Marc and his friend run out of steam! But apart from that, I'm going to help Marc with his little problem before the show.'

Suzette smiled and shrugged. Gaby was scatter-brained, it was part of her charm.

'You won't need a lift to the Folies Bergère with me then?'

'No, *chérie*, I shall be at Marc's. It is too sad to think of him sitting there holding that marvellous big hard thing in his hand and giving himself a lonely thrill. I shall do it for him, that will be much more satisfactory.'

'You'll open your legs for him to make sure he stays limp and small in his flashy *cache-sexe* on stage? That's devotion!'

'No, no!' said Gaby. 'Not before a performance, it takes the sparkle out of my dancing. I never do it before going on stage, you know that. It will be by hand.'

Later that day, in Suzette's flower-filled star dressing-room backstage at the Folies Bergère, so many of her friends crowded in to wish her well for the performance there was hardly space enough to stand. There were bouquets from everyone – even from Charles Desjardins, though he was not present. The little card with his flowers had a suitably intellectual quotation from the writings of Henri de Montherlant, of whom Suzette had never heard. The words Charles had scribbled were: *Most affection is a habit or a duty we lack the courage to end*.

'But what does it mean?' Simone the dresser asked, throwing her hands in the air.

'Perhaps that his wife has returned permanently to him and he has accepted her,' said Suzette. 'What does it matter?'

Many friends were there to wish her well and everyone of them understood why she was making this appearance. She had returned in triumph to sing on the stage where not so long ago she was a bare-breasted show-girl. Whatever international successes would be hers in the future, none would please her as much as this.

Michel Radiguet was there, the heart-broken poet who adored her, a champagne glass in his hand. He had written a new song for her to sing this evening after her standard repertoire. It was called *Jardins des Tuileries* and told of a man and woman deeply in love walking in the sun in the gardens, holding hands. They stop under the trees to kiss for a long moment. They both know that love brings misery as well as happiness – but who can live without it? Michel had composed the words lying on a white leather sofa in Suzette's sitting-room on the day when she and Gaby were sharing Robert between them in her bedroom.

Antoine Ducasse was there, of course, the rising young French film star, looking suave and dashing in a new dinner jacket of midnight-blue silk. He posed with Suzette for the cameras. They were both very interested in preserving the newspaper myth that they were madly in love and would eventually marry. Dalmas the journalist had created the myth originally and now had a vested interest in keeping it going for his readers. He scribbled down a few words of Antoine's to the effect that he adored Suzette – and a few words by Suzette saying she found him fascinating.

They had been lovers once, these two, Dalmas was correct in that. But never serious lovers. And from time to time, when they had no other arrangements, he took her to dinner in great style an with maximum publicity for the occasion. Afterwards Suzette always invited him to stay the night with her.

Robert Dorville looked in for a moment – he dare not stay any longer. He had arrived early with Marie-France to see the show and slipped away from her for five minutes to wish Suzette well and kiss her on the cheek. One who was also out in the audience – who had also sent flowers but did not risk going backstage to present his compliments – was Didier Gruchy, who had intruded upon Michel while he was writing the words of the new song. Simone's threat of exposure had made Didier wary. However, these flowers he had sent were a sure sign that he would eventually try to insinuate himself once more into Suzette's favour.

Gaby dashed in for a minute to embrace Suzette before heading for the big dressing-room the dancers shared with the show-girls.

'Devastate them, *chérie!*' she said. 'Get it into their thick little heads that you're the biggest star Paris has seen since the days when Mistinguett was queen of the stage!'

'I mean to,' said Suzette, she hugged Gaby cheek to cheek for a moment and then grinned and asked if there would be a sparkle in her dancing that evening – or had it been sacrificed to save Marc's blushes on stage?

'I have preserved my sparkle,' Gaby assured her, 'but Marc is unable to go stiff for the next hour or two. It was very funny. I'll tell you about it tomorrow – it will make you laugh.'

'You'll bring him to my party after the show, I hope? You're not to disappear with him to be ravished in the dark by two men – not before we've celebrated together.'

'But of course,' said Gaby. 'There's not a man in the world I would miss your party for! And I'll bring Marc along with me – his friend must wait patiently until we arrive. If we stay all night at your party, poor André must console himself alone.'

With a final hug, off she went to get ready, lively and happy and bubbling. She had left Suzette's apartment on the Boulevard Lannes early, to give herself half an hour with Marc, before it was time to leave for the theatre together. On the way she had made a stop at a theatrical costume shop and bought a male *cache-sexe*.

Poor Marc naturally thought she was there to make love before the show. He'd drawn back the curtain and tidied the room – he had even made the bed. It came as a surprise when she made him strip and put on the tiny stage garment she had brought with her.

It was not like the white glacé leather one he wore on stage. It was of soft black suede, with strings to tie over the hips. And it was small. The problem was that Gaby was helping him put it on, and her long fingers flitting so close to his loins made him start to go long and hard. Gaby was laughing while she and he struggled to cram his stiffening flesh into the suede pouch.

When she tied the strings at his narrow hips, he stared down in dismay – he'd got harder and bigger all the time and the little suede pouch was impossibly tight!

'Very good!' said Gaby, standing back, hands on hips, to see the result. 'It bulges out most impressively, *cheri*.'

She was fully dressed, wearing a thin white pullover tucked down into a slim blue skirt. Marc put his arms about her and kissed her. He got his hand under the skirt and up between her slender thighs. Immediately she pushed him away.

'But, but . . .!' he stammered.

'Don't think you're going to make love to me,' she said. 'Not before a performance, never! Sit in the chair.'

He sat and she perched on his knee and pushed his legs apart to cup her hand over his bulging *cache-sexe* and squeeze. Not just once – she kept on doing it until Marc was groaning. When she at last untied the knot at one hip to let the *cache-sexe* fall he almost sobbed at the sudden feeling of release. His male part, cramped in too small a space and hot from the pressure of the suede was agonisingly hard. It sprang upwards, quivering.

Cool air met his leaping part – ah, the relief of it! But it did not last, this blessed respite. In two seconds Gaby's scarlet-nailed fingers closed round his shaking length of hard flesh and begun a rhythmic up-and-down movement.

She leaned close to press a kiss to his mouth, her hand still moving steadily.

'We must make certain nothing embarrassing happens on stage, she murmured. 'Think of all those bare *nichons* bouncing about, including mine – to say nothing of the show-girls showing their bottoms! This enormous thing of yours would soon be sticking his head up out of the top of that little white *cache-sexe* you wear, *chéri*. We can't have that. I think the black one suits you better than the white – which do you prefer?'

Her smile was unrelenting and faintly malicious as she spoke. Her hand moved faster, drawing out his marrow – Marc wailed and spurted his passion up at the ceiling.

In the star dressing-room Simone was keeping a careful eye on the time. Gradually she began to ease the congratulatory friends toward the door, collecting their empty glasses as they went, edging them out into the corridor. It was not easy for they were all in such good spirits. The journalist Dalmas proved the most difficult to get rid of, he was scribbling in his notebook after everyone had gone although there was nothing to report. He was making his own story up, of course, inventing details to please his readers.

Simone eased him out at last and closed the door – and turned to find that Pierre-Raymond Becquet was still there, sitting close to Suzette at her dressing-table.

'It is necessary to leave now, monsieur,' Simone informed him politely but firmly. 'I have to dress Mademoiselle Suzette. The performance is beginning – listen, you can hear the orchestra! She must be on stage soon.'

'I asked him to stay for a minute after the others had gone,' said Suzette. 'It was impossible to talk properly with all that chatter going on. Leave us alone for five minutes, Simone *chérie*.'

'If you say so,' said the dresser, not pleased, 'but no more than that, there isn't time.'

Pierre-Raymond was looking even more distinguished than usual – his handsome face was suntanned, his eyes were bright. He had been on vacation for some weeks, lying on a beach on the island of Corsica, eating good food and sleeping alone. He'd returned to Paris especially for Suzette's opening night at the Folies Bergère. And here he was, wearing an elegant dinner jacket, his hair smoothed back and his hands perfectly manicured.

If the truth were told, which it almost never is, he had gone away to escape from Giselle Picard. She had pursued him avidly, by day and by night, in his studio and out of it. She was drawn to Monsieur Ten-Times by his reputation as a fantastic lover. A week of trying to satisfy her, a week of lying on her belly and thrusting into her ever-welcoming *joujou* and he had fled from Paris with his back aching, his body crying out for respite – and his male part limp and useless.

Now he was back, refreshed and strong. He meant to stay well clear of Giselle. He was, after all, desperately infatuated by Suzette. She was leaning forward to see her face in the mirror, renewing her make-up before going on stage, a yellow silk scarf tied round her head to protect her glossy raven-black hair. She had taken her frock off when the others left the dressing-room and was sitting there with an eyebrow pencil in her hand, wearing only black lace knickers and a matching bra.

Naturally, Pierre-Raymond couldn't take his eyes off her. She felt no discomfort at being stared at, that he knew, her years as a show-girl had accustomed her to being ogled by heavy-breathing men. But he couldn't resist asking her about it.

'No,' she said with a quick smile, darkening an eyebrow with a skilful hand. 'When you earn your living by posing in a tiny *cache-sexe* and five kilos of ostrich-plumes, you soon cease to be troubled by hundreds of eyes staring at you. To be truthful, it becomes almost exciting after a time, this mass-observation.'

'But surely not!' Pierre-Raymond protested.

'You are a man,' she said. 'Your imagination works in another way, you are a starer, not one of those stared at. But for me, it sometimes felt as if invisible hands slithered over my body, stroking my breasts and sliding between my legs. That hot stare between my legs was like fingers trying to snatch my *cache-sexe* off and bare my last secret! And then caress it!'

'This is monstrous,' said Pierre-Raymond, jealous of the many thousands of unknown men who had sat in the audience and stared at Suzette's body in her show-girl days. 'Thank heaven all that is past now.'

'But it's not,' Suzette said, running a fingertip along her top lip. 'Do you suppose it is any different now that I sing in an expensive frock? Even with my clothes on, I can still feel that intimate gaze on my body from the other side of the lights – the audience like my singing, but the men are thinking how it would be to uncover my *nichons* and feel them.'

Pierre-Raymond thought of denying it, but he knew it was true. Every time he saw Suzette he thought of exactly that – of how it would be to kiss her bare breasts. And to touch between her thighs . . .

Suzette reached behind her back and undid her lace brassiere, she took a large powder-puff and dabbed it on the upper slopes of her breasts, where the frock she meant to wear would expose them to view. Pierre-Raymond sighed inaudibly – she acted as if he were not there, or as if he were a dresser. She seemed to be unaffected by his attractions as a man. He was not used to that in women, normally they could hardly wait for him to slide his hand up their skirt.

Suzette pulled a drawer open to reveal several pairs of fine black silk stockings. Pierre-Raymond took the top pair and with a grin he recalled the fantastic day when she had asked him put her stockings on for her – in his studio, when she came to have new pictures taken for promotion, perhaps for a record. He had the most distinct memory of babbling like an idiot as he knelt down to take off the stockings she was wearing and put on the black ones.

Almost dizzy with emotion, Pierre-Raymond asked the question that had been in his mind for weeks.

'Do you always go on stage without knickers?' he said with smile that was half-apologetic.

'Always,' Suzette answered, her tone serious.

She was smiling at him in the mirror as she spoke, the tip of her wet tongue running over her short upper lip.

'For luck?' he asked.

'Of course for luck – so long as I sing bare-bottomed I shall always be a great success.'

'If your fans knew that!' said Pierre-Raymond, a smile on his face, 'they would love you the more.'

'But no one will ever know except you and two close friends,' Suzette said quickly. 'If the secret were known the luck would disappear, I'm certain of it. You must promise me you'll never tell anyone.'

'I swear it!' he said solemnly.

'Then you may take them off for me.'

Pierre-Raymond held his breath, almost unable to believe his own luck.

She got up from her chair and took two steps toward him, bare breasts bouncing a little. She put her hands on his shoulders and kissed him briefly, a gesture of friendship rather than of passion. He held her waist between his hands and pulled her to him until he felt the warm press of her belly and the fullness of her breasts against his chest. He returned her kiss a little incredulously, then hooked his thumbs in the sides of her black lace knickers and slid them down her thighs.

'We have very little time, *chéri*,' she murmured, her hand down between their bodies to grasp his upright part through the thin material of his black evening trousers.

As if to stress the urgency of the situation, she sank to her knees. Instantly she had his trousers open, his hard flesh in one hand and his hairy pompoms in the other. A spasm of delight shook him – she was lightly kissing the purple shiny head.

'I've been wondering what it looked like, Monsieur Ten-Times, and now I know,' she said, smiling up at him, while her fingers moved easily up and down.

'*Je t'aime*, Suzette,' Pierre-Raymond moaned, '*je t'aime* . . .'

Her red-painted mouth pouted to allow the swollen head of his stiffness to push its way in and his knees shook under him.

'And I adore you, Pierre-Raymond,' she said, tipping her head back to free her mouth, 'but it seems that you are available to anyone who asks. It is impossible to be the friend of a man who has that reputation. You understand me?'

Something must be done, Pierre-Raymond knew, this opportunity would never return! He must show Suzette he was a man who knew his own mind, a man of honour, a lover to be proud of . . . though was any of it true? Couldn't it be said that he only responded to the sexual desire of his female clients? How many years was it since he had really pursued a woman – instead of waiting in his studio for a woman, any woman, to slip her hand between his thighs? And so many did!

He put his hands on Suzette's bare shoulders and helped her to her feet.

'What are you doing?' she asked, and her voice was high with excitement. 'There is no time for what you want, *chéri* – I must be on stage in two minutes!'

Pierre-Raymond held her by her waist, her flesh soft and warm beneath his fingers. He turned her to face the make-up table.

'Lean forward,' he said forcefully. 'Hurry!'

'But this is absurd,' she murmured, head turned to stare

over her shoulder at him. 'There is only a minute before my call . . .'

Absurd or not, she put her hands flat on the cluttered table between the bottles and the jars. She leaned forward, supported on straight arms, the diamond bracelet on her wrist glinting in the light, her feet spread well apart on the floor. A long sigh of pleasure escaped Pierre-Raymond when he gazed at her bottom the firm-fleshed cheeks were so beautifully shaped!

He wanted to feel those cheeks and to kiss them, to nibble at them but time was against him but he was unable to stop himself, whether there was time for it or not, from slipping a hand between Suzette's superb thighs. His male part jumped as his fingers caressed the soft petals of her smooth-shaven mound.

But only for an instant. In the little time left he must show Suzette he was the man, the initiator, the penetrator. He heard her gasp when he opened her wide with his thumbs and pushed his hard flesh up into her. She gave a shriek of pleasure when he forced deeper. She shuddered and sighed to his urgent thrusts.

'Do you truly like me, Suzette?' he demanded. 'Tell me!'

'Oh yes, yes!' she gasped.

His hands were on her shoulders now, holding on tightly while his belly smacked against her bare bottom. What did it matter if she flung him out after he'd made love to her, what did it matter if she never wanted to see him again? This once, this one wonderful evening, he was her lover, her master, a man taking a woman as was his right! This was the moment of truth of his total infatuation with her, his hardness throbbing inside her, she was his!

Her stockinged feet were well apart as his hands slithered

down her smooth flesh to hold her round hips. The lunge of his loins drove his stiff flesh into her in strong strokes and Suzette felt herself being overwhelmed by sensation. She surrendered totally to the throb and slide of the stiff flesh ravaging her.

Pierre-Raymond stared over her shoulder at her reflection the make-up mirror – into her velvet-brown eyes gleaming with emotion, her beautiful face beneath the yellow scarf around her jet-black hair. He stared at the reflection of her superb bare breasts swaying up and down to the rhythm of his thrusting. She was open to him, her long legs splayed, her bottom pressing to his belly.

'Pierre-Raymond,' she moaned, 'finish!'

He tightened his grasp on her hips, his breath rasped in his throat. Spasms of delight shook him. *Oh Suzette!* he sighed in deep adoration at his moment of crisis.

Suzette was swept into shuddering ecstasy and gave a sob of delight. In the mirror he saw her eyes and mouth were wide open as he spurted his desire into her. Then it was over – there was a discreet tapping at the door, a voice calling Suzette's name.

It was Simone, come to remind Suzette she went on in five minutes. Pierre-Raymond sighed in content and eased out of her. He tucked his wet and dwindling part away and zipped up his trousers. Suzette turned round and put her arms about his neck to kiss him warmly.

Both were still trembling from the sensations they had shared together. Pierre-Raymond slid an arm about her waist to return her kiss with great tenderness as Simone came bustling into the dressing-room and stared at them with a knowing grin.

'You must go now, monsieur,' she said. 'Mademoiselle

Suzette is not dressed – as we both very well see! I must get her into her frock and put her make-up right – I fear that you have made her perspire a little, monsieur.'

'I shall be here after the show, waiting for you impatiently, to escort you to your own party,' Pierre-Raymond promised as he kissed Suzette's hand gallantly. The dresser shooed him out the room and returned to remonstrate with Suzette.

'You let Monsieur Pierre-Raymond take liberties with you five minutes before you go on to sing!' Simone said, not concealing her disapproval. 'This is folly – does it mean you are in love with him?'

'No, no!' said Suzette as the dresser handed her the bra and stood ready with the wispy little black frock that exposed her long beautiful back down to her magnificent bottom. 'Of course not – but I shall take him as my lover because I adore him.'

'You know his nickname?' Simone asked, raising one eyebrow. 'They call him Monsieur Ten-Times but I do not know whether it means ten times a day with one lady or once a day with ten – he has a certain reputation.'

'It is of no consequence. From now on his love-making will be directed entirely to one lady – me.'

'Very good,' said Simone, with a little shrug, 'but you ought not to experience these strong emotions the very moment before you go on stage to sing. Your voice could be affected, however slightly – or you may still tremble a little.'

'What nonsense!' Suzette said firmly. 'I shall be marvellous this evening. I shall sing better than ever. I always do when I make love first.'

She was thinking of the cellar in Montmartre, and the

doorway where the young poet Michel Radiguet had influenced her career without realising what he had achieved. Simone knew nothing of this incident.

'I believe you then,' said the dresser, hearing the confidence in Suzette's voice. 'You will be superb. Tonight is going to be another triumph for you! They will beg you on their knees soon to sing at the Lido on the Champs-Elysées – name your own price! They will come knocking all day at your door with offers to put you in movies! And, deny it if you like, but I believe you must be a little in love with Monsieur Pierre-Raymond.'

'Ah, God forbid I should ever fall in love with him,' Suzette said with a smile. 'We know what disasters that can lead to. My new song says all that – *love brings misery besides happiness – but who can live without it?*'

'Yes, very true,' said Simone with a shrug. She wondered how long it would be before Suzette was bored with her new admirer.

Maria Caprio

INFIDELITY

Exploring the boundaries of sensuality...

Experiments between the sheets

Count Otto von Hellmuth takes a scientific view of human nature, that is – he likes to experiment with people. Such as Emma and Jonathan, the young honeymooners just arrived in Palma. The Count picks them up at the airport and they are impressed by his wealth and status – just as he is impressed by Emma's blue eyes and long legs.

The funny thing is, for a newly married couple, they are already a trifle jaded with each other. They are seeking excitement, adventure, a few new amorous thrills. And they're guaranteed to find just what they're looking for as volunteers in one of the Count's little experiments...

Maria Caprio's previous erotic entertainments – BIANCA, TWO WEEKS IN MAY and COMPULSION – are also available in Headline Delta.

FICTION/EROTICA   0 7472 4406 5

Headline Delta Erotic Survey

In order to provide the kind of books you like to read - and to qualify for a free erotic novel of the Editor's choice - we would appreciate it if you would complete the following survey and send your answers, together with any further comments, to:

Headline Book Publishing
FREEPOST (WD 4984)
London
NW1 0YR

1. Are you male or female?
2. Age? Under 20 / 20 to 30 / 30 to 40 / 40 to 50 / 50 to 60 / 60 to 70 / over
3. At what age did you leave full-time education?
4. Where do you live? (Main geographical area)
5. Are you a regular erotic book buyer / a regular book buyer in general / both?
6. How much approximately do you spend a year on erotic books / on books in general?
7. How did you come by this book?
7a. If you bought it, did you purchase from: a national bookchain / a high street store / a newsagent / a motorway station / an airport / a railway station / other........
8. Do you find erotic books easy / hard to come by?
8a. Do you find Headline Delta erotic books easy / hard to come by?
9. Which are the best / worst erotic books you have ever read?
9a. Which are the best / worst Headline Delta erotic books you have ever read?
10. Within the erotic genre there are many periods, subjects and literary styles. Which of the following do you prefer:
10a. (period) historical / Victorian / C20th / contemporary / future?
10b. (subject) nuns / whores & whorehouses / Continental frolics / s&m / vampires / modern realism / escapist fantasy / science fiction?

10c. (styles) hardboiled / humorous / hardcore / ironic / romantic / realistic?

10d. Are there any other ingredients that particularly appeal to you?

11. We try to create a cover appearance that is suitable for each title. Do you consider them to be successful?

12. Would you prefer them to be less explicit / more explicit?

13. We would be interested to hear of your other reading habits. What other types of books do you read?

14. Who are your favourite authors?

15. Which newspapers do you read?

16. Which magazines?

17. Do you have any other comments or suggestions to make?

If you would like to receive a free erotic novel of the Editor's choice (available only to UK residents), together with an up-to-date listing of Headline Delta titles, please supply your name and address. Please allow 28 days for delivery.

Name...

Address..

....

....

A selection of Erotica
from Headline

SCANDAL IN PARADISE	Anonymous	£4.99 ☐
UNDER ORDERS	Nick Aymes	£4.99 ☐
RECKLESS LIAISONS	Anonymous	£4.99 ☐
GROUPIES II	Johnny Angelo	£4.99 ☐
TOTAL ABANDON	Anonymous	£4.99 ☐
AMOUR ENCORE	Marie-Claire Villefranche	£4.99 ☐
COMPULSION	Maria Caprio	£4.99 ☐
INDECENT	Felice Ash	£4.99 ☐
AMATEUR DAYS	Becky Bell	£4.99 ☐
EROS IN SPRINGTIME	Anonymous	£4.99 ☐
GOOD VIBRATIONS	Jeff Charles	£4.99 ☐
CITIZEN JULIETTE	Louise Aragon	

*All Headline books are available at your local bookshop or newsagent, or
can be ordered direct from the publisher. Just tick the titles you want and fill
in the form below. Prices and availability subject to change without notice.*

Headline Book Publishing, Cash Sales Department, Bookpoint, 39 Milton
Park, Abingdon, OXON, OX14 4TD, UK. If you have a credit card you may
order by telephone – 0235 400400.

Please enclose a cheque or postal order made payable to Bookpoint Ltd to the
value of the cover price and allow the following for postage and packing:
UK & BFPO: £1.00 for the first book, 50p for the second book and 30p for
each additional book ordered up to a maximum charge of £3.00.
OVERSEAS & EIRE: £2.00 for the first book, £1.00 for the second book and
50p for each additional book.

Name ....

Address ....

....

....

If you would prefer to pay by credit card, please complete:
Please debit my Visa/Access/Diner's Card/American Express (delete as
applicable) card no:

Signature .... Expiry Date ....